More Than Tempt You

MORE THAN

Tempt

YOU

MORE THAN WORDS SERIES BY

SHAYLA BLACK

MORE THAN TEMPT YOU
More Than Words, Book 5
Written by Shayla Black

This book is an original publication by Shayla Black.

Copyright © 2019 Shelley Bradley LLC
Print Edition

Cover Design by: Rachel Connolly
Photographer: Sara Eirew Photographer
Edited by: Amy Knupp of Blue Otter

ISBN: 978-1-936596-55-3

PRAISE FOR *MORE THAN WANT YOU*

"Amazing! Everything I didn't even know I needed or wanted in a romance novel. Hot. Spicy. Addicting."

—Rachel Van Dyken, #1 New York Times Bestselling Author

"Sexy, passionate and oh-so-clever! An intriguing love story!"

—Lauren Blakely, #1 New York Times Bestselling Author

"You'll hate him and then you'll love him! A sexy read with a surprising twist."

—Carly Phillips, New York Times Bestselling Author

PRAISE FOR *MORE THAN NEED YOU*

5 Stars! "I adore Shayla Black! She masterfully delivers story after story full of passion, love, heartbreak, and redemption."

—Chasing Away Reality

5 Stars! "I love this book!!! It has all the elements that takes you on an emotional rollercoaster."

—Romance Between The Sheets

PRAISE FOR *MORE THAN LOVE YOU*

5 Stars! "The perfect blend of romance, lust, love and standing in your own way. I love the story."

—Alpha Book Club

5 Stars! "One of the best books I've read in months! I love this book!"

—Magic Beyond The Covers Book Blog

PRAISE FOR *MORE THAN CRAVE YOU*

5 Stars! "With beautifully written characters and a storyline that I could not put down this was a fabulous read. It needs more than 5 stars!!"

—The Overflowing Bookcase

5 Stars! "…fun, hot and really hard to put down…loved it!"

—Sissy's Romance Book Review

ABOUT *MORE THAN TEMPT YOU*

I romanced her for revenge…but what if she's not the enemy after all?

I'm Clint Holmes. I was an ambitious guy with a busy life and a growing business. Sure North Dakota wasn't a tropical paradise, but I was happy enough—until tragedy struck. Now the only thing that matters is finding the person responsible and making her pay. But Bethany Banks is a Harvard-educated shark used to swallowing her enemies whole while playing dangerous corporate games. How can a blue-collar oil man like me possibly beat her?

The moment I lay eyes on my beautiful nemesis, the answer is obvious. I seduce her.

On Maui, where she's fled, I get to know the man-eater who caused my family so much pain…only to find she's not the brazen ballbuster I assumed. She's skittish, secretive, vulnerable. For some reason, my instinct is to protect her. I can't abandon my plan…but I can't stop wanting her. Night after night, I pry her open with my touch until I'm drowning in our passion. Soon, I'm questioning everything, especially the fine line between love and hate. But when the past comes back to wreak vengeance and the truth explodes, can I prove that I'm more than tempted to love her forever?

There are infinite ways to tell someone you love them. Some of the most powerful don't require words at all. This was the truth rolling through my head when I first conceived of this series, writing about a love so complete that mere letters strung together to make sentences weren't an adequate communicator of those feelings. Instead, for this series, music was my go-to choice.

I *love* music. I'm always immersed in it and spend hours a day with my ear buds plugged in. I write to music. I think to music. I even sleep to music. I was thrilled to incorporate songs into the story I felt were meaningful to the journey. I think of it this way: a movie has a sound-track. Why shouldn't a book?

So I created one.

Some of the songs I've selected will be familiar. Some are old. Some are newer. Some popular. Some obscure. They all just fit (in my opinion) and came straight from the heart. I listened to many of these songs as I wrote the book.

For maximum understanding (and feels), I seriously recommend becoming familiar with these songs and either playing them or rolling them around in your head as you read. Due to copyright laws, I can't use exact lyrics, but I tried to give you the gist of those most meaningful to Clint and Bethany's story. I've also made it simple for you to give these songs a listen by creating a Spotify playlist.

Hugs and happy reading!

BEER RUN – Garth Brooks featuring George Jones

DON'T STOP BELIEVIN' – Journey

STRONGER (WHAT DOESN'T KILL YOU) – Kelly Clarkson

DARE YOU TO MOVE – Switchfoot

HAPPY – Pharrell Williams

SOMEWHERE OVER THE RAINBOW – Israel Kamakawiwo'ole

I WON'T GIVE UP – Jason Mraz

FORTRESS AROUND YOUR HEART – Sting

PLEASE FORGIVE ME – Bryan Adams

DIG – Incubus

To my beloved. Without you,
nothing would be possible, Coke Zero.

PROLOGUE

June
Rural North Dakota

CLINT

"COME HOME."

I groan as I glance across the room at my father. Not again... "Dad, we've talked about this."

"No, you've talked about it. I haven't said my piece."

"But I know your spiel. Look, I've transplanted, and my roots are here now. My business is growing again. I'm still a newer kid on the block in the oil industry around here, so it's taking time." I lean back in my chair and grip my cold beer. "But I'm okay with that. Besides, you don't need me; you still have Bry at home."

My father huffs, then takes a drag of his cigar. "Until he goes off to college in the fall. Besides, when do you think your youngest brother is ever home? He's a seventeen-year-old boy who's just graduated from high school and has his own wheels. At that age, when were *you* home?"

He's got a valid point, but... "I know it's been hard since Mom's death. The last eighteen months have been an adjustment for everyone."

"It's not that. Open your eyes, son. The oil boom will likely bust again. Five years ago, this was a great business, and you were in the right place at the right time. Even Bethany agreed," he says of his investment advisor, whom he constantly raves about. "But now, it's time to cut your losses before they go any deeper. OPEC wants to put US oil production out of business, and they have the resources to make that happen. They did really well at choking your business last year."

I can't deny that. Twelve months ago, I was lamenting high costs and dismal profits. "This year has been better so far."

"Slightly. C'mon, Clint. Do you really want to eke out a living? Sell this thing. You'll get a pretty penny for the business, even if the industry isn't at its hottest right now." He hunkers back in my favorite leather chair and takes a sip of his whiskey. "If your mother's death taught me anything, it was that life is even shorter than people warn you. Forty-nine was way too young to die, but that didn't matter. Her number was up. Watching her go through all that breast cancer treatment just about killed me."

Me, too. I wasn't there for the worst since I moved to North Dakota at nineteen and went straight to work, eventually building my own oil services business from the ground up. But I came home for the end. Seeing her so frail and wasted devastated me. Losing her gutted my family. "I know, Dad."

When I reach across the space to take his hand, he squeezes mine. "Look, I want to retire. I want to do all the things your mother and I planned to before I pass on. We were going to get season tickets to one of those fancy theaters. We were going to drive up Pacific Coast Highway to San Francisco and see the sights. Hell, we were going to take a Hawaiian vacation. We didn't follow through on any of those plans because we had three growing boys and always thought there would be time. And now...she's gone."

When my father chokes back emotion, I squeeze his hand again. "I'm sorry."

"It's not your fault. She would have chosen keeping you kids happy over a vacation any day."

"But she worked all her life and didn't get to enjoy the quieter years. That upsets you, I know."

"Yes, but it upsets me more that I promised her I'd do all those things after she was gone. So far, I've done nothing but grieve and try to figure out how to carry on."

Guilt tugs at me. If I stay in North Dakota, I'll be following my own path. If I give that up to return to La-La Land, I'll be helping my family, yes. But I'll also be assuming a business that never interested me and putting myself smack-dab in the middle of crowds, congestion, and smog—all the reasons I left LA—again.

"What about Bret? He's going to graduate from UCLA next year with a business degree. I never went to college. Would he be better equipped—"

"You think he's ready to leave the frat house and walk straight into a multimillion-dollar-a-year business? Hell, as far as I can tell he hasn't pulled his head out of a keg in the last six months." My father sighs. "I'm not trying to guilt you. I'm simply hoping you'll see the wisdom of this idea. Your business might be drying up, depending on the price of oil per barrel. Mine is thriving, but it's too much for me to handle these days. I'm just getting too old."

"You're only fifty-three."

"After your mother's passing, I feel ancient."

He's not his usual, robust self. I know he's not sleeping well, and I guess that's age. But he seems more fatigued than I would have thought. Two years ago, he walked to my favorite fishing spot without any trouble. Today, he was short of breath on the same short trek. Even now, hours after our return, a fine sheen of perspiration beads on his forehead. Granted, it's almost ninety degrees and humid as hell outside, but it's comfortable in the air-conditioned house.

"Dad, you just got here yesterday. Enjoy your vacation. Maybe you'll feel refreshed at the end of two weeks and—"

"I've been thinking about this for months. Now I want you to think about it. Please."

How can I say no to that?

"All right. I'll consider it."

My father smiles wide. "Great. I worry about you out here, you know."

"Why?" I love the wide-open spaces and the down-to-earth people. Sure, it gets colder than a well-digger's butt and summers can be miserably hot, but I appreciate the beauty of nature—something you see almost none of in Los Angeles.

"I didn't see many pretty single girls while we drove through town. There don't seem to be any way out here, just a bunch of prairie dogs and cows. And I know better than to think they're keeping you warm at night."

Admittedly, that's one of the biggest drawbacks to living in the middle of nowhere. I've already dated all the single women within a hundred-mile radius. None of them are for me. When I want to feel a warm female, I have to go to Williston or Bismarck, hit a bar, and hope I get lucky. Most often I do, but sometimes I strike out. It happens. North Dakota is one of the few states where males outnumber females, especially in the western half of the state, where the surge of oil workers has made the odds of hitting a home run shittier.

"No. I'm definitely not into anything with four legs, Dad."

He laughs, absently rubbing at a spot under his right shoulder. "Come back to California. The timing is perfect. You can run my business. It's booming. It will make you rich. You can stop getting your hands dirty every day." He peers at the grease that seems permanently embedded under my fingernails, no matter how hard I scrub. "You can spend more time with me and your brothers. And I want to introduce you to Bethany."

"I don't need a financial advisor right now." Especially not one in a state I don't reside in.

"Maybe not. It never hurts to start investing, in my opinion. But that's not what I meant."

It takes me a minute to realize what he's saying. "You're trying to hook me up with her?"

"She's beautiful and smart and sweet. You'd like her, son. You'd like her a lot."

I know zero about this woman, and since I don't want to move to LA, I'm interested even less. "You date her, Dad. You're single."

"Oh, no. No. She's way closer to your age than mine. She's ambitious, on the quiet side, very direct. I trust her. At least let me introduce you next time you're home…"

If I keep refusing, he'll only keep wheedling. Like his entire proposition that I move back to LA and assume his business, it's better to defer than refuse. For all I know, he may change his mind again tomorrow.

"I'll think about it."

He pastes on a big smile and whips out his phone, then presses and swipes until he finds his photos. "We took this last month when we got together for our quarterly meeting. She even brought me a bottle of my favorite whiskey for my birthday. I asked, and she's single…"

To humor him, I lean in to look at the display. The smiling blonde looks chic and, I admit, stunning in a fitted, feminine gray sheath. Her rosy-pale coloring looks almost icy in the photo, but her eyes are a warm mossy green.

If I met her in a bar, I'd definitely try my luck. And I'd probably keep trying until she said yes. She's hot.

"Well, I can't fault your taste in women."

He laughs heartily, then darkens his phone. Before he can pocket it, the device rings. Thank goodness for WiFi-supported calling. Out here, the cell service is shit.

Dad glances at the display. "It's Brenda. One minute."

His secretary. Probably work. I take that as my cue to head to the kitchen for another beer. When I turn back, my dad is rubbing at that spot just below his shoulder again. Did he pull a muscle?

"Another whiskey?" I ask just before he answers the call.

"Hello?" He presses the phone to his ear and shakes his head.

As I head out of the room, I zone out from their conversation and flip on the kitchen radio. Garth Brooks and George Jones are singing a familiar, up-tempo song about a beer run. Grinning, I grab another brew from the fridge, pop off the cap, and take a swallow.

My dad has visibly aged recently, and I think it's because his business runs him. It's high demand. I guess that makes sense for insurance. But being a desk jockey would make me insane. I like spending time outdoors too much and I don't mind getting my hands dirty. Not much call for that in his line of work. I definitely don't want to talk all day about premiums and car accidents.

As I toss the little metal disc in the nearby trash can, my father's voice booms. I hear the shock. It's a tone I've only heard once—after my mother's doctors told my parents her breast cancer was terminal. This blow is every bit as gut-deep and stunned.

I flip off the radio and go running, only to find my dad sheet-white and blinking as he clutches the phone. "Everything?"

"What?" I ask.

He waves me away with a scowl and begins rubbing at the spot under his shoulder even harder. "Everything. I don't… That's thirty-five years of work. Of savings. Oh, shit. And he was arrested yesterday?"

What the hell is he talking about? And who? "Dad?"

He shakes his head again. "Keep making phone calls. I'll do the same and I'll be on a plane home tomorrow. If you find out anything else… Yes. Of course. I'm going to call Bethany right now. Thank you."

The moment he hangs up, I'm beside him. "What happened?"

"According to Brenda, Barclay Reed, the head of my investment firm, was arrested yesterday. He's been charged with running a giant Ponzi scheme, and every penny of his clients' investments is gone." He blinks as if he's in total disbelief. "I've got to call Bethany. He's her dad. Barclay, I mean. I'm not supposed to know that. She's illegitimate. It's hush-hush, but… She'll tell me what's happening. She's honest. There must be some explanation. I saw her less than four weeks ago, and everything was fine. She showed me all the reports. My money was growing. It can't suddenly be gone…"

He rises unsteadily to his feet. I ease him back down. He looks almost gray now. Shock, I suspect. But I'm worried. He's sweating more and seems short of breath.

"Dad, sit here. Rest. I'll get you packed and reserve you a plane ticket back to LA. If you get there and you need my help, I'll fly out."

"Thanks." He nods almost absently. "I'll call Bethany."

Since I want to hear this conversation, I pretend to gather our personal effects around the room. I try to stay calm, but my thoughts are racing. My father has worked his ass off and sacrificed for decades to save a few million dollars. He's well off, but he's earned it. I'm mad that thieves ever steal from anyone, but for scammers to swindle the life savings of a man nearing the end of his money-earning years? Yeah, I'm furious.

"No answer." He presses the button to end the call. "I'm going to try again."

But three attempts later, the "beautiful, smart, and sweet" financial advisor is nowhere to be found. How convenient. If Barclay is the prime suspect and Bethany is his daughter, odds are good she was involved, too. How dare that very pretty shark in a sheath look a lonely widower in the face and prey on his trust?

My father now looks waxen. He's rubbing at his chest in earnest.

"Dad, are you all right? Are you in pain?"

"Indigestion." He waves me off. "Happens all the time. Maybe Bethany isn't in the office. I'll try her cell."

I'd tell him to wait, but in his shoes, I would want to get to the bottom of this shit, too. Still, I'm worried.

I grab my phone to dial Gary, a buddy who happens to be the local family practitioner. Maybe he can tell me what's going on or prescribe something for Dad's anxiety.

"Her phone went straight to voice mail. Oh, god." He presses a hand to his chest as if he's trying to keep it from falling apart. "She's never not answered me. Ever."

His expression tells me that he's crushed. Shattered.

"I've got to… I have to get…" My dad stumbles to his feet.

I pocket my phone and rush back to his side. "What?"

Now, he looks disoriented and pasty. I'm no longer concerned; I'm downright alarmed.

As I wrap my arm around my father to steady him, he grabs his chest again, eyes flaring wide as he makes an animal sound of pain and crumples to the hardwood floor.

"Dad!"

"Hurt," he gurgles. "Ambulance."

Holy shit. He's having a fucking heart attack. The signs are all there.

And it will take an ambulance at least forty minutes to reach me.

Cold fear fills my veins with ice as I fall to my knees beside my dad. My fingers feel as if they're moving in slow motion as I fumble for my phone, trying to unlock the display so I can dial.

It seems to ring forever before a woman answers. "Nine-one-one. What's your emergency?"

I quickly fill her in and ask what I can do to help. Yes, he's lying on the floor. Yes, he's conscious—barely. No, he's not breathing.

Oh, shit.

After advising me an ambulance is on the way, she asks if I have any aspirin in the house. I do, thank god.

"Dad." I grab his hand. "Can you hear me?"

He makes a squeaking sound and grabs weakly at my hand. I try to stay calm. My head keeps telling me this can't possibly be happening. My eyes tell me in living, horrific color it is.

"I'm going to grab an aspirin from my bathroom. Stay here. Stay with me. I'll be right back."

No response. I pocket my phone and flat-out run across the house, into the master bathroom, then tear into my medicine cabinet. My hands are shaking as I try to open the bottle, but the fucking child-proof cap won't come off. Finally, I manage, spilling one tablet in my fist, then dash back down the stairs, panting, heart racing.

"Dad?"

He doesn't respond. Son of a bitch. I have to try CPR. I haven't practiced this since I did the lifeguard thing at the local pool when I was sixteen. But I do my best to screw my head on straight and start chest compressions and breathing.

I have no idea how long I press and exhale, trying to force air into his lungs and prompt his heart to pick up its own tempo. All I know is that I'm dizzy and exhausted and wondering if I'm making any headway when the EMTs pound on my front door.

As much as I hate to, I tear myself away long enough to answer the door. I can't acknowledge that my father still isn't breathing. The professionals are here. They'll get him going. He'll be all right.

He can't die here today.

A trio of uniformed ambulance attendants storm the house with bags and a rolling stretcher.

"Where is the victim?" a capable-looking African-American woman asks in a calm voice.

"Living room." I point.

The other two EMTs waste no time rushing to my father's side. I try to follow, but the woman blocks my path. "Tell me what you've done so far."

I trip over my words as I try to explain, but all I care about is reaching my dad's side. I shove my hands in my pockets. I need something to do. I can't stand here and merely watch. I come up with the aspirin he was never conscious enough to chew and swallow.

"Do you need this?" I ask her.

She glances over her shoulder. I follow her line of vision. The other two medics have hooked my father up to some sort of heart rate monitor.

The sharp, persistent sound rattles my head and pierces my calm. He's flatlined.

"No!" I take off to reach his side.

The woman holds me back. "Let them do their job."

"But..."

I'm not sure what to say. I have zero medical knowledge. Logically, I'll only be in the way, but... He can't be dying. And if—oh, god—he is, he can't be doing it with only strangers to comfort him. He needs family.

"Sir—"

"I have to be with him," I blurt. "At least let me hold his hand."

To my right, I hear one of the EMTs sigh as he rises to his feet and approaches me, regret softening his eyes. "I'm sorry."

"No." I shake my head. "No! I was talking to him less than an hour ago. We were making plans…"

In the back of my head, I realize I'm speaking nonsense, but I can't process what's just happened. I don't know what to say.

My father can't be dead.

"Can't you defib him?" I've watched enough medical dramas on TV to know what that means.

The female shakes her head. "That's not how it works. A defibrillator can't jumpstart a stopped heart. They stop a heart in an irregular rhythm and try to reset it. But your father is in asystole. There's no longer any electrical activity, so there's no tempo to restore. We're very sorry."

I stand rooted. In shock.

Dad is gone.

What the hell happened? What the hell am I going to do?

Pain rips through my chest. I can't breathe.

I have to call Bret and Bry and break their hearts. I'll have to go to California and bury my father. I scrub a hand down my face. Oh, god. I'll have to take care of my seventeen-year-old brother, at least until he's no longer a minor.

I'll have to face my life without the man whose love and counsel I've relied on every one of the twenty-four years of my life.

I clench my fists. Something bites into my palm. I uncurl my fingers. The aspirin.

Gritting my teeth, I'm suddenly choked by grief and anger. I toss the little disc across the room and ignore the female who offers me a sedative. *Fuck that.*

It seems like hours pass before they lift my dad onto a stretcher and cover his face. It's all I can do to hold myself together. I feel so fucking brittle. And lost.

Overall, my father was in decent health. I don't understand.

I grab the arm of the male medic who first pronounced my father dead. "How could this happen? He's never had any history of heart trouble or disease. He was fit and still young and…"

The thirty-something guy with the goatee shrugs. "I don't know the exact cause." He drones on about heart fitness, medication, cholesterol, and other shit that didn't apply to my father. "Or a shock. Did something happen today?"

It did. His investments. His life savings.

Fucking Barclay Reed and his "honest" daughter, Bethany Banks.

This is her doing, and if I have to crawl to the ends of the earth, spend every minute and every last dime, they will pay.

CHAPTER ONE

December 26 (Six months later)
Los Angeles

"YOU'RE WELCOME."

I know the self-satisfied voice on the other end of my cell phone, but I'm confused about his greeting. "Ash?"

"Yep."

We met in the oil fields of North Dakota a few years ago. The back-breaking work and the unrelenting winters weren't for him. After a couple of years, he succumbed to wanderlust and left, but we've remained tight. If I have a best friend, it's Asher Grant.

His tone tells me he can't wait for me to ask. "Okay, what am I thanking you for?"

"A gift. Granted it's a day late—how was your Christmas, by the way?—but I'm calling to give you one hell of a present."

Honestly, Christmas was rough. I did my best to keep it as jovial as possible, but it was our first season without Dad. Bret barely spoke, even to a gorgeous girl who stopped by and offered her condolences in whatever form of comfort he wanted. He's got one semester of college left…if he finishes. I've counseled him—coaxed, cajoled, and threatened, too. Bret seems to be majoring in booze, not so much economics. It would have crushed Dad to see my middle brother throw away his chance to be the first in the family to graduate. The youngest, Bryson, seems hyper-determined to act as if he's not grieving at all. He helped me decorate and cook. He ran from one party to another. Friends, music, revelry, and good times. I know Bry, now eighteen, wanted it to be like every other Christmas. It's simply not. And it never will be again.

"It was about as expected. Yours?" I ask.

"Tough without your dad, I'm sure. Sorry, man. My Christmas was fine. Great actually. I'm in Maui."

"Vacation?"

"Nah. I moved here about three weeks ago. I've been meaning to call you."

"I guess that explains why the card I mailed to Colorado came back to me," I say wryly.

"Yeah, the weather got too cold. You know I hate that. So when I was flipping through channels one night and I saw a show about house hunting in Hawaii, I thought…hell yeah. So here I am, tending bar."

"Like it?"

"Love it. I mean, the gig is decent, but this place has lots of pretty beaches and pretty women… What more could I ask for? But that's not why I called. Seriously, you should thank me now."

I'm betting Ash will say he's found some backdoor, barely legal way to fly me to Hawaii so I can celebrate the New Year with him. I can't do it. I hate to leave Bret and Bry now. I'm not Dad…but at the moment I'm the closest thing they've got. I'm also in the middle of selling our father's business. Negotiations paused for the last few days, but I expect them to resume shortly. My brothers and I are still talking about whether to sell the house here in LA. On the one hand, we're not sure any of us will live in it since I'm planning to go back to North Dakota this spring, and both of my brothers are away at college now. On the other hand, we all grew up here. It's the last vestige of our tight-knit family memories, even if it feels empty without our parents.

"Dude," I say to Ash, "if you've got some scheme…"

"No. You'll appreciate this a lot more. I assume you haven't made any headway in the Bethany Banks department?"

"None."

Ash knows how much I want to nail that woman to a wall because, while her father is still on the hook for the crime, she's getting off free. She had the nerve to send a flower arrangement to my father's funeral, but she only answered my calls to inquire about his money via email. Oh, she was incredibly sorry about everything, and she was looking into the situation. That was months ago. Until recently, she maintained her facade in the office. More than once since Barclay Reed's arrest, she's stated publicly how innocent her boss is and how she's sure he'll be vindicated. I kept thinking she'd eventually be charged, too. As his right hand and the face of Reed Financial, how could she not be?

Then, nine days ago, the FBI declared they had arrested all suspects in the case. Bethany is still roaming free. The woman who looked my father in the face in May and told him that his fortune was growing isn't complicit in this giant scam? I call bullshit.

After the feds' announcement, I drove to her secure office building in San Diego to demand a face-to-face explanation. I damn well intended to hold her accountable for what happened to my father. But Reed Financial was locked up tight. A security guard told me the business had been permanently shut down the previous week. Bethany hasn't been around since.

Furious but undeterred, I drove home. After some digging, I figured out where the woman lives. Early this morning I drove to her place, but her apartment was fucking empty. An elderly neighbor told me she left late on Christmas Eve with two bulging suitcases. She's collecting Bethany's mail for the foreseeable future since she has no idea when the shark will be back.

I'm livid.

"She fucking skipped town," I tell Ash. "I'll have to track her down again, and god knows how long that will take."

"Zero minutes, brother. Ze-ro."

My heart stutters. "You know where she is?"

"I'm looking at her right now."

His assertion is so crazy I can hardly grasp it. "She's drinking in a bar in Maui?"

"She's *working* at a bar in Maui. She started waiting tables here about…two hours ago."

My jaw drops. "Are you fucking kidding me?"

"I'm not."

Still, what Ash is telling me…it makes no sense. "Bethany Banks is serving drinks to tourists right now? This instant?"

"Yep."

"You're sure it's the same woman?"

"It's why I waited two hours to call. I wanted to be positive."

"The one who graduated summa cum laude from Stanford with a double major in business and finance at seventeen? The one who got an MBA from Harvard at twenty? You're telling me *that* woman is slinging beers at some island dive?"

"Hey, this isn't a dive. Well, not a total one. And I don't know about her pedigree. You're the guy who's memorized her bio. But I double-checked her face with a picture online. The woman I'm looking at is definitely her. To be honest, if I'd known the body she had to go with that face, I would have been motivated to find her sooner. Whoa…"

I grit my teeth. I give zero fucks about Bethany Banks's body. I only care about holding her responsible for her actions. "Before I chase her halfway across the ocean, I need to be sure it's her."

Ash tsks. "I figured you'd say that. She introduced herself as Beth. And I can tell she's never waited tables in her life. But if you want absolute proof, I'm texting you a picture right now. I took it ten minutes ago while I pretended to look at my phone as she was picking up drinks. See for yourself."

A few seconds later, an image pops up in my text messages. I tap on the thumbnail. My entire body flares hot at the platinum blonde with the green eyes, delicate face, and revealing-as-hell bikini top. Who cares if she's banging when she's a cold-hearted bitch?

I force myself to compare this picture to others I've snagged from the Internet. Then I turn arctic cold. "That's her."

"Like I said… You're welcome."

"Oh, my god. Thanks, man. You saved me weeks of digging and probably a few thousand dollars in private investigators. Hiring one was my next move."

"No need. Just hop on over to Maui. And bonus? Tropical New Year."

The timing is terrible. But I have to go. I can't let the little scam artist disappear again.

Holy shit, am I really going to jet on the first plane to Hawaii? It's crazy and impulsive. And my last recourse.

But once I get to Maui…then what? Somehow, I have to prove Bethany Banks is no angel. If I charge in like a bull and make accusations or demands, will she even speak to me? Or will she simply vanish when the pressure gets too intense again?

In the back of my head, I remember my father telling me how much I'd like Bethany, what a wonderful woman she is, and that I should date her. Blah, blah, blah.

I'm not sure what to do or how to handle the situation, but I shout for my brothers, both of whom are nursing hangovers. When they finally stumble downstairs and give me groggy what-the-fuck glares, I sit them down.

"I'm going to Maui for a few days. I'm trusting you two to behave and not burn the house down. No parties. Keep the loudness to a minimum so the neighbors don't freak. I don't care if you have a girl over. I don't care if you drink. But if you do, don't drive. I'll call you when I can."

I've got my head in my phone, already looking for the next available flight, when Bry stands. "You're just leaving us for some tropical vacation? It's the fucking holidays."

"This is business. I found Bethany Banks and I'm going to get some goddamn answers so that Dad can hopefully rest in peace." *And I don't have to live with the regret of failing him.*

IT'S AFTER MIDNIGHT when I land in Maui. Thank God there was one seat left on a flight that departed LAX just after eight p.m. I had barely enough time to throw a few things in a duffel and prod Bret into dropping me off at the airport. I raced onto the plane as the flight attendant called for final boarding.

After a long but uneventful flight, I trudge off the aircraft and into the airport that's not like one I've ever seen. It's almost quaint. And after I leave the arrival area, it's open to the tropical night air.

Ash is waiting for me in baggage claim with a wide smile and a tan that people don't usually have in December unless they're getting it chemically…or living in the tropics.

"Hey, man," he greets me with a shoulder bump and a back slap. "You look like shit."

"I feel like shit. Long-ass flight."

"You've been flying back and forth between LA and North Dakota too much, trying to juggle a pair of demanding businesses."

I nod. "And dealing with my crazy younger brothers."

"When was the last time you got drunk?"

"I can't even remember. Labor Day, I think."

"We'll have to fix that pronto." Then he leans in and drops his voice. "Do I dare ask the last time you got laid?"

I huff. "Even longer. All I've done since Dad died is work and solve a never-ending string of problems."

"We'll definitely have to fix that, too. Because I don't know how you're not going crazy or blind."

Despite the tension, I laugh. Ash has been a good balance for me lately. I can usually find the humor and fun in almost any situation. But for the last six months, I've sucked at it.

"I don't know, either." I shrug. "But you're probably right."

He glances at my duffel. "Any other bags?"

I shake my head. "No time. I figured I could pick up anything I forgot on the island."

"Totally. And like I said earlier, I don't have a big pad, but you're welcome to crash on my sofa while you're here."

"Thanks." I clap him on the back. "Really. I was willing to spend whatever time and money I needed to find Barclay Reed's accomplice. You saved me a lot of both."

"You should have seen my face when she walked up to the bar and introduced herself as Beth. She probably thought I was stupid or lust-struck because I gaped like an open-mouthed mute." He laughs at himself. "But I didn't let on that I knew who she was. I figured that would send her running."

I nod. "That's why I have to devise a plan. I'm here. To get closure, I need to be. But I'm not sure how to proceed. I can't bust in and start demanding answers."

Ash nods. "You've already done that over the phone."

"Exactly. She knows my name, so the minute I get in her face and tell her who I am…"

"She'll shut down and sneak out again."

"Yep. If she hadn't fled San Diego and left all my questions unanswered, I might have believed she'd cough up information—if not own up to her crimes—when cornered. Now? I'm sure she'll only slither away. I can't risk it."

Ash strides beside me, obviously thinking. "So you need another angle."

"Yeah, something she won't see coming. After working with her today, do you know anything about her? Did she talk about herself at all?"

"No. She was standoffish. I tried to engage her once or twice while she waited for me to mix her drinks. The only thing she divulged was that she'd never been to Hawaii and that she's staying with family."

"Family?" I try to think back through everything I know about this woman. I've studied her life. I know her history. I don't remember anything about relatives except her mother. "That's bullshit. Her mom finally married for the first time two years ago and lives in Salt Lake City."

"What about her dad?"

Barclay Reed. That Bethany is his daughter is a fact they've somehow managed to keep mostly under wraps for three decades. But I seem to remember the douchebag had kids by his wife.

I pluck out my phone and start surfing. "Okay, you're right. Her dad has three kids. And they all live on the island. Oh, shit. Her half sister is married to Noah Weston."

"The famous quarterback?"

"Yeah."

"Wow. That's cool. Think that's who she's visiting?"

I shrug. "I'll find out."

I'm not entirely sure how the knowledge will help me, but learning as much as possible about my enemy can't hurt. But to get her to confirm that—or even have a conversation with her—I'm pretty sure I only have one unpalatable option.

"How are you going to do that?"

"Paste on a smile and make nice with her. Eventually gain her trust and encourage her to confide in me."

He scowls. "Can you act that well?"

Great question. "I have to."

Ash shakes his head as we hit the front of the airport and emerge into the breezy Maui night. It's warm and slightly sultry. I've spent my last four Decembers in North Dakota, so this is a huge change. And I admit, not an unwelcome one.

He leans closer. "Maybe you should kill two birds with one stone and seduce her."

I look at him as if he's gone crazy. "I'm *not* touching that woman."

"You're going to take one look at her and want to. I guarantee it. You can warm her up faster and end your dry spell all at once. Getting your pound of flesh—literally—is a genius idea. Damn, I'm full of holiday gifts."

I want to refute Ash, but I've seen pictures of Bethany. I can't deny she's gorgeous. If she was any other woman I didn't already hate, I would relish the chance to tempt her into bed.

I drop my duffel in the trunk of Ash's beat-up sedan. "Not happening. I'll think of something else."

He shrugs like I'm crazy. "Good luck with that. She didn't want to make nice with anyone yesterday. You really should consider giving her big *O*s. Nothing opens a woman up faster."

Even if she's the most attractive female on the planet, I refuse to give Bethany Banks an ounce of pleasure. "Nope."

"Did you come this far to fail? Seriously, I don't see her cozying up to anyone. That woman is determined to succeed at whatever she does, almost like she has something to prove. Yesterday, she was terrible her first two hours on the job. Then my manager came out and gave her a few pointers. She excused herself for five minutes, came back reading her phone, then... After that, it was as if she'd been waiting tables for months. She learned *fast*."

I'm not surprised. "She's seriously intelligent. Hell, she's a Mensa member."

"Huh. So she's smart and stunning. Does the woman have any flaws?"

"Her moral character, dipshit. She swindled dozens of people out of hundreds of millions of dollars."

Ash scowls. "Are you sure? If she made all this money off of her victims, why isn't she living the high life somewhere? Why is she waiting tables?"

It's a fair question, one I've considered. One I admittedly don't have an answer for. Sure, the feds still have her legal bank accounts frozen, but if she's got the stolen cash parked offshore, why isn't she living the high life now? "I'll find that out, too."

Because if I can track down other people's money, maybe I can track down my father's. And I can prove Bethany Banks is guilty so she can go to jail—where she belongs. I don't know how or why the FBI overlooked her as a suspect. Did she somehow con her way out of prison time? I don't know, but I'm going to figure it out and right this injustice.

CHAPTER TWO

WHEN MY PHONE rings at two in the afternoon the following day, I answer Ash's call immediately. "Well?"

"Brush off your rusty bartending skills. You're in. You start in three hours."

I let out a sigh of relief. *Game on.*

Last night, Ash and I stayed up, plotting the best tactic for me to interact with Bethany. If I'm going to win her over and be her pal, I can't pose as a customer who buys a drink or two. I need time with her. Working together seems like the smartest ploy. Since Ash is in good with the manager, he can give me the same shifts as Bethany. She and I will have being new on the job and new to the island in common. After those conversation starters, I'll figure out how to build from there.

"Thanks, man. I owe you."

"No sweat. I'll be by to pick you up in an hour. We'll grab a bite and head in to work."

"Great."

I get cleaned up, check in on my brothers and Howie, who's running my business back in North Dakota. Then pace while I wait for Ash. I try to nail down my opening approach—what I'll say to coax her into talking to me, how I'll thaw her ice.

By the time Ash arrives, I've got a rough plan in my head, and it starts with flattery. Don't most people like to be buttered up? Then I'll give her some aw-shucks, fish-out-of-water crap while I play on whatever sense of adventure she has about exploring our beautiful surroundings. By this time tomorrow, I'm hoping she sees me as a budding acquaintance who may soon become a confidant.

After a quick lunch at Zippy's by the airport, we head to Lahaina. "This place is tourist central, being near the hotels and right on the beach. We'll be busier as the night wears on. But you'll have a few hours to acclimate to the bar—and sidle up to your victim."

"She is *not* the victim." My father was, and he's no longer here to defend himself. That's my job.

Ash winces, contrite. "Sorry. Bad choice of words. I meant your target."

"I know. I'm just…" Touchy? Nervous? No, uncomfortable.

The truth is, I'm not loving any of this. Deception goes against my grain. I'm usually honest, even painfully blunt at times. I try to stay friendly about it, but I make my point without mincing words. Hell, I work in oil fields, so that wouldn't fly anyway. But I can't handle Bethany Banks as if she's a fellow oil man. She plays cunning corporate games like an expert. The only way I'll have a chance to beat her is to convince her I'm no threat at all.

I try to quell my irritation. I have to do this. For myself. For my brothers. But mostly, for Dad. He deserves justice.

When we pull up to the bar, two things hit me right away. First, despite Ash's protests, it's a dive. Granted, it's a dive with charm, but the place looks as if it's been here at least forty years, most of them without significant upgrades or improvements. Second, every single person appears to be having a great time—except the petite blonde who's carrying a serving tray, wearing a strappy white bikini top and denim short-shorts, walking in my direction with shoulders squared and strides economical.

Her wide-set eyes, surrounded by a thick fringe of dark lashes, hit me like a sucker punch of green. Wisps of platinum hair manage to soften the sharp angles of her face, but her full mouth pressing into a severe line shouts a silent keep-away. Her cleavage, however—which looks one-hundred-percent real—lures me closer. I can't help but gape as, chin raised, she strides past me, heading for the bartender on duty with purpose.

"*That's* Bethany Banks?" I whisper to Ash, fighting my instant erection.

He merely sends me an I-told-you-so grin.

Damn. She's fucking hot. Not just kind of. Not just a little. She's smokin'. She's a full-blown, five-alarm, inferno-inducing blaze. As much as I hate to acknowledge that, why lie?

Her pictures did *not* do her justice. They all made her look like a corporate drone. This woman… Whoa.

I don't stop to consider all the reasons I shouldn't. I turn and watch her walk away.

The view from the back is equally stunning. Delicate strands of her pale hair tumble from a loose bun and brush her slender nape. Her intricate bikini top crisscrosses her shoulder blades and wraps around her narrow rib cage, the white fabric emphasizing the faintly peachy glow of her skin. Her hips, wrapped snugly in well-worn denim, flare below her tiny waist and sway enticingly with every step.

"Put your tongue back in your mouth if you're not going to seduce her," Ash whispers in my ear.

I rip my gaze from her to glare at him. But why bite his head off when he's right?

"Yeah. I just…" I blow out a breath. "You warned me."

"And you didn't believe me. We need to get you laid."

I suspect Ash is right…but suddenly I'm wondering who the hell will divert my attention when Bethany so thoroughly snagged it. She's the enemy…and my dick doesn't care.

"Why don't you show me the ropes for now?" I suggest.

We head to the back and meet Andy, the manager. He's nice enough. My guess is that he runs this bar because his real passion is surfing and this pays the bills.

"Glad to have you on board. We always need seasonal help around the holidays, and I'm expecting New Year's to be a zoo. How long can you stay?"

"A couple of weeks. I'm flexible." Not really, but I have to be.

"Awesome. Glad you were able to start today. Terry is going home sick," he says of the bartender on duty now. "He claims he's getting the flu. I'm hoping he's just hungover. I'll let Ash give you the quick tour since you're buddies and he's the best."

"Thanks for hiring me on short notice." I hold out my hand. "I'll work hard."

And I will. I hate half-assing anything, and bartending is usually fun.

"Holler if you have any more questions Ash can't answer." He nods dismissively and turns back to a stack of papers on his desk, so we head for the door. "Oh, hey. Wait."

We turn to face him again.

"What's up?" Ash asks.

"Can one of you keep an eye on Beth? She's getting hit on a lot, which I told her to expect. But one creepy guy who was here last night is here again today. He seems awfully determined."

"The one in the loud Hawaiian shirt with the matching personality?" my buddy asks.

"That one. He parked his ass in her station as soon as we opened. He's been messing with her ever since."

"I'll take care of it," I chime in.

First, when I bartended on the side in the past, I saw a lot of the girls struggle with dirtbags who refused to understand that no means no. Second, coming to her rescue will be a great way to meet Bethany and start gaining her trust. I refuse to think about how excited my libido is to spend time with her.

"Thanks, Clint."

With that, Andy dismisses us. Ash and I file down the hall.

My buddy laughs. "You in the role of Bethany's protector. Oh, the irony…"

"Hey, I'm not out to hurt her. I just want justice. I have no doubt she helped to swindle those people, so she deserves to pay as the law provides."

"Fair enough. But, um…she clearly flips your switch. How are you going to keep your paws off her?"

Bethany Banks turning me on visually is fucking inconvenient. I'm sure that once I start talking to the woman, her personality will quickly turn me off. "I'll work it out."

I follow Ash behind the bar, where he claps Terry on the back in greeting. The guy turns, looking pale and clammy, mumbles that he feels like death warmed over, then drags his ass out of the place.

"I don't think that's a hangover," I mutter.

"Nope. If Terry is down for the count, the next few days are going to be insane." Ash sighs. "Ready for the madhouse?"

"Let's do it."

It takes me less than ten minutes to learn how the bar is set up, where the spare supplies are kept, and who's responsible for what. Since Ash and I have also bartended together before, this won't be hard. Then he introduces me to the other waitress on duty, Montana. She's a sultry brunette with dark eyes, golden skin, and big tits. Honestly, she's usually my speed in women.

And yet as we're chatting and she's flirting, my gaze keeps straying to Bethany. What is it about her? She's beautiful, but what else? Is it her aloofness? Maybe. I want to figure her out so I can understand why a brilliant woman, surely capable of making her own fortune, would help her father fleece people. The angry part of me wants to grasp how she managed not to get caught. Mostly, I fear the attraction is chemical and, regardless of what logic tells me, I want to nail her.

Fuck.

When a customer calls for a refill, Montana jaunts off with a wink. Ash pulls me to the front of the bar. "Are you that rusty? Montana would totally do you, and you blew her off."

I know, and the fact I'm not interested annoys me. "I'm not here for sex. Introduce me to 'Beth' and let's get this farce going."

As we approach, she sets a beer down in front of a guy who's fortyish in a Hawaiian shirt—like a lot of the tourists here. He eyes her with

25

excruciating intensity. She meets his gaze with an arched brow raised.

Since I know Bethany's vitals, I know she's already thirty—now five years older than me—so this guy might be her thing. He's in great shape. The little bit of graying at his temples makes him look distinguished, rather than old. My gut tells me, however, she's not only *not* interested, but she's silently rebuffing him.

Now I'm glad I told Andy that I would make her customer interactions my business.

Mug delivered, Bethany turns to leave. The man grips her wrist hard, his muscles flexing, veins popping, knuckles white. When she winces and tries to wriggle free, he clamps tighter and stands, jerking her toward him.

Fuck that. Even if Bethany Banks is guilty of a multitude of sins, she doesn't deserve to be manhandled by this jerk against her will.

I barge my way between them, shoving her behind me. "Do we have a problem here, sir?"

Fury pinches his mouth. He narrows his eyes. "This has nothing to do with you. Butt out."

"You don't have permission to maul the staff. I'm going to have to ask you to keep your hands to yourself or leave."

Beside me, I see Ash ready to jump in. I'm not surprised since he's never backed down from a fight.

"Do you have your head so far up her twat that you don't see she's a fucking bitch?" The guy scoffs and rolls his eyes. "Yeah, and you deserve everything you get when she chews you up and spits you out."

With that, the asshole tosses down some money and starts to walk away.

I'm furious. In part because he accused me of wanting her when I do. But mostly I'm pissed on Bethany's behalf. "That was uncalled for. You're not welcome back here unless you apologize to her."

"Fuck you."

"I'm serious. Just because you pay for your drinks doesn't give you the right to abuse any member of the staff."

He grits his teeth, upper lip curling up with contempt as he turns to

Bethany. "Fine. A thousand apologies."

The douche doesn't mean a word of that, and I want to pound his face. No, I'm not looking to become Bethany's knight in shining armor. But this kind of guy always grates on my nerves because he thinks he can treat all women like trash, and the only thing that matters less than them are their feelings. I hate pricks like him.

Unfortunately, I can't do anything else right now without ramping up the incident, instigating a fight...and probably getting fired. Instead, once he leaves, I turn to Bethany. I'm pissed all over again when I see she's gone tense, as if she's trying to hold herself together, and sporting a big red handprint around her small wrist.

"You okay?"

She nods. It's shaky at first, then she drags in a steadying breath. "Yeah. He might be the first to think he can demand something more than a drink. But like Andy said, he won't be the last. I'll get used to it. Thanks for stepping in. I'm Beth."

When she holds out her hand, I have to admit I'm impressed by her backbone. I've seen new waitresses shrink, cry, and ultimately quit when confronted with a customer that vile. Bethany simply picked herself up and now looks determined to carry on.

"You're welcome. I'm Clint. It's my first day." I shake her hand.

We touch. Heat flares and rolls through me, instant and scorching. If I wanted to fuck her before, it's nothing compared to the lust burning me now.

Damn it to hell.

As I stare, her pleasant smile fades. She stares, blinks. Is she feeling the jolt, too?

That thought makes the fire in my body rage even hotter.

She pulls her hand free. "It's my first week, too. You'll get the hang of it."

I clear my throat. "Yeah. Ash will help me. We've been bros for a long time."

Beside me, my buddy waves at her. "Hey."

She manages a muted smile, crossing one arm around herself as if she's seemingly uncomfortable.

"You want an ice pack for your wrist?" I ask.

She rolls it gingerly. "It will be fine."

Maybe but… "That dude needs his ass kicked."

"It won't solve anything. Besides, I'm a big girl. He won't surprise me again. I'll handle him next time. I've dealt with worse."

Like what? By her own admission, she's never been hit up waiting tables before this week.

"You don't have to do it alone. I'm here. Ash is here."

"Yeah," my buddy cuts in. "No one will let anything happen to you on the job."

"Thanks, but I've got it. Excuse me."

Bethany turns away to check on her tables. It feels as much like she's eager to get away from us as she is conscientious about her customers.

"And…that's exactly how she behaved yesterday. Polite but not friendly."

"With everyone?"

"Everyone. Andy, Montana, me, Terry, Samantha…"

Winning her over and earning her trust might be harder than I thought, but I won't let that deter me. "Well, the evening is young."

"Yep, but after five o'clock we'll start getting too busy for chitchat. If you're going to work on her today, you better do it fast."

Point taken.

"Anything else that needs to be done before the rush starts?"

Ash shakes his head. "I got it. You go do that."

When he points Bethany's way, I nod and look across the room to find her lifting a tray piled with empty glasses and plates above her shoulder, balancing it on one upturned palm. She clutches a folding serving stand in her free hand and heads for the kitchen, determination stamped all over her face.

"Let me." I stop in front of her and start to pluck the heavy tray from her grasp.

She swivels away from me, bristling. "I'm capable."

And clearly touchy. Did someone along the way imply that she wasn't? "Yeah. I just had a spare hand and thought I would help."

She softens. "It's unnecessary. You have a job to do, and so do I. I appreciate your help, but you can't rescue me all the time."

"How about just when you need it?" I try to joke.

She doesn't think that's funny. "I don't date co-workers."

I take a step back. "I don't, either. In no way am I propositioning you. I just don't know anyone on this island except Ash. Is there something wrong with me trying to be friendly? Did I insult you somehow?"

For a moment, she closes her eyes and hands me the tray with a sigh. "No. I'm sorry. I... Forget it. I won't let that jerk upset me again. I get what you mean about not knowing anyone on the island. I only know a few people myself."

"Exactly. Back home, I had a lot of pals and drinking buddies."

"Where's home?"

"North Dakota."

Her mossy eyes flare wide. "Being here must be a huge change for you."

"I haven't even been here twenty-four hours yet, but so far that's an understatement." I head toward the bar and set the tray down. "Back home, it would be below freezing. Our nights would be in the single digits, if not in negative territory. There would be snow, and the wind would threaten to cut me in half."

"That sounds horrible. But I grew up in California." She deposits the stand on a hook in a nearby alcove. "Other than the few years I went to school back East, I've lived in warm climates my whole life. What brings you to Maui?"

A few random details about myself shouldn't tip her off about my identity. Why would she jump to the conclusion that a guy with my name and background would be here for retribution, rather than a mere job? "I lost my dad recently, and Ash convinced me that winter here would be better than winter there."

Her face softens. "I'm sorry. Losing your father can be hard."

"Did yours pass away, too?" Will she lie to my face?

"No. We're…estranged. It's complicated." She waves off the questions she must see on my face.

Subject closed—for now. Though I can't say I'm surprised. We've only known each other for ten minutes. But it's all I can do not to scoff. Estranged? Is that how she describes distancing herself from the man who's taking the fall for her part in their crimes?

"So what about you?" I ask instead. "What brings you to Maui?"

The thaw in our conversation suddenly catches another chill. "I wanted a change of pace. Some well-meaning people convinced me to come here and give this place a try…"

She's being intentionally vague, and a million questions pelt me. I should look for the right lead-in question to steer the conversation toward her last job. But I don't because I already know she'll tense up even more and cut our chat short.

"Like it so far?"

She shrugs. "It's pretty. What I've seen, anyway. I got here late on Christmas Eve. I managed to get this job the day after Christmas. I've been working ever since. So I haven't seen much."

"Seems like a shame, to come all this way and not take in paradise."

She winces. "That's what all the people who suggested I come say."

"I have plans to see this island on my days off. My parents always wanted a second honeymoon here, and they never took it. I'm going to see it for them," I say truthfully. "That probably sounds cheesy—"

"It sounds thoughtful, actually."

"You're welcome to join me if you want. No pressure. I won't hit on you. It just might be nice not to see the sights alone."

Bethany nibbles on her lip for a long moment. The gesture shouldn't be sexy. It shouldn't make me want to run my thumb across the swell of that lower pout. It absolutely shouldn't make me want to kiss her.

But fuck, it does.

"I'll think about it."

"My first day off is Monday."

"Mine, too. I guess we're both going to work a killer New Year's Eve before we get a break."

"Looks that way. If you decide you want to come along, I was thinking about driving down to Wailea to see those beaches and maybe catch a bit of the southern end of the island."

"Thanks. I'll let you know. I'm staying with some…distant family right now. One of them has a baby due this week, so everything is a little up in the air."

I wonder who she's talking about or if her story is even true. "Totally. Like I said, no pressure. But I'd enjoy the company. It would keep me from thinking too much about the fact my mom and dad aren't here to see the island for themselves."

She nods, and I see sympathy flit across her features before she shuttles it. "I should get back to work." She glances across the room to find a couple looking for a refill. "Duty calls."

As I see more people filing in through the open-air entrance from the beach, I nod and head behind the bar. "When you need drinks poured, holler. I'm your man."

Shit, that came out wrong. Flirtier than I intended. A little flush stains her cheeks. "Thanks. I'll keep that in mind."

MY FEET ARE screaming uncle by the time the bar shuts down and we're cleaned up for the night.

"Holy shit," I mutter to Ash. "I don't remember hurting this much when I bartended a few years back."

"Eh, you've just gone soft. The calluses on your soles will come back."

I refrain from pointing out that working the oil fields is no posh job because Ash knows it and is simply yanking my chain. Besides, I haven't gone soft in any way. Staring half the night at Bethany made sure of that.

"Hey," he murmurs as he leans in. "Montana was asking earlier if we wanted to come to her place for the rest of the night."

I raise a brow at him. "Both of us?"

"I guess she's adventurous." He grins.

"No. Thanks, man. You go ahead."

"You're sure?"

The notion of sex sounds great…but I just can't get excited about this proposition or her. "Yeah, I'll pass."

Ash shrugs and yanks his car keys from the pocket of his shorts. "All right. Take the car back to my place. I'll ride with Montana and have her bring me back before our shift tomorrow."

"Sounds good. Have fun. Don't forget to glove up."

With a waggle of his brows and a flashy smile, he tosses down his dish towel and heads toward the flirty waitress. Seconds later, he slings an arm around her, and they're gone. Samantha, whom I just met tonight, shoots them an envious stare as she clutches her keys and heads out with a sigh.

I wonder if Ash knows that shy Samantha is interested in him.

Bethany emerges from the hall that houses the employee break room and lockers, slings a little purse over her shoulder, and heads for the parking lot. Instead of walking to her car, she stands under the awning and pulls out her phone. I follow her with a frown.

"You're heading home?"

She turns to me and nods. "As soon as I call for my ride."

Who is coming to pick her up at three a.m.? Family? A boyfriend she failed to mention? "I'm not sure it's a great idea for you to stand outside and wait alone. That guy who gave you a hard time earlier? I wouldn't put it past him to come back and harass you some more."

"You're right, but…" She looks behind her to find Andy locking up the bar, pocketing the keys, then sauntering toward his truck with a wave.

She can't go back inside. This is my opportunity.

"I have Ash's car if you want a ride home."

That contemplative lip-biting move tells me she's considering my offer. It's also wreaking hell on my restraint.

Why do I have to find Bethany Banks sexy?

"I don't want to inconvenience you…"

But she didn't mind "inconveniencing" people by taking hundreds of millions of dollars from them?

"Aren't you waking someone else up in the middle of the night to come get you?"

She hesitates, then nods reluctantly.

"Beth, I'm already awake. I'm already driving myself home…"

"But where I'm staying… It's not close."

"The island is only so big. How far can it be?"

"A good thirty minutes."

That would give me time to work on her, see if I can get her to start opening up to me.

I shrug like it's no big deal. "I don't mind."

She glances down at her phone, then back up at me. "All right. Thanks."

"Happy to help." I lead her to the car and hit the fob to unlock Ash's serviceable wheels. "It's messy, I warn you. Ash thinks organization is a four-letter word."

Bethany sends me a faint smile. "I'll pretend not to notice since you're doing me a huge favor."

As I back out of the parking space and exit the lot, I glance her way. Shadows cling to the feminine angles of her face. The silhouette of her long lashes curls against the night. She clasps her hands in her lap, looking nervous.

"You okay?"

She shrugs. "Fine."

Bullshit. "Beth…"

"Just tired."

I'm still not buying it but before I can say anything, her stomach rumbles. "And hungry?"

She gives me a self-deprecating grin. "Sorry."

"Don't be. I'm starving."

"I just never had time for dinner."

"Ditto. I've tended bar before but never in a place this hopping."

"I've never even waited tables, so this whole week has been a shock. It's really busy."

"Yeah? What was your last job?"

Let's see how she answers that.

Instantly, she draws up tight. "It was all paper pushing behind a desk. Something I'll probably never do again. Um, where I'm staying is past the airport. When you reach there, keep heading east."

Her change of subject isn't even subtle. I wonder why she thinks she'll never work in investment banking again. From her perspective, she got off scot-free. Why wouldn't she set up shop somewhere else, ride out a few years to let the heat die down and gain new clients' trust, then repeat her scam all over? But clearly, the subject is closed.

"No problem. Hey, we're driving past Zippy's. They're open twenty-four hours. What about a quick bite?"

"Oh, that's not necessary. You don't have to—"

"I could use the food." And the extra time alone with her. Who knows when I'll get it again?

"In that case…all right."

We're there in twenty minutes. The restaurant is small and well lit. Inside, there aren't many places to sit, but we order—she insists on paying for her own breakfast bagel—then we grab an open table and wait for our food.

The initial silence is awkward, and I wrack my brain for another conversation starter that won't get her back up. "Who was going to pick you up?"

"My oldest brother."

Maxon. I remember reading he's a real estate shark. "I thought you were staying with distant family."

Bethany doesn't answer for long moments. "I'd never met him until five days ago. It's complicated."

That shocks the hell out of me. Granted, Maxon is her half brother, but she'd never met him until this week? "Wow, I guess so. I have brothers. We're really tight."

"That sounds...nice."

Her voice is soft, almost wistful. Like she's envious? Like she wishes she had a close-knit family?

"Do you like him?" I ask.

"Yes."

No further elaboration. She's choosing her words carefully. But she's still talking, so I keep gently prying.

"Do you have other family here?"

"Two more brothers and a sister, along with all their spouses."

Two more brothers? My research indicated Barclay only had one other son, Griffin. But why would she lie?

"And you're just now meeting them?"

She nods. "On Christmas Eve, yes."

What the... "Tell me about them."

"I don't really know that much. The two oldest are real estate partners. They seem fantastic. Incredibly ambitious. They worked two massive deals right up until midnight before Christmas. Their wives are both sweet. Funny. Interesting. Perfect for them, honestly. And very pregnant. My younger brother is... I don't even know how to describe him. A genius. And incredibly driven. We all have that in common. Socially, he's a little awkward, but it's because he's always thinking about something technical. He runs a data storage corporation. He and his wife got married a few weeks ago and are officially moving here tomorrow. My sister is..." She sighs and I see the obvious admiration cross her face. "She's vivid, confident, snarky, full of life. She's pretty amazing. And she's married to a former pro athlete who couldn't be nicer. I'm just...trying to fit in with this big, loud clan." Then color splashes across her cheeks. "And I'm talking too much."

"Not at all," I assure her. "I'd love to hear more."

It's fascinating to see this woman I sense is usually self-assured feel so out of place. Clearly, this isn't a common experience for her. My head tells me I should be happy to see her squirm. Instead, inconvenient pity pricks me.

"Not much more to say," she demurs.

"How did you all finally find each other?"

She gnaws her lip again. She does that whenever she's not sure if or how she should proceed. "I actually met my younger brother in Seattle right after Thanksgiving. It was a business discussion. It didn't lead anywhere, but when I asked for his help about three weeks later, he bailed me out of a tough spot. When my siblings discovered I planned to spend the holidays alone, they invited me. Actually, they kind of insisted."

The snarky side of me wants to point out that it's no surprise she had no one to spend this season with. Who wants to spend time with a scam artist? But I'm human, too. I can't imagine spending the holidays utterly alone. It was a somber Christmas, just me and my brothers. But I would have gone batshit if I hadn't had them.

"Your family sounds awesome."

"They are, but I'm hoping tips continue to be lucrative so I can stop imposing on them and get a place of my own. I don't want them to think I'm taking advantage of their hospitality."

Is she pretending she has a moral compass? Or does she think that sounds like the right thing to say?

"You didn't have any more family left in California?"

Bethany doesn't answer for a long while. "Like I said, it's complicated. Who did you spend Christmas with?"

Just like that, she's done opening up. I count it as a win for now. I know more about her than I did when we walked into this place, and it's only day one. I knew before I started this ploy that I would have to be patient.

Even though it chafes to tactically retreat, I do it with a smile. "My younger brothers. They're in college and they're a pain in my ass, but I love them."

"So what did you do in North Dakota?"

"Besides freeze my balls off?" I joke, both to lighten the mood and to distract her from the fact I'm not answering that question.

My dad never told me too much about Bethany. He probably didn't know a lot about her personally—likely by her design. She's interesting…but not warm. My dad, on the other hand, would probably have told her all about his three sons, and probably more than once. I doubt she absorbed the information; I know her type. She would have efficiently taken notes about his family and tucked them away in his file, then peeked at them just before each meeting to make sure she appeared engaged and interested. If I mention Bret's and Bry's names, that might ring a bell. I haven't told her my last name yet—not that she's asked. If it comes up, I'll lie.

She smiles. "Besides that. I assume you tended bar?"

"Some. I did a little of a lot of things." All oil-related. Becoming a jack of every trade tends to happen when you own your own business. "Since my parents are both gone, I've been running their company, but I'm selling it. Not what I wanted to do with my life."

"Then what? Will you give up bartending?"

"I don't know what's next. I should get back to North Dakota, but…" Let her think I'm torn and lost and could use a friend.

"But maybe you'll wait until spring? To preserve your balls and all," she teases me.

"Which will damn near be Memorial Day, but maybe."

As she nods, silence falls again.

Our food is ready, and an employee kindly brings it to us. I grip my hot coffee and study Bethany as she plucks a napkin from the dispenser and lays it across her lap. She's avoiding my gaze now. She's nervous.

"What's wrong?"

Her startled stare bounces up to me. Is she surprised that I can read her? "I'm just out of my element. When I lived in California, work kept me really busy. I never had time for friends or…"

Dates. Boyfriends. Lovers. That's what she means. I frown. Her claim makes no sense. She has to be lying. A woman as sexy and intriguing as Bethany must have had men crawling after her since puberty.

"Anyway…" she goes on. "It's nice to talk to someone. Thanks."

I'm going to have to decipher her statement later in detail, figure out how her assertion is even possible. For now, I smile. I'm making progress. And I need to set her at ease. "You can talk to me anytime."

She takes a delicate bite of her sandwich, chews, then swallows it down with some water before cocking her head at me. "Why are you being so nice? If you were hitting on me, the answer would be obvious. But you haven't—thank you for that—but I'm confused."

By the fact we're relative strangers chatting amicably? Or because we're people who have no particular agenda in mind except getting to know each other? "Why? My motto is that you can never have too many friends. When we first met, that guy hounding you pissed me off. And I guess it's the protective older brother in me—"

"I'm pretty sure I'm older than you."

"Doesn't matter. Maybe it's the man in me. Either way, I don't like bullies. I especially don't like bullies who prey on women."

She smiles softly. "Your parents raised you right."

"I like to think so. Speaking of parents, where were yours this holiday?"

"My mother married not long ago, and I'm giving her and her husband some space." Bethany looks away and shuts down. "My father and I…"

Nearly a minute passes before I resign myself to the fact that she doesn't intend to finish that sentence. "You said it's complicated?"

"Very."

"Do you know where he is?" I know he's out on bail, but where is he living until the trial?

"Not exactly."

They aren't in contact? After being his accomplice for years and scamming their clients with him, now that he's been implicated and arrested, is she cutting him loose? If so, that's cold…

"Did you speak to him at all?"

"He left me a voice mail."

"And?" I want to demand an answer right now, but she's stiff and definitely uncomfortable. We'll come back to this line of questioning later, when I've gained more of her trust, made inroads. I can't expect that she'll spill all her secrets to me after a few hours.

"And that's it. How's your burger?" she asks.

Another dead end. I fight not to grit my teeth and nod instead. "Good."

She sends me a little smile, and I chow down a bit more, give her time to relax. I even volunteer to fetch her more water after she empties her cup.

When I return, I realize she's almost done with her sandwich. So am I. My limited time is ticking by too quickly. I need to try to push again, this time from a different angle.

"So I hear that barfly bugging you yesterday has been hounding you since you started working at the bar. Is he just trying to get you into bed? If so, calling you a fucking bitch isn't going to win him any brownie points."

"He's a jerk." She sidesteps my question.

"Absolutely. I wanted to punch him in the face." I can say that with all honesty.

When I glance at her wrist, I'm a little shocked to see bruises forming in the shape of his fingers. I don't think twice before I reach across the table and take her hand in mine.

There's that fucking jolt of awareness again. Across from me, I hear her smother a gasp.

I swallow down my hot rush of renewed lust. "Beth, this looks horrible. You should have let me get you some ice."

With a shrug, she tugs her hand free. "I'll be fine. I'm getting really tired and I'd like to get home."

In other words, I finally crossed the line and shoved her out of her comfort zone. She's done for the night.

Fuck.

"Sure."

Silently, she rises and cleans up after herself, then lifts her purse onto her shoulder. She looks nervous again.

I send her a smile I hope has some charm and motion her to the door. "This way…"

Bethany heads to the parking lot. I wish she hadn't thrown a baggy T-shirt over her bikini top. I wish I didn't notice her smooth, firm legs and her gorgeous ass sway with every step. Weirdly—and not merely because I need information—I wish she'd stop shutting me out.

In the car, she settles into the passenger's seat and closes her eyes with a sigh.

"Tired?"

She turns to me. "Confused."

I start up the car and head east down the road. "Why's that?"

"I know Montana propositioned you tonight."

She does, huh? "Why would you think that?"

"She told me she was going to. She asked me what I knew about you."

Oh, this is interesting. "So why are you confused?"

"You turned her down, but you're driving *me* home? I don't get it. She was willing to…"

"Have sex with me?"

And Bethany isn't. That's her subtext as she nods. We're both fully aware of that fact, so why bring it up? Because, maybe, she's thought of me as more than a potential pal? If so, maybe refusing Montana will earn me more of Bethany's trust.

"I know. The truth is, I'd rather drive you home," I say.

Honestly, I'm not sure why I said no to Montana. She's fun, easy on the eyes, and even easier to get into bed. What's not to like? Back in North Dakota, she would have been the blessed cure for a blah Friday night. But now? Maybe I'm too into justice to give a shit about an uncomplicated lay.

Bethany blinks at me. "Thanks for making the sacrifice. You didn't have to."

"It wasn't a sacrifice." Spending time with Bethany is way more important than mindless sex. "I'm here on the island for a reason, and it's not to get laid."

"Wow. That's a refreshing point of view," she says, sounding even more surprised. "Can you head down Highway 36?"

"Sure," I murmur. "Refreshing, huh? Someone in your life a man-whore?"

"You could say that." Under her careful reply, there's a story. I want to hear it. But her demeanor tells me this is another closed subject—for now.

She spends the rest of the drive giving me directions until we pull up at a place that's seemingly in the middle of nowhere. I see a sign that reads SUNSHINE COAST BED AND BREAKFAST.

"You're staying here?"

She nods. "This is Keeley's business." I must look confused because she rushes to add, "My oldest brother's wife. She's got a whole yoga, organic food, and happy times approach to running this place. I think what sells most people on coming here, though, is the killer view and the charm. They haven't been open long, and she's already attracting some famous people. My sister and her husband, Noah Weston, were married here, which put it on the map. Since then, one of President Hayes's best friends, Dax Spencer, and his bride, Holland, honeymooned here. Rumor has it Shealyn West, that TV actress, and her new husband are coming here for their honeymoon, too. Keeley is really excited."

"That's great." It's impressive, but I'm more interested in the fact that Bethany is perfectly happy to chat—as long as the subject doesn't get too personal.

I make a mental note to broach "safe" topics next time we're together, lull her into letting her guard down.

"I'd give you a tour, but…"

It's dark, and everyone is probably asleep.

"I'd love that." Especially if it means locking her into spending more time with me so I can work her over. "Another time?"

As I pull up to the front and put the car in park, Bethany immediately opens the door like she can't wait to escape. Then she pauses. "Thank you for the ride. I'm sure my brother thanks you, too. He already has to be up in two hours, so I have no doubt he appreciates you letting him catch as many Z's as possible."

"Really, it's no problem. I'll be happy to do it tomorrow, too." I hope Ash will lend me his car again.

"Bethany," I hear a man call somewhere past my left shoulder.

I turn my head to find a figure standing on the lanai. He's tall. Even in silhouette, I can tell he's well acquainted with the gym. I can't make out his expression since he's in shadow, but the warning vibes he's sending my way are hard to miss.

She stands. "I'm here, Maxon. I'm sorry if we woke you up."

"When I didn't hear from you somewhere around two, I got worried. I sent a couple of texts…"

Bethany pulls her phone from her small purse. "Sorry. I didn't hear them."

Maxon steps into the light. Now I can read his expression. He's wondering what I've been doing to his sister that precluded her from hearing her messages ding.

True, I don't know this particular guy, but I know how most brothers think. Even if Bethany is new to their family dynamic, brothers—especially older ones, which Maxon is—are protective. He can either be my ally or my roadblock, depending on how I handle him.

I kill the engine of the car and step out, approaching Bethany's brother, hand outstretched. "I'm Clint." Shit. I need a last name. Obviously, I can't tell her it's Holmes. So I pull my mother's maiden name out of my ass. "Clint Dietrich. Beth and I work together. I offered to give her a ride home."

The expression I shoot him is designed to assure him that I would never hurt her.

He shakes my hand, takes my measure. I meet his gaze. He visibly relaxes. "Maxon Reed."

"Nice to meet you. Great place."

"Thanks."

A redhead with a little ponytail and a big, pregnant belly waddles onto the lanai, shielding her eyes from the headlights. "Maxon?"

"Everything is okay, sunshine." He turns to kiss her forehead. "Go back to bed. Bethany is home."

"Oh, hi." Then she frowns and looks my way. "You brought her home?"

"Yes."

Bethany cuts in, "Keeley, this is Clint."

I give her a friendly wave, less because she's several feet away and more because I have a suspicion that Maxon doesn't want me anywhere near his wife when she's only wearing a slinky bathrobe.

"Great to meet you," she says. "Thanks for saving Maxon the trip to town. Want to come in for some coffee?"

I'd love to talk to these people, see if I can get them to fill in some of the blanks Bethany is refusing to. I don't think Maxon will be too forthcoming, but I'm hoping cheerful little Keeley will be. But now isn't the time. Maxon is scowling, and Bethany looks displeased by her sister-in-law's offer.

"Thank you, but I'll take a rain check. I'll see you tomorrow, Beth. Let me know if you want a ride home then."

"Thanks again." She shuts the car door, then tucks her hair behind her ear, looking a lot more like a schoolgirl than a grown woman who's scammed people out of their fortunes.

Again, I can't escape the fact she looks nervous. Why is that her nearly perpetual state around me?

Interesting question… One I definitely need to figure out soon.

CHAPTER THREE

TWO NIGHTS LATER, Bethany sets her tray on the bar with a clatter and leans on the hard surface with a sigh. "Andy said we'd be busy on New Year's Eve. He wasn't kidding."

"I'd say we're in hell, but I'd be insulting the underworld," I quip. "I've been mixing drinks so quickly for the last hour and a half, I'm not even sure I've taken more than a breath or two."

"Same, brother," Ash chimes in beside me.

"Terry really isn't coming?" That possibility distresses me.

Ash shakes his head. "He went to urgent care this morning. It's definitely the flu."

"Shit," I groan. "The next few hours are going to be like the seventh circle of hell."

Bethany gives me a grudging smile. "My feet already feel like they've traversed rings of fire. I don't know how I'll last another four hours. At least the tips are good."

In part because she's gotten really proficient at waitressing. But also because she looks absolutely stunning with her pillowy lips painted red and a spaghetti-strapped black dress that ends mid-thigh. It isn't low-cut or flashy like Montana's bright red number. But it hugs her perfectly, and I've spent half the night staring at her. So have most of the guys in this place, including loud-Hawaiian-shirt dude. He's back—for the fifth day in a row. His behavior is borderline harassing again, so I've been trying my best to watch over Bethany. I can't deny, though, that I simply like looking at her.

I also can't deny that I'd like to do more than look. In fact, the raunchy fantasies saturating my brain are both making me angry and making it tough to concentrate. I need to snap out of my NC-17 daydreams and focus.

"You doing okay with Mr. Asshole?" I ask.

She shrugs. "About like every other day. He wants another Bud on draft. The honeymooners a few tables over both want Sex on the Beach shots and a fishbowl of the rum punch to share. Then I need a whiskey neat and a dry vodka martini for the two guys at the front who told me they're looking to ring in the near year with a meaningless fling and asked if I'd be interested."

I hope like fuck she said no.

My knee-jerk reaction is a kick in the balls. It's one thing to want her admittedly gorgeous body, but to be jealous?

Fuck.

I'd love to tell myself that I'm simply concerned she'll be distracted by a couple of tourists and stop focusing on the rapport we're building—the one that should soon start netting me the information I need. But I know better.

What the hell is wrong with me? I've known Bethany for a handful of days. We've only talked a few times. I certainly haven't touched her. And I'm not going to. Sure, the horny guy in me would love to peel off her clothes, lower my body over hers, and press her to my bed before I find some relief deep inside her. Even if I don't want to want her, she's attractive and I'm a guy. Lust is easy.

But this feels uncomfortably like more than mere desire.

God, I can't pleasure someone who hurt my family so much. I'm here to give Bethany her just desserts, damn it, not orgasms. But to covet her? No. Absolutely fucking no.

"They sound like douches. What did you tell them?" I do my best to sound nonchalant. "Interested?"

Logic tells me she's not. In fact, she doesn't seem interested in any man, me included. Because some other guy who apparently couldn't keep his pants zipped burned her, so she finds me "refreshing?" Maybe. But one thing I do know? Since we met, Bethany hasn't acted like a duplicitous criminal mastermind. She works hard, does her job, and refuses to fraternize. Then I take her home alone because Ash seems glued to Montana these days. During the drive, I try to coax her to open up to me…but it's as if the bit she confided the other night scared her from revealing more.

I'm hoping tonight will be different.

The last hour leading up to midnight is particularly grueling. Everyone wants a fresh round to toast the new year. Champagne bottles come out of the chiller, bubbly gets poured, glasses get raised. As people start the last ten seconds of the countdown, accompanied by a tape-delayed feed on the TV from Times Square, Bethany drops her tray on the bar, grabs herself a glass of water, and takes a sip.

"Five, four, three, two, one. Happy New Year!" the crowd shouts.

Beside us, Ash leans across the bar to mack on Montana. I look away—and my stare locks on Bethany. Around us, everything is pandemonium. Everyone is kissing, their lip locks somewhere between joyous and passionate. Between us, the air is suddenly and completely still.

The urge to lay my mouth over hers storms my brain. Can she read my thoughts? I don't know. She just gazes back, unblinking. What she's not doing? Putting distance between us.

I swallow. My blood surges. My cock flares to life.

Yes, I want this to be the year I get retribution for my dad. On the other hand, what if Bethany is innocent?

Is that even possible…or is that simply my libido negotiating with my head because I want her?

"Happy New Year," she murmurs softly.

"Happy New Year."

Ash elbows me. "Ring in the New Year right. Kiss her!"

I don't dare. If I start, I'm afraid I'll back her against the bar and seduce her into wrapping her legs around me so I can unzip, and we can get busy.

Finally, I settle for cupping her shoulder. It's friendly without being flirty, right? It's also not enough. Not nearly. Without conscious thought, I shuffle closer, lean in. I'm shocked when Bethany does the same. My heart kicks my ribs. Holy shit, is this going to happen?

Breath held, I bend to her, my face inches above hers. She bites her lip, clearly wavering and unsure. But breathless. Damn it, she looks as if she wants me to kiss her. How can I? Yet how can I fucking refuse when I want to so badly?

Her pouty, rosy lips lure me closer. My body is on autopilot. I keep leaning in, moving closer and closer, heart thundering. Anticipation buzzes under my skin.

I close the distance. But just before I brush my lips across hers, she turns her head. My lips glide across her soft cheek. I inhale her light, sugary scent, then jerk away in disappointment. In frustration. I'm full of recriminations, even though not kissing her is for the best.

Fuck, I need to get my head together. I also need to lighten the mood between us.

"Back to work for me," I quip as I somehow find the will to step back. "I'll get those drinks you asked for."

"Thanks," she murmurs, then gulps down the last of her water nervously before bustling to a nearby table to pick up empty glasses and cash out their tab.

Over the next two hours, the crowd thins quickly. A little after two a.m., Andy locks up while the staff collectively groans in exhaustion.

"Good job, everyone. Beth, Clint, Samantha? I'll see you guys on Tuesday. Enjoy your day off."

"See you." I wave at him.

Predictably, Ash tosses me his car keys and disappears with Montana again.

When I look for Bethany, she's standing at the far end of the overhang and tapping on her phone.

"Ready to head home?"

She hesitates. "I'm sure you're way too tired to drive me. Maxon volunteered—"

"Are you bailing because of what didn't happen between us tonight?"

For a moment, I think she's going to demur, but she finally nods. "I didn't mean to…"

Get that close to me. As much as her last-minute cold shoulder grated on me, I'm glad now it happened. I don't need my head clouded by Bethany. I still have a million and one problems. Fixating on how much I want to fuck her won't help.

"It's cool," I downplay our almost-kiss. "Look, we're friends, right? It would have just been a friendly New Year's peck in the moment. It wouldn't have meant anything."

A little frown steals across her face. "Sure. And nothing personal, but I have a lot happening in my life right now. I don't need anything romantic. Not that you see me that way. I'm older than you, after all."

"Not that much."

"Enough that we probably shouldn't be a thing."

Five years is nothing, and if Bethany were the target of my lust rather than my retribution, I wouldn't give a shit how much older she was. She's crazy if she thinks that matters to me one bit. But if that gives her some false sense of security, fine by me.

I give her a noncommittal shrug. "How about that ride home? There's no reason to wake Maxon when I'm already up."

"Actually, they're awake. All my siblings and their spouses gathered to celebrate the New Year, so…"

"Beth…" I give her my best let's-be-reasonable tone. "You'd have to wait at least thirty minutes until Maxon arrives, and I'd have to stand here and wait with you. I'm not leaving you alone so Mr. Asshole can find you and harass you some more." Then I notice she's sporting fresh finger-shaped bruises on her other arm. Instantly, my temper explodes. "Did he do this to you?"

"It's all right. I elbowed him in the ribs and told him to keep his hands off me or to get the hell out. He backed off."

Maybe, but for how long?

Damn it, I wish I hadn't somehow missed seeing him grabbing her again. What the hell does this douche want? He must know Bethany is not going to sleep with him. "It's not all right. Did you tell Andy?"

Suddenly, her phone dings, then she looks my way with a sigh. "Would you mind taking me home after all? Keeley is having contractions for the third night this week. Maxon can't leave her."

Fate is smiling on me. "Let's go."

Once we're in the car, I crack the windows to let the sultry Hawaiian air caress me. I've got thirty minutes to recover from my earlier slip. But how can I continue to be "just a friend" when it's getting tough to keep my hands to myself? If I tried to kiss her again, would she let me? Maybe. If I did, how much more betrayed would I feel if I proved her wide-eyed behavior is an act and she's fucked me over, too?

On the other hand, am I getting anywhere by being her pal? So far, no. I've been in Hawaii nearly a week and I'm no closer to proving she's a lying, stealing bitch than I was the night my plane touched down. I can't stay here indefinitely…

"Thanks," she says as I pull onto the highway. "As much as you've been driving me lately, at least let me give you some gas money."

When she reaches into her wallet, I stay her. First of all, I've made a few million dollars of my own, and if we ever find my father's money, I'll have another million or so on top of that. Second, I'm a little old-fashioned, thanks to my dad. Even if we're not dating, I wouldn't take money from a woman simply for doing her a favor.

"No need. I got it."

"I insist. Gas on the island is expensive."

True. But why would a thief be so adamant about repaying me? I don't have an answer for that, just like I don't have an answer for why someone who's just stolen hundreds of millions of dollars is working like a slave at a dive bar rather than enjoying the spoils of her scam. Is it a ploy designed to throw investigators off her scent? But if the FBI has publicly stated they've already arrested everyone they intend to, does she really need to be duping them?

"Nope. But if you want to give me something, talk to me. I like conversation with you."

It's probably shitty to assure her she's not beholden to me, then use her feelings to get closer. But I have to step up my game, work faster. If I don't, if I can't prove who Bethany Banks is and what she's done quickly, I have a terrible feeling life will pull me away from Maui before the job is done. Or…I'll get weak, kiss her, get her naked, and stop caring about her past. I can't live with either outcome.

"I don't know why." She shrugs. "I've said nothing interesting."

"I get the feeling you run deep. Honestly, I don't find that often."

She looks uncomfortable with the thought that I might be digging into her psyche. "I think almost everyone who reaches of age of thirty has had experiences, some that have left scars. I'm not unique in that."

No, she's not. But since I need her to open up fast, maybe if I offer something up personal she'll feel like reciprocating.

"I hear you. I've got scars, too. Do you know how awful it is to live with guilt?"

Bethany falls very quiet and drops her stare to her folded hands on her lap. "Yes. Every day."

Oh, now we're getting somewhere… But now what should I share to encourage her to open up?

"My mom died of cancer, and I was away from home for most of her illness," I blurt. Once I realize what I've said, I'm horrified…but I'm stuck. I have to roll with it. "Up until the end, I kept telling myself she wouldn't die, that she was too young and too healthy. That she would beat this. She'd always been such a go-getter. She tackled everything in life, so I convinced myself this was just a bump in the road. She was always upbeat when I talked to her on the phone. My dad tried to tell me it was serious, but I didn't hear him." I pause, frustrated that I'm choked up. "It wasn't until I came home to surprise Mom for her birthday that I saw how much the cancer had ravaged her and I realized I'd pissed away most of our remaining time together with my denial. I stayed another three weeks. I told her I loved her as she took her last breath." Tears sting my eyes. *Jesus...* "Burying her just about killed me. Even as they lowered her casket in the ground, I couldn't believe she was gone."

Bethany turns to me, tears shimmering in the dark as she reaches for my hand and squeezes it. "I'm sorry. Have you ever told anyone that?"

I can't speak, so I just shake my head and squeeze her hand back.

"Not your father or your brothers?"

"Dad was going through enough. My brothers were dealing with their own grief. I listened to them. I knew they needed it, but..." I couldn't unload on Bret and Bry.

"You don't have to be that strong for everyone. You don't have to be alone." She bites her lip as if debating the wisdom of her next words. "I'll listen."

"Thanks. I'm sorry for bringing up something that's so fucking personal." I sniffle back the threat of tears that just aren't manly. "I'm supposed to be driving you home, and here I go, bringing up a downer of a topic. If I keep talking about it, I'll embarrass myself."

She squeezes my hand again. "Then I can sit here while you get yourself together. You've done a lot to help me. This is the very least I can do."

I give her a tight smile. "Tell me about your mom."

"She had me young and raised me as a single mother. A couple of years ago, she married a great guy—a widower—and they moved to Salt Lake. It's been good for her."

"You two close?"

Bethany doesn't answer right away. "Not as much as I wish we were. She was twenty-one when she had me. I think she resented me a little bit for forcing her to adult before she was ready."

"No one held a gun to her head and made her have sex with your dad, I presume."

She shakes her head. "I just don't think she realized how much responsibility being a mom would be until I was in her life. When I was a kid, she always looked for ways to ditch me so she could party. I spent a lot of time with neighbors, babysitters, and my dad. He's older. And wealthy—or he was." She turns pensive, frowns. "I think from the time I was little I knew that she enjoyed extorting money from him to pay for my upbringing. Dance lessons, piano lessons, and lots of private schools. Dad wasn't warm, but at least when we were together he wasn't looking for ways to get away from me, so I kind of resented her for being a bitch to him."

Wow. For a woman who's barely opened up, she's suddenly shared a lot. And since we're skirting the topic of her dad, I urge her to go on. "So you're closer to him?"

She shrugs. "Yes and no. He encouraged me growing up. He made me believe I was smart enough to learn everything I would ever need to do great things in life. Up until the last few years, my mom thought the most valuable skill she could teach me was to squeeze money out of a man's balls. Apparently, I was a miserable failure at this. Anyway, I think falling in love finally brought her some peace, because she's a lot better to be around now. She's tried in subtle ways to make my childhood up to me, but I needed a mom when I was three, not so much now that I'm thirty."

That's pretty fucking sad. Through no fault of her own, Bethany paid for her mother's mistakes. She tries to shrug the pain off as if it's in the past, but I see it still haunts her.

I caress her hand with my thumb and squeeze her fingers. "I'm sorry. You and your mom have a lot to work through, it sounds like. You have time, though. You can still do it."

"And you can't. My whining sounds insensitive."

"That's not what I'm saying. I'm giving you the silver lining. She's still here for you to mend the rift. You said the other day that your dad left you a voice mail. Have you called him back? You guys still in touch?"

She shakes her head. "Which also makes me sound terrible because your dad isn't here anymore, either. Honestly, I don't know if we'll ever work our differences out."

"Did you fight?"

Bethany falls really silent. I hold my breath, wondering if she's going to tell me something helpful. Guilt niggles me for luring her into this conversation, but now that we're here, it's raw and stark and real. And I feel as if I'm beginning to understand her in a way I just didn't during our previous conversations.

"Let's just say that I recently came into contact with his unpleasant side."

Like she didn't know he was a douchebag all along? How is that possible? I want to press for more, but Bethany appears to be struggling to hold herself together.

"And you didn't like it," I finish for her. "I'm sorry."

"It was...a shock. I grew up thinking he was so proud of me. He always pushed me to succeed. I was in a gifted and talented pre-K program by the time I was three. I was reading and doing simple math at four. I never went to kindergarten, just jumped directly into second grade. I also skipped fourth grade, eighth grade, and did concurrent high school and college course work as a senior. School was really awkward. I was so much younger than everyone. I used to cry. Dad did his best to convince me that everyone was simply jealous that I was so much better than them and that I should ignore their crap. But the truth is, to those kids, I was a freak."

Shit, the picture she paints of her childhood is bleak. Against my will, I feel sorry for her. I wonder if that's why she had so little compunction about stealing from others. People showed her no compassion or empathy, so she merely returned the favor? Maybe. Is it possible she's bullshitting me altogether? Sure...but it seems unlikely. She'd have to be a really good actress. Not saying it's impossible, but how could she so realistically fake the guilt and sadness pouring off her? Then again, maybe that's how she scammed her clients in the first place.

My gut rejects that.

What if her father was the one responsible for the theft and she was swept up in the scam?

"You're fantastic, not a freak," I assure her in soothing tones.

"I'm pretty sure that, other than my siblings and their spouses, you might be the only person who thinks so. But...thanks." She smiles at me with forced cheer and extracts her hand from mine to wipe away tears.

Real fucking tears.

"You don't have to front for me."

"I appreciate that, but wallowing is no way to start a new year. Besides, we're almost to Maxon and Keeley's place and I'd rather not have them see me upset."

Good call. "Your brother seemed pretty intense."

"Maxon is protective. Griff, too. We might not have known each other long, but they slipped right into family mode. It's been…kind of nice. In some ways, they're a lot like my father. But in the ways that count, they're not."

"So was your dad married when he had an affair with your mom?"

"Yeah. Over the decades, he's had a lot of affairs with a lot of his assistants. I'm not his only illegitimate child. My youngest brother, Evan, came a few years after me. Dad even has a newborn by his last assistant, the daughter of a friend—who's predictably now an enemy." She shakes her head. "I think I overlooked a lot of his behavior for a long time, made excuses for why his wandering penis had nothing to do with his true character. But in the end, it did."

And she's disillusioned. That fact rings in her voice. So not only was her mom not someone to look up to, now she has to deal with the reality of her dad being a tomcatting, defrauding asshole.

The implications of everything she tells me have my head reeling. I need to think.

"Well, at least you have your siblings in your corner now."

"Seemingly, yeah. They've been way better to me than I would have believed or probably deserve. I'm grateful for that."

As we pull up in front of the bed-and-breakfast, her siblings, their spouses, and a few guests all spill out. The lights glow above the lanai. Tiki torches are lit. People laugh. Couples embrace. I see a lot of happiness.

"Speaking of…" she drawls. "Thanks for the ride."

"You're welcome. Looks like they're holding the party for you. Have fun."

She shakes her head. "I'm going to bed. They've got a few guests here this week, and I'd really rather not stay and be the sad third wheel. Again."

I get that. Even at a glance I'm envious of the cheer I see among the small group of people milling around the inn. "I'm sure you're not."

Bethany grips the door handle. "It's fine. They're all happily married, and that's something I'll never be. I've made peace with it. I'm good to let them enjoy their party." She opens the car door. "Thanks for the ride. Good night."

Before I can say anything, a big hunk of a man saunters over with his beefy arm slung around a gorgeous brunette's waist expanding with pregnancy. "Bethany! How are you? I saved you some champagne." Then he peers at me through the windshield. "You're Clint? Maxon told me about you. I'm Noah Weston."

I debate giving Bethany privacy and peace versus making inroads with her family and gaining insider information. It's no contest.

With a smile, I exit Ash's sedan and stick out my hand. "Nice to meet you. I'm a fan. You're killing it with the color commentary this season."

"Thanks. Other than that, nothing to be a fan of these days except the dad bod I might be working on." He pats what appears to be a flat, hard stomach. His arms definitely bulge in a tank top that leaves me little doubt he's stronger than fuck.

The brunette laughs. "You're so full of shit. You're working out harder than ever—and dragging me with you. My thighs hurt after yesterday."

"Hey, watch your language around the baby." Looking slightly tipsy, he presses a hand to her rounded belly. "We don't want her picking up on bad habits. Besides, if you want, I'll really give your thighs a reason to hurt."

When he winks lasciviously her way, the brunette laughs. She turns to Maxon. "Don't give him any more to drink."

"What?" Noah protests. "The night is still young! You want a drink?" he asks me.

"Sure," I say, then I turn to Bethany.

She looks torn.

I take her hand. "I won't stay long. I just…Ash is going to be with Montana, and I'm not ready to be alone if that's okay." I press my lips together and confess something that, even if it's manipulative, has been paining me all night. "This will be my first whole year without my parents and…I'm not sure how mentally ready I am for that."

Her face softens. "I didn't even think of that. I'm sorry to be wrapped up in my own crap. Come on in. Meet everyone."

Within minutes, I've officially met Noah's wife and Bethany's half sister, Harlow. She's just like Bethany described her—confident and full of life. I like her instantly. I can tell she's good people. Maxon shakes my hand, seemingly thawing toward me. Keeley pauses her pregnant walk to hug me and tell me glumly that the labor pains have stopped—again. Griff shuffles up next, seeming to take my measure. As we're introduced, he shakes my hand a bit too forcefully as if to let me know he's watching me and he's got teeth he has no problem using if I mess with his sister. I give him my friendliest smile to assure him that's not a problem.

By the time I've gotten the evidence I need from Bethany and turned it over to the authorities, I'll be long gone and none of these people's opinions will matter.

As unwanted guilt twinges me, Griff introduces me to his blond wife, Britta, who is also very pregnant. She's very sweet, too.

A tall, intellectual guy saunters up next. He might be smart, but he's clearly logged a lot of hours at the gym, as well. He introduces himself as Evan Cook. I've heard the tech genius's name. I had no idea he's Barclay Reed's son. Then he wraps a long arm around a beautiful African-American woman and introduces me to his wife, Nia, whom he says is also pregnant. Apparently, all these newlyweds decided not to waste any time before starting their families.

Next, I meet a few of the inn's guests just before they thank Maxon and Keeley for a great time and head off to bed. Single dad Trace, Noah's brother, picks up his sleeping son in his infant carrier, waves at us, and heads home.

Last, Evan's friend and CFO, Sebastian, comes out of the house with a cold one and passes it my way. "Beer?"

"I have to drive home," I say with a shake of my head.

"Just one," he says. "If you don't feel comfortable driving, someone will take you or let you crash on a sofa somewhere."

I hesitate. I probably shouldn't stay long. I don't know how Bethany will handle it. But I need to make inroads, get information. Plus, the idea of going back to Ash's crappy apartment to spend the rest of the night alone really does sound depressing.

"All right. Thanks." Then I scan the lawn for Bethany and see she's talking to Keeley and Harlow, but she's empty-handed. "What does Beth drink?"

He raises a brow. "I don't know. We've only met once."

"It's cool. I'll figure it out." I take a swig of the ice-cold beer, then sidle up to Maxon. "What does your sister drink?"

"Sauvignon Blanc. I've got a good one from New Zealand chilling in the fridge for her."

"Mind if I grab her a glass? She's had a rough night. It was killer at work."

Maxon nods as we head inside, toward the white, bright kitchen. "I told her she didn't have to take the first job that came along when she got here. She's so damn determined to earn some money so she can 'get out of my hair,' as she puts it and get her own place. I've told her there's no rush, but she's so damn stubborn and independent."

"That sounds like Beth."

"Beth, huh?" He frowns. "Look, I appreciate you giving her a ride home after her shifts, but man to man? She's not in a good place right now. If you're cozying up to her simply to bang her—"

"I'm not. We're…friends."

"I see the way you look at her."

That's not good because if Maxon can tell I'd like to fuck his sister, what else can he read from me? "I won't deny she's beautiful. But she's already let me know that she's not into dating right now and that I'm apparently too young for her."

"Pfft." Maxon rolls his eyes. "It's not as if you're sixteen, but like I said, she's not in a great place mentally to be dating…or anything else."

Personally, I think that's Bethany's decision and I wonder if she'd appreciate Maxon butting in. But I don't rebut him since I'm not actually looking to hook up with her, just make her pay for whatever sins she might have committed against my father.

Her oldest brother shows me where the wine tumblers are and opens the fridge to extract a bottle of vino when Griff walks in. He looks over his shoulder and spots his petite wife talking to Keeley and rubbing her back helpfully.

Then he focuses all his attention on me again, brow raised. *Cue the interrogation.*

"You're not trying to scam Bethany into bed, I hope."

I choke on my beer.

"Dude." Maxon rolls his eyes. "I already asked and I was way more subtle."

"Fuck subtle. I want information. And what's with the bruises around her wrists?" He sends me a pointed glance.

"That's not me. There's a persistent, handsy patron who keeps coming back to the bar. I've tried to intervene when I can, but it was so busy tonight that I missed his latest stunt."

"Why hasn't anyone thrown this guy out?"

"I'm going to talk to Andy about it on Tuesday because it's not right. But I gotta ask, why does Beth seem reluctant to stand up for herself?"

Maxon and Griff exchange a glance before the older takes over with what I assume is the more carefully crafted reply while he pours her a glass of wine. "She's in the middle of a rough patch now. She needs to work through a few things."

As answers go, it doesn't tell me much, but we're talking. It's a start. "Beth mentioned that she and her dad recently had a falling-out."

They look stunned by that admission.

"That's one way of putting it," Griff snorts.

Maxon hands me Bethany's glass, then elbows his brother. "Yeah. Our old man is a massive, bleeding asshole. It was just a matter of time before she figured that out the hard way, too. We should get back to the others."

Clearly, they aren't going to divulge more, but it's interesting that these two have an even less glowing opinion of their father than Bethany. Of course, I never assumed Barclay Reed was a great guy. He's been arrested, and the victims' stories circulating online of the clients who had trusted him for decades are heartbreaking. But he's going to get what he deserves, so I'm focused on Bethany.

"Whatever you do, though, go easy on her," Maxon murmurs. "She may not seem like it, but Bethany is fragile right now."

Griff grabs my arm. "And if we find out you've hurt her, we'll be all too happy to rip your balls off. Are we clear?"

CHAPTER FOUR

WITH THAT WARNING pinging around my brain, I head outside toward the people spilled across the lanai. Evan and Sebastian seem to be deep in an office-related conversation. Noah opens another bottle of beer, takes a swig, then wraps his arm around Harlow, who is talking animatedly with Keeley, Britta, and Nia. Bethany hovers in the periphery, hands clasped in front of her. The women do their best to draw her into the conversation. She smiles, clearly listening, but says nothing. I think that's less because babies aren't her thing and more because she feels out of place.

"Hey." I approach with a cold drink in each hand before I extend the glass of wine her way. "Have a drink. You've earned it."

"Thanks. I've got to sit. My feet are still killing me."

I wouldn't mind that, either, so I let her lead me to some patio furniture clustered on the corner of the lanai. She sinks onto a love seat, probably because it's closest. I ignore the chair a few feet away and sit beside her, following suit when she props her feet on the low table.

"Hell of a night," I say.

"I have a whole new respect for waitstaff. It's a hard job."

"It is. Bartending is also tougher than I remember. Or maybe I'm just rusty."

"It might feel that way, but you have the right touch. I heard nothing but compliments on the drinks tonight."

I smile. "Good. Since I started again, I've been telling myself that it's like riding a bike."

A smile floats across her face. "Probably. Like a lot of things, I guess."

"Yes." The first thing that comes to mind is sex. In fact, whenever I get close to Bethany, it's always on my brain.

It sucks being so suspicious of the woman I'm dying to fuck.

As she sips her wine, I scoot closer—until she stiffens.

Biting back a curse, I settle back against the cushions and remind myself that I should be focused on what to say next to Bethany, how to get her to open up like she was on the drive over. I have to stop fixating on how to get into her pants. Something has raised her reserve again, damn it, and I need to relax her.

Thankfully, I know just how…

"Let's play a drinking game."

"Like we're at a frat party?" She raises an arched brow at me.

"Like we're trying to forget our problems, be silly, and have a little fun."

Bethany glances around the gathering. "The rest of the women are all pregnant. They can't play."

"I meant just the two of us. We've got our cozy corner and some fresh drinks. Why not?"

"Or we could just call it a day and get some much-needed sleep." She sighs tiredly.

"Where's your New Year's spirit?"

With a shake of her head, she laughs. "All right, but only because it's New Year's and only because I graduated college at seventeen, so I missed all the usual party stuff."

"Excellent. We're going to play a game called Drink or Dare."

"I've never heard of that."

Because I just made it up. "It's like truth or dare, but if you don't tell the truth, you're daring yourself to take a drink."

She shrugs. "Sounds simple enough. But I'm going to bore you. I've led a pretty sheltered life."

I haven't, so this should be interesting. "I'll ask you a question first so you get the gist of it. Um…drink or dare. Have you ever had a one-night stand?"

Bethany presses her lips together. "I'm pleading the fifth."

I shoot her a grin, but wonder why she won't answer. "Then you have to drink."

She lifts her glass in salute, then takes a dainty sip of the vino before setting it on the table again. If I let her play like this, we'll be here all night.

"Nope." I hand her the wine glass again. "You have to drink all of it."

Her eyes flare wide. "Are you kidding?"

"Hey, every time I defer I have to drink a whole bottle of beer." And after a few, I'll probably be drunk as hell. But I'll cross that bridge if and when I come to it.

"I'm a total lightweight," she pushes back. "This is going to be a short game."

That definitely skews the odds in my favor, along with the fact that I probably outweigh her by nearly a hundred pounds.

With a little frown, she lifts the glass to her lips and starts imbibing. At first, the sips are small and controlled. But when she eases the tumbler from her mouth and sighs at how little she's managed to drink, she tries again, this time gulping the wine until she manages to drain every last drop.

"Fantastic. Wait here!" Before she can ask what I'm doing, I dart into the kitchen, past Maxon and Griff, who are strolling out to meet up with the others, then grab the bottle of Sauvignon Blanc from the fridge. When I return to the lanai, I refill her glass and set the half-full bottle on the floor beside the love seat. "Now you're ready for the next question."

She narrows her eyes at me. "Isn't it my turn to ask you a question?"

"Sure."

Her jaunty little smile surprises me. "Hmm… Drink or dare. How old were you the first time you got drunk?"

She's keeping things light, which makes this game easy on me. Me? I'll be pressing hard, but she probably won't figure that out until it's too late.

"Thirteen. I went to a cousin's wedding, and when the adults all got busy socializing and dancing, I dipped into the punchbowl. No one told me it was spiked. My mother was so pissed when my dad had to pull me out of the men's bathroom because I'd gone in there to pee but I was too drunk to find my way out."

Bethany laughs out loud, an artless smile brightening her face. She's always stunning, but this expression makes her beyond beautiful. The tinkling sound of her amusement is light and feminine, and for the first time, she's responding to me without first thinking. Right now, she's natural. She's real. This is *her*.

It's arousing as hell.

"I can picture you as a bleary-eyed teenager stumbling around to find the exit. Oh, that's hysterical."

"When I recovered from the horrible hangover the next afternoon, I found the humor in it. When my dad was explaining what had happened to my mom, he was trying really hard not to chuckle. But he wasn't terribly successful." I take a swig of my beer. "Now it's my turn. Drink or dare… Have you ever stolen anything?"

Instantly, her face closes up. I grit my teeth, mentally berating myself. That question was too much, too fast. Damn, I need to be more patient.

"That's a terrible thing to ask."

"Sorry. It was just random," I lie. "I'm usually better at this, but it's been a long day."

"Then why don't we end it?"

I take a risk and grab her hand. "Please. I'm enjoying my time with you. Would you rather have another question?"

"No, it's fine." She waves me away. "I need to stop making assumptions and being insecure."

"About what?"

"Nothing." She shakes her head. "You asked me about stealing. I'd rather drink."

Because she's guilty and she doesn't want to admit it?

"Living dangerously?" I taunt.

"That's one way of looking at it. Bottoms up." She lifts her wine and downs the entire glass in seconds.

Coupled with her almost nonexistent dinner, I wonder how much longer before she's feeling the alcohol.

As soon as she sets the empty glass down, sinks back to the cushions, and shoots me a slightly unfocused glance, I have my answer. The booze is hitting her. Now we might get someplace.

"What did you steal?" I whisper conspiratorially.

"I never said I stole anything."

"You drank to avoid answering me."

"Which means I'm not talking about it."

I slip into flirt mode. It's not conscious. I can't help but *want* to flirt with her. "Did you steal someone's heart?"

Instantly, she scoffs. "I wish. I've never really been in a relationship. I always put work first—and I was fine with that. Hell, I was great with that since my dad was my only real example of what marriage was. If that was supposed to be happiness, I wanted no part of it."

"Never?"

She shakes her head.

"You've never been anyone's girlfriend?" I can't fathom that. She's beautiful and obviously smart and surprisingly easy to be around.

"In high school, I was the age of an average freshman when I was a senior. The upperclassmen ignored me. The underclassmen were intimidated by me. When I got to college, all the guys referred to me as jailbait. No one wanted anything to do with me." She shrugs. "As soon as I finished my MBA, my dad put me to work. I wasn't about to date clients and I didn't have a lot of opportunities to meet other men. I didn't have any girlfriends I could go barhopping with, either. And online dating never held any appeal. Besides, I was too busy."

"But you've had sex?"

"Yes." She glares at me.

I want to know how old she was, who with, why she gave her V-card

64

to someone she didn't even have a relationship with. But my last too-fast question taught me that I need to slow down. So I'll keep a lid on my curiosity—for now.

"What about you?"

"I've had sex," I assure her, tongue-in-cheek.

"A lot of it, I'm sure. You're smooth. You look like the kind of guy who knows what to do with a woman. One of my first thoughts when I saw you was of your hands."

"My hands?"

"They look capable of stroking a woman and making her very happy."

Okay, that's the booze talking, but it's interesting to know that she's thought about me, even in passing, as more than a friend.

"Oh, yeah. What else did you think?"

"Hey, it's my turn to ask you a question. And since you sneaked in a few extras, you can answer me. Ever been someone's boyfriend?"

"Not since high school, but yeah."

"Why not since then? Why not now? Did something happen to swear you off relationships?"

Good question, one I haven't given much thought, to be honest. "No, nothing happened except I got busy with work and figured I had all kinds of time to find the right woman. And I want what my parents had. They were married for twenty-eight years, and I never saw two people more in love. A couple of my buddies put a ring on the first piece of steady ass they got, and now they barely talk to their wives because they have nothing in common and they're miserable. I want more."

She nods slowly. "I want what all my siblings have. I didn't know that until I saw the way they care and compromise. They tease and help each other and share everything." She sighs. "But I'll never find that. I grew up warped and I'm not sure I'm wired for relationships. Damn it, how did we end up talking about me again? No." She shakes her head. "Drink or dare. Who was your first girlfriend?"

"Well, if you mean the very first one, that would be Reah, whom I met in church camp when I was thirteen." I lean in and whisper, "We kissed behind a tree when we were supposed to be working on a camp production about the Nativity story. Then we got caught…and we both got sent home. My mom was pissed. That was a running theme during my teen years. But if you mean my first semi-serious girlfriend, the first one I had sex with, Demi and I dated our entire sophomore year. Over the summer, she took Driver's Ed and ended up falling for some douche of a football player from our rival school and broke up with me. I was pretty crushed for a while."

"But you rebounded, I take it?"

"Yeah, I did. With one of Demi's friends, Catherine. That was ugly for a while, but a couple of months into our junior year, I figured out I was dating her as a fuck you to Demi and let her go. I dated another girl while I was a senior, but when she got accepted to a college on the other side of the country and I decided to move to North Dakota to tackle a whole new way of life, we decided mutually to end things." I shrug. "That's it. She was my last 'girlfriend.' Now it's my turn. Who was your first sexual partner?"

"That's personal!" she protests, her voice slurred, her eyes glazed.

She's definitely well on her way to drunk.

"All our conversation tonight has been pretty personal, don't you think? I'm not asking you to share anything I haven't shared myself." I brush my mouth against her ear and have to restrain myself from letting my lips linger on her neck. "Don't worry. Your secrets are safe with me."

As I pull back, her eyes are closed. She shivers delicately. Am I getting to her? Is she thinking about having a relationship—sexual or otherwise—with me?

I shouldn't like that thought. But suddenly I'm hard as hell, so I do.

Bethany shakes her head. "I'd rather drink again."

"You passed on the last two Drink-or-Dare questions. The rule is that you can't pass on three in a row."

"You're making that up."

Totally. But I manage to keep a straight face. "Seriously, you have to answer…"

She frowns. "Fine. His name was Dalton. I was twenty and fresh out of grad school. My father set us up."

The tense way she's suddenly holding her body tells me it wasn't good. "Did you like it at all?"

"No."

Her answer is so quick and sharp, I'm worried. "Did he hurt you?"

She takes a long time answering. "Doesn't the first time always hurt?"

That isn't what I asked, and now I'm downright suspicious. "Did he force you?"

"No."

But something about the way she utters the word tells me it wasn't exactly her choice, either. I'm dying to know what the hell happened, but even as I sit beside her, Bethany starts pulling into her shell and putting distance between us.

I squeeze her hand. "I'm sorry if I brought up bad memories."

"Not your fault. You didn't know. I just…try not to think about it."

"We all have those moments in life we'd rather not remember."

Like my dad dying on my living room floor and me being wholly unable to save him.

Fuck. I need to get my head back in the game.

Still, the next thing that comes out of my mouth is way flirtier than it should be. "Have you ever found a lover who made you feel good?"

Bethany extracts her hand from mine, tosses back another glass of wine, then crosses her arms around her middle. "I'm passing on that question. Can we talk about something else?"

"You know what, sweetheart? We don't have to talk at all. Come here."

I extend my arm to curl it around her shoulders before easing her close. She's stiff, but she doesn't protest, merely sits beside me in oddly companionable silence as I drink the rest of my beer.

To my surprise, she lays her head on my shoulder with a tired sigh.

"You okay, Beth?"

"Yeah."

That's good. As much as I need the information and I wonder constantly if she's guilty, I feel so reluctant to hurt her. Or believe the worst about her. What seemed like such an open-and-shut case of criminal activity when I was packing my suitcase in LA to hunt her down in Maui now feels a lot less obvious.

Is there any chance the scheme to steal all their clients' money was purely her father's? That she somehow didn't know? Or am I hoping so because she's shown me her fragile side and I feel this irrational urge to protect her, even as I'm dying to take her to bed?

I don't know.

Still, I can't stop myself from opening my big mouth. "Sex should never hurt, sweetheart. It should only make you feel like the goddess you are. And if you've never found the right man to prove that to you…I'm here if you want me."

Silence.

Is she trying to decide what to say to me? How she feels about my offer? Is she shocked? Upset? Or intrigued?

After a few dozen tense seconds slide by, I risk a peek at her face—and realize she's fallen asleep.

Damn…

When I look up, I realize that everyone else has gone to bed. The lanai is empty. The house is dark. We're totally alone. And I don't want to leave Bethany's side, so I curl her closer, lay my head back, and shut my eyes.

SLOWLY, I BECOME aware of sunbeams dancing on my lids. My neck is bent at an odd angle and propped against something hard. I try to move, but I'm too damn stiff to do anything but wince. On the plus side, someone soft—definitely a woman—is curled up beside me, her head on my chest. My arm wraps around her small waist as I press her to my side.

At the feel of her, my morning wood becomes more than automatic and nothing less than insistent.

I risk opening one eye, my fuzzy brain scrambling to remember who the hell I spent the night with and where. The sound of the waves crashing on the nearby beach registers at the same time I look down to find Bethany plastered against me. We're still on the lanai, where we apparently spent all night cuddled together. And even though the sun is up, I'm in no hurry to let her go.

Except…I'm wondering if getting so cozy with her is a giant tactical mistake.

On the surface, I should be pissed at myself for sleeping with the enemy. After all, when I boarded the plane to Maui, I had no doubt Bethany Banks was guilty and needed to pay. Now, nothing is that simple or obvious anymore. Nothing is black and white. She's human. She's real. She's been abandoned, ostracized, and hurt. Some people might use that as a justification not to care about anyone else—and as a rationale to commit crimes. It's still possible Bethany did that. But the stories she shared about herself and the compassion she showed me last night after hearing about my mom…

Fuck, I'm torn. Who is she really?

I study her as if staring will answer my question. All I see is her pale hair tumbling from its messy bun in a silken cascade down to her plush breasts. Dark lashes lay curled against her rosy cheeks. Soft lips are gently parted in slumber. Her face looks so at peace, she appears guileless, like a sweetly mussed female, not a criminal mastermind.

Appearances can be deceiving.

Still, the Bethany I'm coming to know seems too human to treat hardworking people so inhumanely by scamming them out of their every last dime. For the first time, I'm giving serious consideration to the possibility that she might truly be innocent.

I don't like this indecisive gray area. My head keeps telling my libido to back the fuck down and stop trying to make it okay to want a criminal. My gut tells my head to stop being so quick to judge.

It's frustrating to be this unsure what to think.

Maybe it's time to examine the facts again. I first convicted her mentally because she was my dad's financial advisor. It seemed logical that she knew where his money had gone and how it had been stolen. But the feds arrested and charged Barclay Reed, not Bethany. She admitted last night that she'd recently encountered her dad's "unpleasant side," even admitting she'd made excuses for him. Yes, in the context of his wandering penis, not clients' financial transactions. Did she really mean both? I don't know.

It's possible Bethany was Reed's accomplice and that she escaped jail time because she's a cooperating witness. If so, that doesn't change anything. Helping to commit a crime still makes her responsible. But I keep wondering if she, too, was somehow duped by her father's scheme.

No clue.

And I'm right back to the beginning of this argument with myself.

Beside me, Bethany stirs, rolling toward the sun as her lashes flutter open. She turns to me, brows knit in confusion before her eyes flare wide with a gasp. "We spent the night out here?"

"Looks that way. I only figured that out when I woke up a few minutes ago."

"Oh, my god. I had too much wine. I never get drunk and—"

"It's okay." I cut into her panic. "You were tired, it was New Year's, and I twisted your arm into playing that drinking game. How much do you remember?"

"Some…"

Does she recall telling me about her first lover? About the first thing she thought when she looked at me?

"Don't worry. You didn't embarrass yourself."

"If you have to assure me of that, I probably did." She winces.

"You hungover?"

"No, thank goodness. And I know you're not because you barely drank. Have you seen anyone else this morning?"

"Not a soul."

She cocks her head as if she's listening for sounds from inside. "The house seems awfully quiet this morning. I wonder where everyone went... Do you want coffee?"

As she rises to her feet, I follow suit, scowling when she won't meet my gaze. Is she embarrassed that she spent all night pressed against me? Does she suspect on some level how personal last night was?

"Sure. That would be great."

Without even thinking, I drop my hand to the small of her back and guide her inside. She bustles away from me, almost running for the kitchen.

Yes, she knows exactly how personal last night was. She's feeling cautious again. Her walls are up.

As she turns on the coffeemaker and retrieves a pair of mugs from the cabinet, she looks decidedly nervous. I lean against the island and regard her with a considering stare. "Beth, in case you're wondering, we spent last night together platonically. I'm not going to jump on you this morning."

"I never said you were."

"But you act as if you're worried I might."

She retrieves the cream and sugar. "It's just...I don't make a habit of spending the night with anyone. Maybe waking up next to someone you've only known a few days is normal for you. For me, it's not."

I wonder how much sex she's actually had beyond Dalton the First, who apparently sucked in bed. Is it possible her experiences have been few and far between?

As sexy as she is, that possibility blows my mind.

"It's not normal for me, either," I admit. "But this isn't a big deal. We're friends."

"We are."

The quick snap of her agreement makes me think she's also thought about us being more. My cock perks up again at the thought.

Ignoring it, I lean closer and murmur softly, "I won't touch you if you don't want me to, I promise."

She shoots a skittish glance my way. I see the wary question in her eyes.

But what if I do?

"Thanks." She turns her focus to the brewing java instead. "I'm sorry. I'm handling this badly. I'm not a morning person, especially before coffee."

"And you're not looking for someone right now. Neither am I."

But the suggestion is between us now. I know we both feel it.

Her face softens. "Clint, it's not you."

"No worries. After coffee, I'll leave you to enjoy your day off."

I'll use the time to regroup and figure out how to approach her from a different angle, one that skirts the sexual tension brewing between us. I don't have a choice.

"No rush." She hands me a cup of steaming joe, then sets about making her own.

After a few sips in the awkward silence, she sets her mug down and scans the bottom floor of the house. "Hello? Anyone home?"

No answer.

"Maybe Maxon is at the office and Keeley went somewhere?" I suggest.

"It's New Year's Day. He and Griff both planned to take the day off. Keeley isn't going much of anywhere these days since she keeps having labor pains."

I shrug. "Did they text you? Leave you a note?"

"Good question." She goes in search of her purse and retrieves her phone. "Oh, they're at the birthing center! Keeley's water broke at six this morning. They want me to come when I wake up so I can be there when their daughter is born and I become an aunt again. That's so sweet." Tears fill her eyes.

There's no faking how genuinely touched she is that they included her.

"Finish your coffee, and I'll take you where you need to go."

"It's your day off…" And she clearly hates to impose.

"It's okay. This is more important than random sightseeing."

"Let me grab a quick shower and… There's an outdoor facility if you want one, too. I can get you a towel. Maxon has some clothes you can borrow."

A shower would clear my foggy head, and I need to be at the top of my game around Bethany. "I'll take the towel. I stashed some clean clothes in the gym bag I keep in the trunk."

A few minutes later, she's putting herself together in the cottage out back, which they call an ohana in Hawaii. That's where she's staying. I wish I could get into the place to search her personal belongings, maybe find proof of her guilt…or innocence. But there's no time now, so I enjoy the hell out of the hot spray and the morning breeze on my skin.

When I finish putting myself together, I wait for Bethany in the kitchen. A few of the inn's guests mill in for pastries someone left on a plate on a nearby buffet table.

When I hear the back door open, I turn to see Bethany enter. She's wearing a lacy white tank and faded jeans that hug her sleek thighs—and make me want to be sure she knows I'm a man. She's arranged her hair into a loose braid that tumbles over one shoulder. Platinum wisps surround her face. She's tossed on some mascara and lip gloss, and she looks amazing.

I don't realize I'm staring at her until she frowns. "Is this the wrong thing to wear to a birth?"

"No. You look great. Just marveling at how fast you were," I lie to cover my reaction. "My mom used to take forever, change clothes four times, redo her hair, paint her nails… We waited a lot when I was a kid."

She smiles and slings a small pink purse over her shoulder. "I've always been busy, so I learned how to make the most of the minimum. Ready?"

"Sure."

I lead her outside and we get on the road. The drive to the birthing center takes twenty minutes, and she fills most of the time by texting Harlow and passing the updates along to me.

"Keeley is dilating quickly. They think she'll be delivering in another hour or so."

Bethany looks worried we may not make it in time, so I drive a little faster.

"Is your whole extended family going to be in the waiting room?" Maybe I can use some of the time to discreetly talk to them.

She shakes her head. "In the delivery room. Keeley picked a midwife who believes that families should welcome babies together. So that's what she wants us to do."

"Wow." Thankfully, Bethany said family, which excludes me. I'm happy I won't be witnessing a virtual stranger give birth today.

"It's great that Keeley and Maxon want you there. Did you expect to be treated like family when you first arrived?"

"Hardly. I expected to be grilled at the least. Maybe even blamed and reviled. But they've been amazingly inclusive and understanding."

They seemingly have. Which brings up another question... Would these people really welcome a criminal with open arms? What are the odds she conned all of them, too?

"When did you first find out about your siblings?"

"I've always known. Dad never tried to hide them from me." She frowns. "Of course, he described his children by his wife as useless and ungrateful, so I never had any desire to meet them. I wish now I hadn't taken him at face value about Maxon, Griff, and Harlow. Well, about a lot of things, really."

"Evan, too?" I know she purposely didn't include him, but maybe since I tossed out the question, she'll take the bait and give me more information.

Bethany shakes her head. "Dad knew of Evan, called him 'the weird kid,' but they didn't meet for the first time until last summer, at Harlow's wedding. He always told me that Evan's mother was a money-grabbing whore and that if he paid any attention to his son, she'd try to extort him for more. I didn't learn until recently that Evan's mother died when he was five and, instead of claiming him, my father allowed Evan to be a ward of the state and shoved into foster care until he turned eighteen."

Her carefully arranged expression slips. I see glimpses of her disillusionment. She looks so much like she's hurting...

I steel myself. I need facts, not feelings.

"Beth, did you two have a falling-out because he lied to you so much?"

She nods. "You have no idea."

Before I can ask her to elaborate, Bethany's phone dings again. "It's Harlow. They've revised the timeline up. Keeley might be delivering in thirty minutes!"

"We'll be there in less than ten," I promise.

Bethany seems distracted for the rest of the car ride, so I don't pry anymore. I make a mental note to come back to the subject of her father, try to find out whether it's possible he lied to her about the scam, too. Now just isn't the time.

As promised, we pull up to the birthing center in eight minutes. I drop her at the door and thankfully find a prime parking spot close by. Not long after, I run inside the pseudo-medical facility, asking a maternal woman behind a desk where to find the Reed birth. She points, and I catch up to Bethany just before she disappears behind a set of double doors with Harlow.

"Thanks for bringing Bethany here—and so quickly," the pregnant brunette says.

"My pleasure. Where can I wait for Beth? I'm happy to take her home whenever she's ready."

Beside Harlow, Bethany's expression softens. She's surprised I'm willing to wait around? I don't mind. Sure, I have other things to do on my day off, but Keeley and Maxon may well spend the night here. It would be out of everyone else's way to take Bethany back to the inn. The logistics of the situation help me take every moment I can get with her.

"I hate to inconvenience you," she murmurs.

"You're not," I assure her. "Go be with your family. I'll find somewhere to wait."

"Harlow!" Noah sticks his head out the door. "You're here, Bethany. Good. It won't be long now…"

"No time," Harlow shrieks. "Come with us!"

She grips my wrist and gives me a surprisingly strong yank before she starts sprinting toward the open door, swelling belly leading the way. Bethany follows, shooting me a wide-eyed stare and a shrug. I start to sweat. Am I really about to witness a woman I've only met a couple of times give birth?

When we round the corner, the obvious answer is yes.

With one eye open, I wedge myself against the back wall on one side of the room. Thankfully, a discreet sheet covers everything I'd rather not see. Maxon holds Keeley's hands. Harlow scoops ice chips into her mouth. Britta gives her last-minute advice.

Over Keeley's rhythmic pants and the monitors she's hooked up to, the atmospheric music overhead abruptly goes quiet. Journey's "Don't Stop Believin'" takes its place seconds later, suddenly blaring from the overhead speakers.

"Who changed the music?" the redhead demands with a scowl between contractions.

"I did," Maxon offers. "That meditative crap wasn't working—"

"It's supposed to help me focus."

"Screw that. Journey will help you push like a champion. And it won't put the rest of us to sleep while we wait."

Keeley grips his hand tighter and leans in with a scowl, teeth bared. "So this is about you?"

"No, sunshine." He backpedals. "Of course not. But you're always making mixes for everyone else to encourage them. I've been putting this one together for a while. To show you that I'm thinking of you and our daughter. To tell you both that I love you."

Another contraction hits. The pain seems to ramp up. Keeley groans and sobs at once. "That's wonderful and terrible. I practiced my breathing to the other music."

"It sounded like whales humping."

Everyone erupts into laughter, including me. Before it dies down, Keeley bows as the contraction seizes her. She grips Maxon's hand with all her might and screams.

The midwife, a Hawaiian woman in her fifties who looks both efficient and calm, rushes in and makes a beeline for the mother-to-be. "I'm going to check you now, Keeley. You're probably close."

The redhead nods. "I think so."

Journey's rock anthem slides into the Kelly Clarkson tune "Stronger (What Doesn't Kill You)." It was one of my mom's favorite songs. She worked out to it while she could. She fought death to it. At the end, she told me that even though cancer was getting the last laugh, the tune had definitely helped her stay as strong as she could during her last days. For that, she was thankful.

I really wish she was still here. She would be able to read Bethany so much better than me...

"Nine centimeters," the midwife says happily.

Suddenly, Keeley tenses and squeezes Maxon's hand in a death grip once more as she growls out in agony. "Are you kidding me?"

"No," the midwife assures. "You're almost there."

"I meant my husband. What were you thinking with this song?"

I can't see Maxon's face but I swear I can hear him swallow audibly. "Giving you encouragement, sunshine. From one lady to another. Kelly has had kids. Birth didn't kill her, just made her more badass."

Keeley rolls her eyes, and I'm thinking Maxon made a decent save of the situation—until he opens his big mouth again.

"Of course, Kelly didn't wait until January first to go into labor and bypass a whole year's worth of a tax break..." he grumbles.

Harlow leans across the distance and slaps her oldest brother upside the head. "You just keep digging yourself a deeper grave, fidiot. Shut up while she's still letting you breathe."

Griff nods. "I admit that I can sometimes be oblivious, but—"

"You mean insensitive," Harlow cuts in.

Britta represses a smile and nods, sending her husband a fond glance.

"Whatever." Griff waves her away. "But even I wouldn't say something that douchy."

"But you thought it," Maxon contends.

When Griff doesn't answer right away, everyone laughs again.

Keeley giggles, too—until another contraction wracks her, her entire body jolting.

Maxon leans in. "Breathe, sunshine. You got this."

"You fucking breathe! I'm trying to—*ahhhh!*"

"You're doing great," the midwife encourages. "I see the top of the baby's head."

Evan pokes Maxon in the back. "Don't lock your knees. You've lost the color in your face. Medically speaking—"

"Save the explanation, babe." Nia caresses his arm, then turns to Maxon. "Breathe, buddy."

Evan frowns. "But if he understands what he's doing that may cause him to faint—"

"Don't you *dare* faint on me!" Keeley shouts, huffing in between her words. "Do you hear me, Maxon Miles Reed? If you pass out, I'm going to—" She jolts again. "*Oooh!*"

"One more good push, Keeley." The midwife nods enthusiastically. "One more, and you'll be a mother."

"And I'll be a father," Maxon mumbles. "This is really happening. Oh, shit…" He loses more color.

"What doesn't kill you makes you stronger…" Griff parrots the song still playing overhead.

"Bite me," Maxon growls back.

"How about you hold my hand?" Keeley demands of her husband.

"I am. Sunshine, could you let up a bit? I think you're about to break it."

"Giving birth is breaking my vagina!"

It's taking everything I have not to howl with laughter. Britta doesn't even try to stop herself. Neither does Harlow or Nia. Even Evan looks as if he's repressing a roaring guffaw.

Noah starts to sweat, then leans over to his wife. "Is this how you're going to be when you give birth?"

"No." She shakes her head. "Keeley is much sweeter than I am. You probably ought to wear protective gear the day I have this big boy. Especially a cup."

Half the color leaches from his face. "You wouldn't really kick me in the balls. Right?"

"I can't guarantee what I'll do if you get too close. That looks painful."

"It is," Britta put in. "My labor with Jamie felt so long I barely knew what day it was by the time I pushed him out."

"Are you kidding me?" Harlow looks terrified, then turns to her husband. "If that's the case, that's a definite yes on the cup."

He nods adamantly, then no one speaks again because Keeley wails out in a primal howl of pain that makes me wince and feel really damn sorry for her.

"Did anyone give her drugs?" I ask Bethany, who's beside me, looking wide-eyed and stunned by the birth playing out live and in color in front of us.

"Keeley wants to do this naturally." She swallows and clutches my arm like she needs help balancing. "I'm thinking she's crazy."

"Don't remind me!" Keeley snaps between contractions. "If there's a next time, I want *all* the drugs."

"You'll forget about the pain," the midwife assures.

Maxon scowls. "Of course there will be a next time. Sunshine..."

"Now isn't the right time to talk about having another baby..." Britta shakes her head at him.

The midwife motions Maxon to get behind Keeley and help her brace.

"Ha! I won't forget an instant of this," the redhead hisses out as she grits her teeth and bears down.

"That's it!" the midwife coaxes. "Just one more push and—"

Keeley keens out an ear-piercing shriek that bounces off the walls and fills the room. It's low and pained and seems to last for fucking ever. I tense and hold my breath. Bethany eases toward the bed, still gripping my arm. Suddenly, she gasps and squeezes my hand, too.

Personally, I can't see much of the birth—and I'm happy with that. I get peeks of the midwife's profile, since the Reed clan has all gathered around Keeley in front of me. I've got a glimpse of some sheet, the mom-to-be's left calf and foot, along with her forearm and damp, flushed face.

Suddenly, the midwife pulls and tugs, then lifts the infant above the sheet, little by little, until her entire body is nestled in the woman's arms.

"Oh, my god…" Maxon breathes, seemingly fixated on his daughter. "She's…"

"Beautiful," Keeley finishes, staring at the infant like she's a miracle. Then the new mother bursts into tears.

"Amazing." He bends to his wife as the baby starts to cry in protest. "Thank you. She's perfect. God, I love you."

The redhead looks at him with absolute worship in her eyes. "I love you, too. We did it."

Then she buries her head in her husband's shoulder. He wraps his arms around her and strokes her damp hair as she sobs. I have absolutely no doubt how strong their marriage is. They're committed the way my parents were. I feel the love, thick and tangible in the room, which now includes the child they made together.

"Would you like to hold your daughter?" the midwife asks after wiping her down and briefly checking her out.

"Please." Maxon sounds choked up.

I am, too. I never realized that witnessing a birth and being surrounded by this much joy would impact me.

Suddenly, the overhead song switches and a male vocalist croons, "Welcome to the planet. Welcome to existence…" As Switchfoot fills my ears, the love in the room swells even more, including the baby's sniffling aunts and proud uncles. I can't remember the last time I've been around a family that functioned like a family. I'm doing all I can to hold my brothers and me together, but I'm not Dad. We all miss him and Mom. But they're both gone, and this—right in front of me—is the circle of life.

What's in front of me is something I really want someday—real family.

Bethany turns to me. Tears run down her face. I crowd in to stand beside her and comfort her. She cries harder when Maxon and Keeley invite her closer to see the infant.

"She's beautiful," Beth whispers. "Congratulations."

Then Nia and Evan step in to get an in-depth glance at the newborn, and Bethany approaches me, chin trembling, wonder and envy all over her face. It seems like the most natural thing in the world to open my arms to her. It feels even more natural when she walks in and I enfold her against me.

Without hesitation, she lays her head on my chest. I cradle her neck and press kisses to her crown. We don't speak words, but I know we've both been touched by what we've witnessed together this morning. She's lowered more of her walls and shown me her softer side. I can't unsee that. It's impossible to unknow how caring she can be.

In the span of a few hours, for better or worse, everything between us has changed.

CHAPTER FIVE

WHEN WE REACH the inn a few hours later, we're alone. Maxon, Keeley, and baby Kailani, whose name was chosen because it's Hawaiian for sea and sky, will be home sometime tomorrow.

Bethany has been quiet since we left the birthing center. Not sad, just contemplative. Judging by the fact she's barely let go of me since Kailani made her way into the world, Beth is as impacted by the infant's birth as I feel. I wish I knew what was going on in her head.

"It's midafternoon, and you never got breakfast. I'm sure you're starving," she says as we enter the bright kitchen at Maxon and Keeley's place. "At least let me cook for you before you go. I owe you that much."

"You don't owe me anything. I was happy to drive you there."

"But you stayed. That was above and beyond. I'm already cooking for myself. So unless you have someplace to be…"

"I don't." My mission is her.

She grabs a few things from the pantry, then opens the fridge. "Allergic to anything?"

"No."

"Hate anything?"

"My palate is pretty open-minded."

She turns and smiles at me. "Perfect."

I try not to let the warmth on her face affect me. No such luck.

In a few short minutes, she's diced an onion, sliced off some soft white cheese I can't identify, chopped sweet cherry tomatoes, then grabbed a couple of skillets from the drawer beneath the stove. She's proficient, methodical, and strangely fascinating to watch.

"You're good in the kitchen. I can, um…boil water."

"Seriously? Then what do you eat?"

"A lot of stuff that's frozen or out of a can. Where I live in North Dakota, there aren't many restaurants nearby, so I learned to fend for myself…but it wasn't pretty."

"Your mom never taught you to cook?"

"She liked taking care of 'her boys,' as she called me, my dad, and my brothers. I never imagined a time she wouldn't be here to do it." Thoughts of my parents and years we should still have together always drag me into a pensive mood. I can't go there right now. This is my alone time with Bethany. I have to take advantage of it. "In fairness, she did teach me some basics before I moved out of the house, so I can scramble an egg, make tacos, even toss together a no-frills lasagna. That's about it. Who taught you? Your mom?"

Bethany shakes her head. "Since Mom wasn't around much, an older neighbor taught me. Patti lived alone since her jerk of a husband left her for a friend of their daughter's and the other kids had moved away. She and I spent a lot of time together when I was in junior high since she loved to cook, and I enjoyed learning. She was kind. It was nice."

Though their mutual loneliness tossed them together, I can tell Bethany was genuinely fond of the woman. "Where is Patti now? Still in your old neighborhood?"

For a long moment, she doesn't answer. "My freshman year of high school, I went to her house to tell her that I'd been invited to a slumber party by this really popular girl and to ask if she'd help me bake awesome brownies to take. When I knocked, she didn't answer, even though her car was out front. I waited a few minutes in case she was in the shower or something, then I let myself in with my key so I could check on her."

Dread tightens my stomach. "Was she dead?"

"Yeah." Sadness mutes her expression.

"Heart attack?"

Losing my dad decimated me, and I'm a grown-ass man. I can only imagine how traumatic losing a maternal figure as a kid must have impacted Bethany.

"No. She'd hung herself."

Oh, shit. Being left behind sucks. So does the hurting, grieving, and clinging to happier times. But to lose a loved one to a death so preventable?

"How old were you?"

"Eleven."

"You must have been devastated."

Bethany nods as she sautés the onions. I can't see her face since she's focused on the stove, but my money is that, on top of an already emotional day, she's fighting tears.

"I'm sorry, sweetheart."

"The worst part was, she didn't leave a note. She didn't say goodbye. She just…"

The squeak in her voice tugs at my heart. As much as my head tells me I shouldn't empathize with her until I figure out how guilty she is, I can't be unmoved. At the moment, I can't even bring myself to care whether she scammed clients' money or not.

Maybe the big picture I've been missing is that Bethany Banks endured a childhood full of disappointments, thanks to the adults around her. How was she supposed to learn to care about others when she had almost zero examples to follow? How was she supposed to truly understand the trauma she'd leave in her swindling wake if no one ever showed her empathy or compassion?

I vault to my feet and cross the kitchen, wrapping my hands around her delicate shoulders. "Beth…"

She sniffles. "I'm okay. I just haven't let myself think about Patti Robbins in years. And watching Kailani's birth this morning was…intense."

"Totally."

"So I'm just emotional. It will pass."

She scoops half the onions onto a spoon and drops them to the heating skillet on her left, then cracks two eggs in each pan. They sizzle. The savory smells begin to meld. My stomach growls. But all my thoughts are with the complicated woman I'm holding in my arms.

"You must think I'm pitiful." She dabs at her eyes. "Every story I tell you about my past is sad. I'm not an unhappy person."

Maybe, but she's not exactly filled with joy, either. I'm trying to decide what to attribute that to. Guilt? Or events far more tragic?

"You don't have to pretend to be all right for me."

"I'm not. I promise." She sets thin slices of the cheese down around the firming eggs and throws the cherry tomatoes into another pan. "It's just that I haven't had time to reflect on anything in…well, pretty much a decade. Until I came here, I worked constantly and moved fast. Yesterday's events quickly became irrelevant. My focus was always on tomorrow. Now that everything has changed and I'm…I don't know, getting in touch with myself?…all these memories and feelings are flooding back." A self-deprecating laugh follows. "I promise, I'll get myself together."

"You are together," I assure her, caressing her shoulders. "Can I do anything to help?"

"You are, just by being here and listening to me."

I'm glad that's how she sees the situation, but if she's actually innocent and figures out I've been hanging on her every word simply to gain her trust and use whatever she divulges against her? I'll be another asshole in a long line of them who have used, hurt, and mistreated her.

But I'm here for justice, not to exploit her.

Another nagging voice in my head asks, if Dad knew I felt this much empathy for the woman who may have, even inadvertently, caused his death, would he be rolling in his grave?

That's a question I'd rather not answer. I need to stay on task.

"Beth, something happened to you recently, didn't it? Why did you come to Hawaii?"

She pops two pieces of sourdough in the toaster, then removes the cherry tomatoes from the third pan before dividing them equally between the first two. "We always talk about me, and I never get a chance to ask about you. Why did you move to North Dakota?"

Hard change of subject. I'm not surprised. Bethany doesn't let many people inside her life or thoughts. Learning who she really is—and deciding what she's capable of—is going to require more time.

The one commodity I'm running out of.

Negotiations for my dad's business will probably resume tomorrow since the buyers seem eager. I'll have to head back to California to sign the papers soon and move the last of Dad's stuff out of the offices. While I'm there, I'll visit Bret at UCLA, then try to slip up the coast to check in on Bry in Santa Barbara.

"You'll laugh," I tell her. "I went to North Dakota because I wanted to make money, and I read on the internet—which makes me sound really stupid in retrospect—that I could earn a lot of cash doing industrial work there. I like jobs that require both brains and brawn, and it was a drastic change of pace from where I grew up. I was determined to be independent. At first, everything was great. I have to admit, though, that after the first couple of snows, the novelty of the white stuff wore off."

And the house I built there seems tainted by the ghost of tragedy. Every time I walk in, I see my dad lying dead on the floor. And on the rare occasions I'm there now, I can't wait to leave.

"Still think you'll go back in the spring?"

Though I'm beginning to wonder if that's the right move, where else would I move? "Yeah."

"But no girlfriend back there? I remember that from last night." She gives me a little smile as she plates the toast, slaps on some butter, then sets a bit of spinach on top of our sizzling scrambles. "Can you do your job anywhere besides North Dakota?"

"Not really." I could move to Texas or Alaska or a few other oil-producing states, but I'd only be starting all over again in a business where it's hard to gain a foothold.

"Do you still like your job? Is it what you always wanted to do?"

"I like it, but I'm not sure I see myself doing it forever. The hours suck. It can be backbreaking. And it's hard to find reliable people." I laugh at myself. "Growing up I really wanted to be a rock star. Unfortunately, when I tried to sing…the feedback wasn't super positive. So I had to give that up. What about you? I know you haven't always been a waitress."

"No."

"What was your last job? You said you were a paper pusher…"

"Pretty much. I was good at it, too, but…" She trails off with a regretful shrug. "When I was a kid, I wanted to be a chef when I grew up. My father told me it was a waste of my intelligence."

And never mind what she wanted to do? "Seriously?"

She nods. "My IQ is why everyone I went to school with thought I was a freak."

"Just how smart are you?"

Sliding hot skillets across the stone countertops as spinach leaves curl with the heat is a stall tactic. "Enough to get me into the Harvard MBA program at seventeen."

I already knew that, but when I think about what a feat that is, she amazes me. "Wow."

"So…yeah. Dig in. I hope it's good. High protein, a few veggies, some healthy fat."

"It looks as spectacular as it smells," I praise her in all honesty.

"Thanks. Tabasco? Salsa?" She plucks both bottles out of the fridge before sliding two forks and two napkins in my direction, then settling onto the stool beside me.

"Maybe." I watch her pour a liberal amount of Tabasco on hers. "Are you going to be able to feel your tongue later?"

Bethany laughs. "I like things spicy. What can I say?"

I like things spicy, too. Maybe not food, but women? Yes, please. The one beside me has so many facets, and the longer I spend with her the more of her personality I glimpse. The more I find myself liking her…despite the fact it isn't smart.

"All right." I sprinkle a little on to be adventurous, then I take my first bite. The combination of flavors hits my tongue. I don't even think about what I'm saying before the words slip out. "Mmmm… This is amazing. We should get married."

The light trill of her laughter fills the air. "I'm glad you like it, but marriage seems a bit drastic for food. How about, since we're friends, I promise to feed you if you're hungry?"

"Deal."

Parts south love the notion of her sating all my hungers. But that's lust talking. It would be dangerous to get in any deeper right now.

We eat in silence that feels thick with awareness. She's so close that with every lift of her fork, her elbow brushes my arm. Whether I want to feel it or not, desire simmers in my blood. Why can't I get my head and my body on the same page?

"What are you going to sightsee today?" she asks.

I glance at the clock on the microwave. "The sun will be down in a few hours, so it's probably too late. I'll do it another day."

Bethany places a hand over mine. "I'm sorry you missed out."

"I didn't. I got to spend the time with you."

Her cheeks flush as she looks up at me from beneath the fringe of her lashes. "I'm really glad you were here today. I felt less like a third wheel. And you're really easy to talk to. Thanks."

I quash my guilt. I enjoy talking to Bethany—way more than I should. And I hate feeling disingenuous. "You're welcome."

She bites her lip like she's gathering her words and her courage. "If you don't have plans, I'd like it if you stayed a while."

She's going out of her way to ask for time with me. That's a first. Because she's starting to trust me? Because she's ready to open up?

"I'd like that. It would be more entertaining than going back to Ash's place to warm his sofa alone. He's working tonight. After that, he'll probably spend more time with Montana. What did you have in mind?"

"Would you mind helping me do something for Maxon, Keeley, and baby Kailani?"

"Sure. What are you thinking?"

"They've been so gracious, opening up their house to me when they didn't have to. They're letting me stay in the cottage—sorry, ohana—out back for free, which is the most lucrative room on their property, just so I can have some peace and privacy. It's really sweet, but I feel bad about taking advantage of their hospitality. I've been making my way in life for a long time, and I'm not about to quit. Since I'm saving my money to move out—hopefully next week—I can't buy them anything. They seem to have everything a newborn could need anyway. But I can whip up some dinners for them to reheat next week while I'm at work. That way, they'll only have to focus on the baby."

There's her thoughtful streak that confuses me every time she shows it. Bethany is willing to use her lone day off, stand on feet that surely feel overtaxed, to make the lives of the people around her better. Could this same woman have stolen millions from her clients?

"That's really sweet of you."

She shrugs. "I wish I could do more, but I want help my brother and his wife in some meaningful way so they know I'm thinking of them."

"Then I'm happy to stay." I swallow down another bite and try not to moan in pleasure. "I don't know how much help I'll be since I suck in the kitchen…"

"How are your furniture assembly skills?"

"Much better."

"Good. That's where I'm terrible. Maxon didn't get time to put together the baby's changing table. It was backordered for weeks and it just arrived. So if you don't mind helping, I'd like to surprise them."

"No problem."

We finish up our meal in minutes, then rise from the breakfast bar and head back into the kitchen.

"You start the food. I'll do our dishes," I offer.

"You sure?" She seems surprised.

"Yeah. That's one thing my mother taught me really well."

With her melodic laughter in my ears, I tackle the dirty plates and pans with a grin. Then it hits me that I enjoy making Bethany smile.

That's so dangerous…

When I've finished loading the dishwasher, I turn to find several casseroles in progress. Lasagna, I recognize. Everything else? I have no clue.

I watch in awe as Bethany tosses together seven dishes without once glancing at a recipe. She makes it look effortless, and she manages to slide lasagna, baked ziti, black bean enchiladas, butternut squash and spinach ravioli, a gumbo bake, and chicken Alfredo pie into the refrigerator ninety minutes later with minimal help from me.

"That was impressive, woman!" Even my mother would have been amazed.

She waves me away. "It was fun. And now all they have to do is heat the casseroles up when they want to eat. Should we tackle this changing table before it gets too dark?"

"Lead the way."

Bethany and I hit the garage and find Maxon's tool stash, then we head for the baby's nursery. I stop in the doorway. Soft grays and cheerful white fill the space, accented with a touch of pink and topped off with a chandelier. Everything looks plush and inviting and ready for the arrival of their newborn—except the changing table still in pieces.

We find the instructions. They're written in pseudo-English that's almost impossible to follow. After a lot of confusion—I hate cam bolts—and laughter at the puny Allen wrench included, we finish assembling the changing table. Together, we move the piece to the blank wall by the window and complete the task by filling the appointed cubbies with stacks of tiny diapers and packs of baby wipes.

Clean-up takes less than five minutes. The sun is just setting. Our timing is perfect.

"Everything looks great. They're going to be so happy." Bethany looks my way, wearing a smile. "I couldn't have done it without you. Thanks."

"My pleasure. This baby is going to be so loved, I can tell."

"Yeah." She sounds wistful.

I turn to her. "You okay?"

She shrugs as she flips off the light and leads me back into the great room. "Still emotional, I guess. Since we left the birthing center, I've felt jumbled and I've been trying to put my finger on what's bugging me. My life is a mess. I have no one to blame but myself for that. But this is something else." She tilts her head and regards me with solemn eyes. "Have you ever believed something deep down, then been stunned when you've realized it wasn't true?"

"Can't say I have."

She sighs. "Then what I'm thinking probably won't make sense."

"Try me. Doesn't mean I can't listen." Is she somehow realizing that stealing would, in fact, hurt people? Is she grasping that by swindling her clients with her father she did wrong?

Bethany manages a hint of a smile. "You're a really amazing guy, you know. Tell me again, why aren't you taken?"

"I haven't been looking. What about you? You're smart, kind, and hardworking. Why aren't you taken?"

"I haven't been looking, either."

"So what's bugging you, Beth?"

She sighs. "I hate to dump this on you, but right now you're my only friend. I mean, that I'm not related to."

She sounds as if she's apologizing for having feelings. Or for wanting to share them. That disturbs me. So does hearing that she has almost no one in her life to talk to. Her admission should make me happy because I can exploit her loneliness to my advantage. Instead, I have to fight the urge to wrap her in my arms and assure her she's not alone anymore.

"Go on."

"It's hard to put into words." Bethany shrugs. "Maybe this will sound odd. But I'm still stunned and in awe from witnessing Kailani's birth."

"I feel the same," I admit. "But mostly stunned. I wasn't expecting *all* that."

Her light laughter surrounds me. "I'll bet. Sorry you got way more than you bargained for."

"Yeah, but it was…profound. It's something I'll never forget."

She nods. "The way it made me feel is a lot to process."

"Because?"

"I spent so long thinking I'd never have what Maxon and Keeley or any of my other siblings have. Marriage and babies were for someone else. I had a world to conquer. I had a glass ceiling to raise. I had an empire to learn. Nothing else really mattered. If I ever felt twinges of wistfulness for more, I always had plenty of work to squash them. All that was fine until I came here. My brothers and sister have these great marriages. And to hear them tell their stories, none of them reached this point without overcoming a lot of hardship, conflict, adversity, and fear."

"Fear?"

The curl of her lips is nothing short of self-deprecating. "Apparently all the Reeds are born with an innate aversion to emotion. Well, Maxon, Griff, Harlow, and I probably have growing up with our father to thank for that. But Evan struggled not to reject feelings, too. We've discussed this phenomenon and shared some about our upbringings." She shakes her head. "But I've been intentionally trying not to think about where I'm at in life or where I'm going, long term. Right now, I'm focused on putting one foot in front of the other until life makes sense again. And so far—"

"Hang on. It sounds like your life fell apart. Are you sure you don't want to talk about that?" I try not to fire the question at her, but I'm dying to know if she'll admit the real reason she's in Hawaii.

She shakes her head. "It's a long story full of family drama, and I won't bore you. But today made me realize that feelings aren't wrong. There are more reasons to let someone close to you besides figuring out how you can use them."

"Yes," I confirm, instantly wondering what she means. How did she use people?

Again, she gives me an ironic smile. "That probably sounds obvious to you—and to most people. But it's a new way of thinking for me. If Maxon hadn't listened to his heart, Keeley wouldn't be his wife. Kailani wouldn't have been born today. Griff would still be a miserable bastard who hated Maxon and didn't know his son, Jamie, existed. He wouldn't have Britta or another baby on the way. Harlow would have kept her relationship with Noah to a fling. Evan would have stayed in Seattle, grieving the loss of a wife who didn't love him, rather than letting himself fall for Nia. But every one of my siblings made the choice to open themselves up to new possibilities, and their lives are all better for it. I can't help but wonder if I've been blind and I'm missing out."

Her speech is both a jolt and a gut punch. Did she really tell me all this because she's just now realizing that using people is wrong? Or is she trying to tell me she's receptive to more than friendship because she's fishing to find out how I feel about her?

My heart starts pounding. Hooking up with Bethany would be the most expedient way of getting closer to her. It would allow me intimate access into her psyche and her life. But I'm so conflicted about going there... Sex—even if I haven't stopped thinking about having it with her for days—would muddle my thoughts even more. And I hate the idea of screwing her literally merely so I can screw her figuratively.

On the other hand, if she's willing to open up about anything at all, I need to play along.

"Does the possibility of falling for someone scare you, Beth?"

"Scare? No. It terrifies me. What if they're not everything I think they are? Or need them to be?"

I try to shrug off my remorse. If she's innocent and if she wants me, I'll be the most thoughtful, attentive lover she's ever had. If she's guilty...then she should get what she deserves.

"What if they are?" I murmur.

"I don't know." She shrugs. "And what if I'm not enough for them? I've never stopped to think about what it would require to make a significant other happy."

"Are you thinking about it now?"

"Yes."

I shouldn't ask but... "Are you thinking about it with me?"

"We've only known each other for a few days."

Though she hedged, her face tells me that's exactly what she's thinking.

"That isn't what I asked. Have you thought about it with me, Beth?"

She hesitates, gnawing on her lip. "Yes."

I lean closer. God, this is so dangerous. My heart pounds and throbs. I'm aching to touch her. She has no idea how badly I want to give in…

"Even though you said you don't date co-workers and aren't looking for romance?"

An even longer hesitation. "Yes."

"What exactly are you thinking about, Beth?"

"Stop asking me questions and kiss me."

CHAPTER SIX

H ER WHISPER PELTS my brain, heats my blood, stops my heart—
stiffens my cock. "Are you sure, Beth? I think we should talk about
this."

But talking is the last damn thing my body wants to do.

"Look, if you don't want to…" She ducks her head in mortification
and turns away.

I pull her back to face me. "Oh, I do. But…" I scramble for an excuse
to explain my reluctance. "You and I both need a friend right now. Let's
make sure neither of us is mistaking loneliness for attachment."

"It's a kiss, not marriage."

"You're right. But once we cross the line…" *There's no going back.*
Frankly, that's one of the few things stopping me from backing her against
the wall, laying my mouth over hers, and stripping off her goddamn
clothes.

"Really, just forget I said anything."

"Now that it's out there, I can't. So we need to work through this,
especially since you're not the only one who's been thinking about it."

"Oh." She looks taken aback. "Well…the inn's guests will start wandering in here shortly for the evening wine and appetizers Keeley usually
sets out. Britta's mom is taking care of it today, but if we want to talk
privately, we should head to the ohana."

"Let's go."

As I press my hand to the small of her back—mostly because I can't keep my hands off her—Beth and I make our way out the back door, following the stone path to the cottage on stilts that's adjacent to the main house. Under the structure is a fenced-in lanai with a quaint table and chairs. Bethany makes her way up the stairs and opens the bright turquoise door.

Once we're inside, my gaze sweeps over the cozy space. A plush sofa invites a duo to snuggle. Windows all around provide both mountain and ocean views to enjoy. Exposed ceiling beams and tropical colors relax and soothe. A little kitchenette supplies sustenance when needed. But it's the big bed dominating the place that tells me this room was made for romance.

It's impossible not to picture Bethany lying across the white sheets, half-dressed, breathing hard, and waiting for me to peel off all the rest. I do my best to push the vision aside and focus, but it's not happening. All I want is her.

"This is really nice," I manage to say.

"They've done a great job with the place. Have a seat. Want a beer? Keeley keeps a few up here."

"Sure. Thanks."

As she opens me a cold one and pours herself a glass of white, I scan her room again. It's meticulous. Other than the suitcase on the luggage rack and another standing in the open closet, I would swear the room is vacant. I'm not surprised Bethany keeps the place neat and orderly. It fits her. My personal space is always a little more…relaxed.

Finally, she hands me the chilled bottle, then sinks beside me nervously, clutching her glass. "I'm sorry I pushed you to kiss me. I shouldn't have."

"I'm glad you did. It was bound to come up sooner or later anyway." I sip my brew and set it on the tray across the nearby ottoman. "Because like I said, I've been thinking about kissing you, too, Beth. I've been thinking about it a lot. I know your life is complicated now. So is mine."

"That's another reason I should never have said anything. I don't want to drag you into my problems."

"You're not dragging me. I'm willing to help you work through whatever's bothering you. We're friends, right? That's what friends do."

When we first met, lines like that were a necessary evil, and I had no problem saying whatever would get me into Bethany's good graces. Now? Unless she asked me to help her carry out the Reed Financial scheme, I think I'd do just about anything to ease her load.

Because I don't simply want her; I like her, too.

Fuck.

That inconvenient truth aside, I can't let my questions about her role in Dad's death go unanswered.

What the hell am I going to do? If I refuse Bethany tonight, I doubt she'll give me a second chance to touch her. If I give in, there's no way I'll be able to stop at just a kiss. Either way, she's going to tie me up in knots.

Fucking no-win situation.

"Thanks for the offer. But some things I need to work out myself. They're big and complicated."

I frown. "And I'm too young to understand?"

"No. I'm too scared to share, all right?"

Because of what she'll admit? Or what I'll think of her?

"Okay." I squeeze her hand. I can't push her any more now. "But I'm here for you."

"Thanks."

Suddenly, we're sitting in shadow illuminated by only the faintest hint of dusk eking through the windows. Her green eyes look so wide and uncertain. Her pale skin gleams. Her rosy lips and the way she nibbles that bottom one eat at my restraint.

"If we're really going to talk about this, I should turn on some lights and grab us a snack from the main house."

I suspect she's stalling, but that's okay. It gives me more time to think. "That would be great."

With a quiet nod, she rises and flips on a cozy table lamp before letting herself out of the cottage. She descends the stairs and disappears inside the inn.

The moment she's gone, I realize that I'm alone in her personal space and this may be my only opportunity to search it for clues. I have five minutes—tops—to figure out whether I need to put on the brakes with Bethany...or whether I can give in to the endless fucking need burning me to take her to bed.

I hate this. I wish I had a choice...but I can't pass up this opportunity.

Shoving down my niggle of reluctance, I fling open her suitcases, checking the side pockets and zippered compartments first to avoid ruffling her carefully folded clothes. They're empty. Other than a collection of shorts and T-shirts, I find nothing of note in the rest of her luggage. A few dresses and a couple of light sweaters hang from the overhead rack.

Next, I yank open the dresser on the far side of the bed. Panties in muted colors—some lacy and downright sweat-inducing—line the bottom. Delicate matching bras are nested and stacked beside them. The rest of the drawers net a collection of bikinis, socks, scarves, and tanks. No papers. No thumb drives. No files of any kind. Of course, it doesn't help that I don't know what I'm looking for other than something that tells me whether Bethany Banks is guilty.

She doesn't have a computer that I can see. Maybe she left it in San Diego. Maybe the feds confiscated it. I don't know. But damn it, the clock is ticking, so I keep moving.

Quickly, I sweep the bathroom. She keeps the counter clear of personal items. In the cabinet, I find nothing out of the ordinary—makeup, deodorant, shampoo, shower gel, and the like. There's no incriminating evidence, unless you count tampons and birth control pills.

Darting back to the main room, I visually sweep the cottage again and spot her purse on the kitchenette counter. The display on my phone tells me she's been gone four minutes.

Stop or keep searching? I don't want to be caught, but if I quit now, will I get another chance to inspect her personal space again?

Biting back a curse, I reach for the magnetic closure on her quilted pale pink purse. The golden logo across the front proclaims the bag is Chanel. Inside, there's one main compartment containing mints, a mini hairbrush, a few tubes of lipstick, and a compact—but nothing incriminating, nothing that gives me a reason to mentally convict her.

I also find a small ring with two keys. One I saw her use to let us into this unit. The other... I don't know what it opens, but I know what it doesn't: any sort of safe deposit or strong box. My best guess is that it unlocks her apartment in San Diego.

Next, I troll through her matching Chanel wallet, feeling guiltier by the moment for invading her privacy because it's seeming more and more like she's done nothing...except make me second-guess everything I thought I knew.

Her driver's license, ATM card, and credit cards galore take up all the slots. She doesn't have a lot of cash on hand—mostly small, wrinkled bills people have left as tips, but her posh purse tells me she must have money somewhere. Same with all the plastic. But I keep coming back to the fundamental question: why the fuck is she working as a cocktail waitress when she's way too educated for the job? Either she's hiding here while maintaining a low profile to ensure people cool down and look the other way before she hits up her stolen stash and starts living her bougie life, or she's innocent, the feds and her father have stripped her of everything, and she's just trying to survive.

Which fucking possibility is the right one?

Tucked inside a compartment I nearly missed is a card from an FBI agent, Trevor Forsythe. I've never heard of this guy, but I whip out my phone, take a picture of his digits, then slide it back into place. I'll pursue that later. But there's nothing else of note here, and I have the same damn questions I did before I invaded her personal belongings without her consent.

Finally, I reach for her phone. It's password protected, no surprise. Bethany isn't stupid, and I'm at another dead end.

When I hear soft footsteps making their way up the stairs, I shove everything in her bag once more. I'm not going to make it back to the sofa in time, so I'll have to lie to her. Again. This is really bugging the shit out of me.

Behind me, the door opens. Wincing, I peek in the nearest cabinet. "Hey, I was just seeing if there was a glass I could pour the beer into. Found one."

When I turn, she's looking at me suspiciously. I don't blame her. What self-respecting beer drinker wants their cold beer poured into a room temperature mug?

"Let me put it in the freezer for you, at least for a few minutes." She takes it from my hand.

There she is again, thinking of others. "Thanks."

As I settle back onto the sofa, she handles the mug, then sets a plate of cheese and crackers, along with some fresh pineapple, grapes, and mangos, in front of us. "Help yourself."

I'm not hungry, but I've already been an impolite bastard. I can choke down a few bites to make her effort worthwhile. "Thanks. You should eat, too. You've worked hard the last couple of hours."

She gives me a wan smile as she plucks a grape between her fingers. I reach for a cracker and watch her, shoving down guilt and grappling for conversation, when she sucks the fruit between her lips, closing her eyes as she bites.

Watching her is a sexual experience that makes me instantly hard. And when she lets out an unconscious moan, the urge to kiss her, strip her down, and fuck her hits me even harder. Feeling like a heel, I drag in a shuddering breath.

Jesus, what am I going to do?

She swallows and lifts her wine. "You know, you're the first man who's ever wanted to discuss whether we should kiss before we actually did. I'm not sure if I should be flattered you're taking this so seriously or feel rejected because you put me off."

I need to decide how to proceed, but my head is at war with my gut. Both keep tangling with my libido until I'm one giant clusterfuck. But everything boils down to two increasingly obvious facts: One, the desire I feel for this woman isn't going away. The more I get to know her, the more I want her. Two, though my quick search of her ohana is hardly comprehensive, I haven't seen a single shred of evidence that Bethany is guilty…and everything about her behavior so far says she's not.

It's possible the feds didn't arrest her is because she really is innocent. It's possible she's been through a lot, and I've just been an asshole on a witch hunt. It's possible the quiet, caring woman I've been trying to resist these last few days is the real Bethany Banks.

It's also possible that's what I want to believe because I'm falling for her.

Fuck, I could talk myself in circles all day. I have to make a decision now, so I'm going with my gut. The Beth I've come to know isn't the kind to steal from anyone. So I'm going to stifle my suspicions and believe she's innocent…unless I prove her guilty. Until then, I'm going to treat her not like a suspect but like a woman.

Like my lover.

"When you put it like that, I sound like an idiot," I quip. "If you still want me to kiss you, I'm beyond happy to do it."

Five seconds slide by as she sends me a considering stare.

Whether she means to or not, she's making me wait. Anticipation screams through my blood. The thought of finally touching her is so fucking turning me on.

"If you're sure you want to…"

"Yeah, Beth. I *really* do."

I can say that with all honesty.

With a nervous nod, she tilts her head up to me. Her eyes slide shut as she waits.

My heart thumps as I cup my fingers around her nape and stare. God, she's going to be a sensory treat; I can already tell. Her skin here is ridiculously soft. Her braid caresses the back of my hand in a silky graze. I'll explore every inch of her eventually. Right now, I'm fixated on her delicate jaw in my palm as I caress her pouty lower lip with my thumb.

As I lean in to kiss her, she surprises me by staying me with a palm on my chest. "But Clint? One thing… I've never been vulnerable to a lover. Ever. I'm trusting you. Please don't make me regret it."

Her plea gouges my conscience. "Beth…"

Shit. Maybe I should come clean here and now, explain everything, and give her the opportunity to tell me the truth in turn.

As I'm weighing the pros and cons, she wraps her arms around my neck, pulls herself against my body, and slants her lips across mine.

Then I forget everything.

Her kiss is an instant jolt of lust. My heart stops, then starts to thud dangerously. I drag in a breath to control the hot surge of lust, but it's useless. Desire pours through my veins like lava, scalding every inch with need.

I yank her closer, fastening my mouth over hers, and tumble her back against the arm of the sofa. As my body covers hers, I revel in her indrawn gasp. Impossibly, my desire notches up again. Impatiently, I part her lips with my own and sink into her.

Oh, hell yes.

Against me, Bethany melts, tilting her head to admit me deeper. Groaning and greedy for more, I give her exactly what she silently begs me for.

Fuck, she smells so sultry and sugary sweet. She fits against me, every curve and swell, like she belongs here. She kisses like she's hungry, and I'm her dessert. The way she tastes is something I've fantasized about a hundred times, but now that I *know* her shy, sweet-tart flavor? I'm going to crave it every time I don't have my mouth on her.

The endless kiss goes on. Our tongues caress in a fevered frenzy. I get dizzy. She makes me sweat. Ache. Need. What little restraint I have goes up in flames.

A warning voice in my head reminds me that Bethany merely asked me to kiss her. I should probably leave it there until our situation is less complicated. But now that I've got my mouth and hands on her…I don't have the will to stop.

"Beth, what do you want?"

"More," she breathes.

Her reply goes straight to my dick.

Taking her face in my hands, I angle my mouth over hers again and sweep inside, plunging deeper. God, everything about her is flipping my switch in a way I've never felt. A week ago I would have said this woman wasn't my type. Too quiet, too delicate, too controlled. Now? Every fantasy I'm having is about mussing her up and making her scream.

"Beth… Fuck, yes." I pant as I drag my lips across her jaw to whisper against her ear. "I've wanted to do this since the moment I saw you."

A little smile curls the corners of her lips. "I wasn't sure why you were staring. It unnerved me, so I looked past you."

"All that made me do was want to look more." I kiss her again because I can't help it, but I nearly lose myself when I taste more of her sweetness. "You're the reason I said no to Montana. Even when you were barely speaking to me, I wanted you. There was no way I could think of her. You crowded everyone else out."

She looks stunned. "You said we were friends."

"We were. And we are. But I've always wanted more." I may have been dishonest about the reason I sought her out, but I can't not be honest about that.

"Even though my life is such a mess?"

"You're not the only one."

"Does it bother you that you're younger than me?"

Is she actually hung up on that? "Why should it?"

She considers that for a long moment. "You're right. These days, my dad never seduces a female older than half his age. Why shouldn't I be with whomever I want?"

"He can have all those girls." I take her face in my hands. "I want a woman. I want you."

When I lunge in and crush Bethany against me again, she meets me in a rough, breathless tangle of lips and arms. Beneath me, she unfurls, opening to me, luring me farther inside, sliding her tongue against mine. I'm kissing her as deeply as I can, but I still crave more.

I haven't taken Bethany to bed yet, but I already know that one night with her isn't going to be enough.

Admittedly, over the last decade, I've had a lot of sex with more than a few women, so I know my usual response to a hookup. This isn't it. Hell, this doesn't even feel sane. Right now, I'll do anything to sate the gnawing need to sink inside Bethany and know what it feels like when she's mine.

My hands wander down her back, molding to her sides, clutching her hips, before I cup her ass and lure her against me. Her snug denim is in my way, and I hope she lets me peel it off soon so I can feel the woman underneath. But I have to take this at her speed. As revved up as I am, she might not be ready for more than a blistering kiss or two. And maybe me going back to Ash's place to take a long masturbatory shower to thoughts of Bethany would be for the best. It certainly wouldn't be the first time.

Suddenly, she tears her lips from mine, harsh breaths filling the air as she grabs the hem of my shirt and jerks it halfway up my torso. "Take it off."

She doesn't have to ask me twice.

With one fist, I yank it from my body, then toss it across the room. With another, I grip her hair and angle her mouth beneath mine so I can kiss her deeply again.

Bethany moans and meets me halfway, her fingers digging into my shoulders. She kisses me back as if nothing in the world matters more to her right now than being with me.

I can't keep my hands off her. They roam under her lacy tank, traversing the soft skin of her back. When I reach her bra strap, I want to pry it open so fucking bad. But I hesitate. Is she ready for this?

"Do it," she whispers as she rains kisses on my neck.

"You're sure?"

She cocks a brow. "Would you rather I keep it on?"

"Hell no. I want you totally bare. I want to see your breasts—touch them, suck them, torment them." When a shiver wracks her body, I press on. "I want to watch you writhe for me, hear you scream for me."

"Ambitious?" she pants.

"Confident."

Bethany reacts like a woman who hasn't been touched enough lately. Or maybe ever. Then again, when I'm with her, I feel as if I'm ravenous— and she's my ideal banquet. Our electric, erotic chemistry is no joke. Whatever happens between us is going to be more than explosive.

With a shake of her head, she gives me a shove and peels off her delicate tank to reveal a lacy beige strapless bra. The swells of her breasts rising above her slender waist and her smooth, peachy skin have my eyes bulging and my mouth watering.

Yeah, the bra needs to go—now.

Clutching her hips, I drag her closer, my lips falling automatically to claim hers again as I wrench the hooks of her bra open. The second the garment is free, I toss it in the vague direction I lobbed my shirt. Then I press our chests together, bare skin to skin.

She gasps. "Clint…"

My palms roam the soft flesh of her back. Fuck, she feels like warm velvet. I'm dying to know the weight of her breasts in my palms, in my mouth.

"Yeah?" My voice sounds rough.

She looks into my eyes. "Are you going to do more than kiss me?"

Hell yeah, I am. "I would never keep a lady waiting."

When she sends me a lazy-lidded smile, my heart chugs. Fuck, she's sexy when she's flirting with me. Bethany is usually so serious, so her little tease is a thrill.

Desperate now, I drag my lips down her neck and ease back onto my knees. The sofa isn't going to work for what I have in mind, but I'll worry about that in a minute. Right now, I'm fixated on her breasts.

Holy gorgeous nipples. I like boobs. No, I *love* boobs. They're my thing on a woman. When I first meet an attractive female, I look at her eyes, glance at her mouth, then see what God or her plastic surgeon implanted inside her chest. It's not very evolved, I know…but I'm a guy.

With Bethany, I'm perfectly happy with quality over quantity. I've seen better-endowed women topless, but her breasts might be the most beautiful, symmetrical pair I've ever laid eyes on.

"Oh, sweetheart…" I cradle one in each hand.

At my touch, she jolts, and when I rake my thumbs across the tips, she inhales sharply.

I smile like the ravenous bastard I am. "Do you like your nipples sucked?"

"I guess." She sounds breathless but hesitant. And slightly confused.

Does she not know the answer to my question? The possibility that every man she's ever slept with has been a bumbling dipshit in bed weirdly thrills me. I love the idea of being the first to blow her doors off.

I can't resist toying with her. "Is there any part you don't you like?"

She bites her lip and wriggles as if she's unnerved by the way I'm cupping her breasts and staring. "The part where they lick them like I'm a lollipop. Or when they blow on them. What is that?"

"Ineptitude. Let me try, Beth. If you don't like it, stop me. In fact, any time I do something you don't like, I expect you to let me know."

The sideways glance she shoots me tells me she's surprised. "And your ego won't take a nose dive?"

"No. Every woman likes something different. That's cool. I can adjust because I already know sex between us is going to be amazing. I want to make sure you find it amazing, too."

Her body relaxes. "Okay."

When I focus on her curves rather than the conversation, she tenses. I bet she's expecting me to pounce on her tits, do something that doesn't stimulate her, and ignore the rest of her until I decide to thrust and grunt and come.

Balancing my hands on the arm of the sofa, I lean in and brush a kiss against her lips. Instantly I realize I'm going to need another. But a second buss becomes a long melding of lips. After that, I have to taste her again, see if her flavor is really as addicting as I recall.

The second my tongue slides against hers, I know the answer is yes. I groan and lean in, kissing her in heated sweeps, searching every last corner of her for untapped flavor.

She clings to me, whimpering. I don't know whether she's conscious of her legs gently parting around me or not, but crouched in front of her, I sure as hell am.

Finally, I manage to break the spell of her kiss to trail my lips down her neck, licking and nibbling on the way. I nip at her collarbone, earning an excited little gasp. My thumb brushes one taut nipple before I lave my way down the swell of her breast, then lift her straining tip to my mouth.

I tease her with a hot exhalation before I close my lips around the point and kiss it softly. It beads tighter, the surrounding flesh crinkling and flushing darker. I smile.

"Like it so far?"

"Uh-huh." Her reply is breathless.

"What else?"

"I'm anxious. Waiting. My stomach is in knots. My heart…"

"Is racing?"

She gives me a shaky nod. "The closer you come, the faster it gets."

"Good." I pet her, then press another kiss to the side of her breast. "Let's try more."

"Hurry."

Her answering plea is a rushed breath that makes me grin. Holding her pleasure in my hands, suspending it for my own dirty thrill, makes sweat bead at my temples and my cock throb in need.

"Remember, tell me if you don't like this…"

As aroused as she seems now, there's almost zero chance of that. Vaguely, I wonder if her past lovers haven't bothered much with foreplay or just didn't care about her experience. Then the hard bead of her nipple is against my lips, and I don't care about anything but pleasing her.

Slowly, I open my mouth and ease her breast inside. Her ragged inhalation as I close my lips around the hard crest and give it a gentle pull almost undoes me.

She gasps. Her entire back goes taut. Whether she means to or not, she thrusts her breasts toward me. "Yes…"

I moan in understanding, reveling when she closes her eyes and sinks into the moment.

Then I tug harder, the suction stretching her nipple against my tongue, pulling on it with friction.

Bethany braces her hands on my shoulders, her eyes flaring wide. "Oh!"

So she likes her nipples stimulated and she likes a little edge. We're going to get along so, so well…

Lifting her free breast into my other hand, I pinch the hard point. "I don't want this one to feel neglected."

"N-no. Oh…yeah." Her head falls back, over the arm of the sofa, and she reveals the vulnerable arch of her throat to me. She's trembling and flushing—and she's not doing a single thing to hide it.

God, her reactions are everything I could have wanted—visible, honest, and arousing as fuck.

I give the nipple in my mouth one last hard tug before I release the other from my grip, swirl my tongue around it, and watch her shudder.

She digs her fingers deeper into my flesh. "Clint…"

I give her taut crest a firm, almost savage pull before releasing her. "Something you want to say?"

She gives me a slow, dazed shake of her head. "Just…more."

"Keep doing it? Or do it harder?" I coax. I think I know the answer, but I love the idea of her telling me exactly how to undo her carefully buttoned-up facade.

"Both," she manages to whisper.

"Yeah?"

I nip one tip with my teeth and delight in her indrawn breath. Then I switch to the other, laving it in long, luxurious strokes, prepping and priming it until she's squirming and arching her back in a silent plea.

"Hm-huh." Her affirmative cry is almost incoherent because it's damn near a wail.

Am I the first man to actually arouse her? The way she responds, as if she's surprised by her body, suggests that's the case.

This time, I don't hold back. I give her tender breast a little squeeze, then lift it directly onto my tongue before I close around her. She pants. I take a long draw of her, one suckle after another. She writhes. I nip down with the edge of my teeth. She keens, parts her legs wider, and wraps her hands around my neck to force me closer.

"You're so sexy," I mutter against her flesh. "I want to do this to you half the night. I want to see how swollen and hard I can make your nipples. Then I want to use my fingers and tongue to find out just how wet I make your pussy."

"I'm already drenched," she admits. "I'm aching."

"Good." I keep thumbing her nipples, alternately gliding and pinching. "You ever felt this aroused while your pants were still on?"

She blinks at me, mossy eyes bright, wide, and hazy. "I've never felt like this at all."

Is she actually admitting she's never, ever been aroused?

Holy shit. That's terrible…and yet it turns me on like nothing else.

I brush away a strand of hair clinging to her lips, then kiss her rosy mouth, tasting her sweetness even as I keep toying with the taut peaks of her breasts.

"Still want me to give you more?"

Bethany hesitates for a mere instant. "I don't know whether I'll go up in flames or just explode, but…don't stop."

"Good. I wasn't planning to."

The second my words are out, Bethany surges up, collides into me, then tumbles me onto my back before straddling me. Her lips burn across mine with feverish need. Mashing her breasts against my chest, she sighs into me as her fingers walk across my skin, exploring with inquisitive brushes here, a teasing drag of her fingernails there. "I can't seem to get close enough to you."

Shuddering, I caress my way down the sleek line of her spine. "I can't get close enough, either."

Bethany sits up and slides her way down my body until her ass is perched on my thighs. I gotta say, the view is spectacular. Plush pink breasts sit high above her narrow rib cage and the long, lean line of her torso. Her cute little belly button peeks above the waistband of her jeans that cling to every dip and curve.

But she doesn't notice my perusal. She's too busy gaping at me. "How much time do you spend in the gym? I thought abs like these were for celebrities and bodybuilders."

I laugh. But before I can answer, her finger traces the line bisecting my abdominals from stern to naval. Her jolt of a touch makes my flesh quiver with electricity.

My breaths pick up speed when her fingers wander south of my waistband. Slowly, she drags one curious finger past the button fastening my jeans, then down to my fly, until she's tracing the ridge of my aching cock.

I buck as if she burned me. I'm so aroused that my skin feels as if it's on fire. How can she undo me with one itty-bitty touch? "Fuck…"

"Do you want to?"

When she drags her finger back up my engorged shaft, I can't follow her question. "Want to what?"

"Fuck." She bites her lip, and I can tell she's nervous. "Me, I mean."

Does she think there's any way at all this doesn't end with me on top of her, plowing deep inside her, making her feel every inch of me?

I grab her wrist to stop her wandering fingers. "Oh, yeah. I want you naked, panting, and wailing for me."

With a shaking breath, she wrenches free and attacks my fly, practically tearing away my button and clawing at my zipper.

After my last trip to the gym, I wore my spare pair of clean underwear, so once she yanks my fly open, my bare cock all but springs into her eager hands.

The feel of her fingers wrapping around me is mind-bending, spine-melting. Incredible. "Oh, my god…"

She strokes every bit of my length she can reach, fingertips skimming the sensitive head. A tremor quakes me. I know it's been a long while since I had sex, but even after my longest dry spell, the sensations were never this intense.

"What are you doing to me?" I groan.

"Trying to make you feel good."

"You're succeeding."

Bethany's fingertips dance up my cock again as she gives me a bad-girl grin that makes me shiver.

Shit, no matter how much I'd love to let her have her way with me, I have to take control of the situation. I can't think of another time or another woman who's undone me so thoroughly and so easily. It's a little terrifying.

Gathering my resolve, I wrap my arms around her and haul her closer.

She yelps in surprise, wrapping her arms and legs around me as I stand. "What are you doing?"

"Getting you someplace more comfortable, where I can spread you out and fuck you." I flip off the light by the sofa and make my way to the bed. "Lose the pants."

She licks her lips nervously. "And the underwear?"

I send her a wolfish smile as I kick off my shoes and jeans. "Leave those to me."

With a shaky bob of her head, she complies while I fish a condom from my pocket. I only have two. *Damn it.*

I forget my problem as I watch her shimmy out of her denim. I've seen those sleek thighs in shorts, and the sight is mighty nice. But getting to view the whole package almost fully unwrapped? I swallow. Stare. She's even hotter than I thought.

And her strappy, pale-pink panties are nothing short of a visual sin. Two sets of thin straps crisscrossing under her naval reveal tantalizing glimpses of her flat abdomen. Under those little bands of silk, the garment plunges to a lacy vee, intersecting just above her pussy to—barely—cover the essentials.

My tongue belongs there.

"Say something," she begs. "You're just staring."

It seems impossible that she's feeling insecure, but I hear it in her voice. "Oh, sweetheart… You are sexy as hell. I'm going to eat those panties off your body."

A flush steals across her skin from head to toe. Time to get busy.

After tossing the condoms on the nightstand, I lift Bethany and drape her across the middle of the bed, shoving tropical-colored pillows out of my way and onto the floor. Then I crawl above her, looking down at her gleaming like a pearl in the evening shadows. She's focused completely on me, on us, on what will happen next.

She stuns me when she trails her fingers down my chest, over my abs, and wraps hers fingers around my cock again. "I'm waiting."

"Are you trying to rush me?"

"If you're still wondering, I must not be doing this right." She strokes my length again, harder, faster.

Somehow, I resist the urge to let my eyes roll into the back of my head and lose myself. "You're doing more than fine, sweetheart. Trust me."

In fact, the longer she's got me in her hand, the more I feel my skin go damp and my system buzz with need. If I don't stop her, this is going to be over way before I'm ready.

I twist away from her, tangle my fingers in hers, and pin her wandering hand to the bed. "But I'm a gentleman. Ladies come first."

Her lips part in a soft, open-mouthed *O* as I work my way down her body, pressing kisses to the undersides of her breasts, her abdomen, and between the sexy crisscrossed straps of her panties before I open my mouth over the pink lace covering her pussy.

Bethany wasn't lying; she's drenched. Through the fabric, I smell her. I taste a hint of her essence that only leaves me hungry for more. I feel how swollen and juicy she is.

"So fucking sweet," I moan.

She shudders and cries out as I drag my tongue up the lace, then prod her clit through the lace. "Oh!"

"If you're at all attached to these panties, you should take them off now. If you leave me to do it, I can't guarantee they'll be wearable tomorrow."

"Okay." She wraps her thumbs around the straps at her hips.

Though I want her naked, I resent having to take my mouth off her and I'm even harder-pressed to give her the space to strip. With a curse, I ease up and flip on the closest light so I can see every inch of her, especially her face when I thrust deep and fill her up.

I turn just in time to see her wriggle her panties down her thighs and into a puddle on the floor. Then I get my first view of her completely naked. "Oh, sweetheart... Give that pretty pussy to me now."

I back her onto the bed and wedge myself between her legs. She falls to her elbows, watching me, eyes dark with desire. I prowl closer until I flatten her onto her back. It takes all my restraint not to fit my hips between her spread thighs, probe for her wet opening, and plunge my throbbing length inside her.

Instead, I lave her hard, juicy nipples and draw each, one after the other, into my mouth, eliciting another catch of breath from Bethany. Then I let my lips trail down her body once more until the Shangri-La of her pink, neatly trimmed sex is right under my lips. She's wet and swollen. Her clit peeks out from between her folds, begging for attention.

I cup her with my hand. Her entire body shudders as her eyes close. She lets out a long, agonized breath. "Clint..."

"Hmm, I'm here. And I'm staying here for a good, long while. Spread your legs wider."

She trembles as she complies. "I-I don't need to be more aroused for sex. Believe me, I'm more than ready."

"We're going to get there, I promise. First, I need this perfect peach of a pussy in my mouth."

Thankfully, she doesn't protest.

With a growl, I rake my tongue up her center, lapping at her sweetness and reveling in her shocked little moan, before I settle on her clit.

Her fingers find their way into my hair, and she tugs, hips wriggling, as I work the hard bud.

"Oh, my..." Her back arches. "Oh. *Oh...yes.*"

The sound of her pleasure resonates through every nerve and cell in my body. Once, I swore I'd never give her an orgasm. Now I can't fucking wait. There's something so kittenish and sensual about Bethany. If I had to bet whether any of her former lovers had ever gone down on her, I'd gamble everything I owned the answer is no. Being her first is turning me the fuck on.

Happily, I redouble my efforts. I'm glad now that I've always enjoyed being oral with females. It won't take me long to learn what stroke of my tongue will send her over the fastest. And I'll definitely enjoy figuring it out.

Soon, I settle into a slow, draggy rhythm, teasing her with long strokes before I lazily suck her clit into my mouth and pull, taunt her with a little nip, then release her to start all over again. Soon, she's tensing, holding her breath, squirming and panting and begging.

"Clint… Oh, please. Please. I…" Her next breath trembles, along with the rest of her body. "You're killing me."

"Hmm," I drawl, unwilling to take my mouth off her succulent flesh.

I love the way she swells and blushes and grips my hair, trying to pull the short strands. The sting of my scalp spurs me on, makes me want to taste her on a deeper level.

With my thumbs, I part her rosy folds and peek at all her sweet pink flesh. She's beautiful all over, but hell, this must be the most perfect pussy I've ever seen, especially when I'm watching her whole body twist and writhe with the pleasure I'm giving her. And maybe I only think she's so ideal because I'm in the moment. Maybe she's really not any better put-together than any other woman. But I don't remember similar thoughts ever crossing my mind.

I dip my tongue deep in her well, drawing from the source of her flavor. Fuck, I want her everywhere—on me, around me, under me. Arousing her is pushing me close to the brink. I need to send her over and end my self-torture.

I've got to get inside her.

As I curl my tongue deeper, I circle my thumb around her distended clit in slow circles. She wails in agony, back contorting. Her skin is rosy all over. She struggles to breathe. And she looks so goddamn beautiful in pleasure I can hardly remember why I ever refused to give her any.

"I-I'm…so close."

Fuck, yeah, she is. I can feel it, taste it, sense it.

I grip her hips, sweep my tongue back over her clit, and lap my way into the rhythm I know will undo her. Seconds later, she digs her nails into my scalp, thrusts frantic hips up at me, and saws air in and out of her lungs before she screams like I've devastated her with the kind of pleasure that's changed her definition of the word. And I'm loving every second of her orgasm, the smooth flow of honey, the undulating roll of her body as she tries to wring every last moment of ecstasy out of her climax and share it with me.

Finally, she falls limply to the bed, breathing deep and fast, legs lax. Beautiful satiation transforms her face.

I drink her expression in as I grab a condom before making my way up her body, kissing one hip bone and dragging my tongue over the soft valley between her breasts. Then I settle on top of her.

"Am I alive?" she asks with a loopy grin.

"You are," I assure her. "In about two minutes, I'll happily prove it again."

She shakes her head. "In two minutes, I'll still be lying here with my eyes closed, trying to comprehend what just happened."

I laugh as I peel open the condom and roll it down my aching cock. "Not a chance. Come here, sweetheart."

When I gather Bethany in my arms, she shifts to her side with me, soft and instantly willing to cuddle. It feels good to have her against me, trusting me enough to hold her close when she's vulnerable.

Stroking my palm across her skin, I glide down her back, over the cheek of her ass, across her thigh. Needing more of her nearness, I lift her leg over my hip and press kisses across her shoulder, up her neck, take teasing nips of her lobe. Her eyes flare wide with surprise and rekindling arousal.

I send her a knowing smile before I brush her lips with a kiss. "Hi."

"Hi."

I press my mouth to hers again, this time nudging her open. As soon as she parts for me, I invade deep, fusing our lips together as I roll her to her back and align my cock with her opening. I probe her, gliding inside her—one slick, tight inch at a time. She wraps her legs around me, gasping as I slowly submerge myself all the way.

Oh, damn... Being buried inside Bethany is almost a sacred experience. A shudder wracks me from head to toe. A groan tears from my chest. My hands tighten on her hips. I want to keep her pinned under me for each thrust as much as I want to feel her in my grip and be assured that she's mine.

I tear my lips from hers. "Hold on, this is going to be hard and fast."

"Yes...please."

That's all I needed to hear.

Like a man possessed, I grip the far edge of the mattress and use it as leverage to fuck her in deep, rapid-fire strokes. Her lips trailing across my jaw and her arms wrapped around me like she hopes I never let go does something to me. But the way her pussy grips me is magic. With every retreat and surge inside her, I swear she melts my muscles, ignites my skin, and fries my brain.

"Yes!" I use every bit of my strength to pull myself up and into her, even deeper than before. "Fuck..."

"Clint!" Her lips move in a flurry of frenetic need across my shoulder. "I ache again. How?"

Around me she tightens, wails, fingers digging desperately into me. I can't last much longer. Bethany is destroying my self-control. Being inside her and hearing her climbing cries of passion juices my bloodstream with pure, dizzying euphoria. I can't stop myself from plowing into her one hard, pounding stroke after another.

"Come for me," I growl out. "Come..."

It's my last coherent thought before bliss rolls me. The sensations only grow more intense when Bethany tosses her head back and clamps down on me with a violent, shattering scream. As she comes apart in my arms, I unravel. Blood rushes. My heart pounds. My body grinds, churning closer and closer to a climax that I swear feels cataclysmic and unlike anything I've ever termed an orgasm in my life. It's stripping me down, ripping me up, fucking rooting me to this woman. I should be terrified. Instead, it can't get here fast enough.

When the peak finally hits, it seizes my whole body. My rhythm falters. I try to get impossibly deeper inside her. Even though it's hopeless, I still sweat and growl and charge ahead, pouring out every ounce of need into her. Something thick and unfamiliar backfills its place. I can't identify it, but it's sweet. It attaches me to Bethany in a way I've never felt. It makes me grip her harder, spill the last drops of my soul into her, and cling as if only she can somehow save me.

As if, regardless of who she is or what's happened in the past, with her is where I belong.

CHAPTER SEVEN

D AWN IS A promise on the horizon when I slip out of Bethany's cottage and tiptoe to the main house. She's still sleeping, wrapped in the limp sheets and cozy blankets we shared last night.

Other than Bethany, I can't remember the last woman I actually slept beside for more than an hour or two. I usually don't like touching a lover in my sleep. But, as seems to be the case with a lot of things, she's different. All night, Bethany kept curling away from me on the far side of the bed. More than once, I rolled closer and dragged her body against me, wrapping my arm around her waist and burying my face in her neck. I woke up to her scent, to the feel of her backside against my cock, which stood hard and eager to pleasure her again after a peaceful, uninterrupted night's sleep.

Since Dad's sudden death, that's unusual, too.

I let myself in the main house's back door, hoping not to see anyone, and promise myself I'll start mentally unpacking last night after coffee.

As the brew drips into a spare carafe, I rummage around to find some fruit and a few pastries Keeley keeps on hand. As I toss everything onto a tray I find in the pantry, my phone buzzes. I almost ignore it—until I see the display.

"Bret?" I answer my middle brother. "You okay?"

"Yeah. Just checking in, making sure you're okay. Happy New Year, bro."

"Sorry I didn't call yesterday. Tending bar the other night was a bitch.

I think my feet are still recovering," I try to joke, all the while wondering why Bret is calling so early...and what I'm going to tell him about Bethany. I know how he'll view the situation—and that he'll see what's happening between her and me as a betrayal.

"It's cool. I would have called sooner myself, but man, was I hungover. I'm so glad class doesn't start for a couple of weeks."

"Yeah. Listen, not to nag, but it's time to lay off the booze and start focusing on the future again."

He's quiet for a very long time. "Yeah, I know. And I know you've had it way worse than me, watching Dad die and being helpless to stop it. But I keep realizing that I'm twenty-one, and both of my parents are already gone. Basically, I'm an orphan. And every time I think about doing things like finding my first job, buying my first house, or getting married without them giving me advice or cheering me on, it scares the shit out of me. I've got no safety net."

I understand exactly how he feels, but he's wrong. "I know it's not the same, but you've got me. I'll always be here for you. I don't profess to know everything, but I promise I'll help you figure it out as best I can."

He sighs. "Yeah, and I appreciate it. I'm aware that I need to adult and to stop leaning on parties and vodka to get through this shit. I'm just trying to figure out how. It will be easier once you nail that fucking bitch. How's it going, by the way? Get anything from her yet?"

I wince. What the hell do I say? Bret is convinced that if I pin Dad's death on Bethany, his pain will vanish. Looking back, I pretty much thought the same.

"Listen... Now that I'm here and looking into all the facts, I think we may have gotten it wrong. She's not who you think."

"What does that mean?"

"Based on what I've been able to find, I don't think she was involved with the theft of Dad's money."

"What? How is that even possible?" he shoots back hotly. "She was his financial advisor. She had the pulse on his investments. According to you, she fucking lied to him, didn't care that he died of a massive heart attack after he got the news, then skipped town. What suddenly changed?"

"Bethany and I work together, so I've spent some time actually getting to know her. She doesn't have a greedy or vicious bone in her body. I even had the chance to search her place and found nothing incriminating. I just don't think she did it." When he answers me with shocked silence, I feel compelled to fill the void. "Bret, there are two sides to every story. I don't know all of hers yet but—"

"Oh, my god. You fucked her, didn't you?" my brother growls.

I swallow. "The situation is more complicated than—"

"Bullshit! You got some from her and decided that her pussy is more important than Dad's justice. I can't fucking believe you."

Shit, Bret is pissed, which makes him almost impossible to reason with. Still, I have to try. Yeah, I admit the cynic in me still harbors niggling doubt about Bethany and wonders if I'm being played by a maestro. But I can't admit my reservations to my brother. Innocent until proven guilty, right? Ninety-nine percent of me is not sorry about what happened last night, and I won't let him guilt me into regretting the intimacy Bethany and I shared.

"Stop. Think. Do you want to know what happened to Dad and the money or not? I'm not going to get whatever information she has about the criminal operation at Reed Financial by being an asshole. She may be the only person who can tell us, so don't judge. You're not here. You don't know what's happening. You don't know her. And you don't know what she's been through."

"Whatever. I hope you can live with putting your dick above your family. Just don't cry to me when she fucks you over, too."

Suddenly, I hear three beeps in my ear and scowl. The little shit hung up on me? I shouldn't be shocked. Bret has always been a rash hothead. I wish like fuck he would think things through before he acts.

Gritting my teeth, I shove my phone in my pocket. Now isn't the time to reason with him. Sure, I know why he's upset. I understand what my actions look like on the surface, but he shouldn't judge without the facts. Once I can answer the questions we've all had since the day I told him Dad was gone, he'll come around. For now, I'm going to focus on Bethany and earning her trust so she'll tell me her secrets. No, we probably don't have a future. That sucks because I actually like her, and we seriously had the best sex ever. But someday—soon—I'll have to come clean with her. Hell, she doesn't even know my real last name. And once she figures out who I am, she might even hate me.

Unless we're stronger before I confess… Unless the feelings between us genuinely grow and she's willing to forgive…

Because lying and deceit are totally the ways to persuade her not to lump you in the douchebag category.

Okay, I'll have to try plan B, then—once I figure out what that is.

But what if Bret is right? that annoying voice asks me. *What if she is guilty?* Nope. I can't let myself think about the fact I could be falling for the woman who contributed to my father's demise.

The coffee finishes brewing, and I balance it all on the tray before I head back to Bethany's cottage. Inside, I set everything on the kitchen counter, then tiptoe to the bed.

At my approach, she rolls over and opens her eyes.

The sight of her is a gut punch. Her pale hair splays across the sheets. Her half-closed eyes look slumberous and sexy as hell. But the little smile curling up her lips makes me want to strip down and persuade her to repeat last night right now.

"Morning," she murmurs, voice husky.

Just like that, I'm hard again.

I clear my throat. "Morning. I found some food and coffee at the main house."

She moans, something between acknowledgment and pleasure, then hides a lazy yawn behind her hand. "Thank you. That's really sweet. Would you mind grabbing my robe off the back of the bathroom door?"

It's on the tip of my tongue to remind her that I've already seen it all, but if that makes her feel comfortable, I'll do it.

"Sure." I grab the pale blue satin garment and hand it to her.

"Thanks."

"Want me to pour you some java?"

"Please. Can you add a splash of cream from the fridge and a stevia packet from the cabinet to the left?"

"You got it."

By the time I've done that, Bethany rounds the corner to claim her steaming mug, robe securely belted around her small waist...which only accentuates the fact she's not wearing a bra. I can see the points of her nipples. I remember what they felt like, tasted like. I remember how she responds to my touch.

She clutches the mug, blowing on her brew to cool it, not quite meeting my gaze.

I swallow down a scalding sip of my own and try not to seduce her, at least not before caffeine.

With a sigh, I set my java aside and grab her by the waist. "Come here."

Bethany is stiff until I nestle her against me and press a gentle kiss to her lips. Finally, she blinks up at me. "You make good coffee."

"You make good everything else. Last night was..." I grin at her. "Let's just say I wanted to blow your doors off, but I'm the one dazzled." When she blushes, I can't help but laugh. "We're good together. How are you feeling about it?"

She frowns. "You actually want to talk about this?"

"You don't?"

"I guess we could. It's just that I expected..."

"What? For me to roll you on your back and do you again without saying a word? Or for you to wake and find me gone because I decided to skip out?"

"Either."

I can only imagine she expects that because someone taught her to. "Was Dalton the morning-after jackass?"

"He was one of them." She nibbles on her lip nervously, gaze not wavering from the brew in her mug. "But he was the one who hurt the most."

I tuck a stray strand of hair behind her ear. "Want to tell me about him?"

She shakes her head. "He's not important."

"I'm not trying to make you uncomfortable, Beth. But I need to know what you want to happen between us next."

"I don't know."

"Now that we've had a night of fun, are you having thoughts about kicking me to the curb?"

"I wouldn't have said yes in the first place if I didn't like you enough to want more than a hookup. But I don't have any expectations," she's quick to assure me. "I just appreciate you being so…kind."

I'm not following. "Kind?"

A soft blush stains her cheeks. "Caring about my pleasure. I've only had that once before, and even then—"

"Seriously?"

"That's weird to you, huh? Sex was just never that important. Now I see the big deal." She gives me a nervous laugh.

It's shocking to hear Beth confirm the suspicions I had last night. It blows my mind that a woman as gorgeous and responsive in bed as Bethany has only had one sexual partner before me who gave a shit about her pleasure. I'm not going to ask if she's picked up all her exes at Douchebags R Us. And I'm not listening to that voice in the back of my head—the one that sounds a lot like Bret's—telling me I shouldn't be giving her orgasms now. Because what really matters is what happens next.

"It was a big deal for me, too." And while I'm being honest, I might as well admit something else. "It felt special."

In fact, I'm not only relieved that I need to spend more time with her to find out what she knows about the Reed Financial scheme, I *want* to spend time with her. If she were any other woman, I'd already be thinking this relationship might turn serious.

Instead of smiling, she nods pensively. "It's almost too bad we can't have more than sex."

Frowning, I sit and pull her onto my lap. "Why can't we?"

"Like I've said, there's a lot going on in my life. I don't know how long I'll be on the island. Or how long you'll be here, for that matter. Still…" She squirms. "It's only fair of me to tell you that…I'm not exactly who you think I am."

I try to act completely casual, as if I'm not thrilled she might be on the verge of admitting something useful. "What do you mean? You're not Beth?"

"You've heard my family call me Bethany."

"Yeah, I figured you liked using your nickname at work or something."

"It's…more complicated than that." She presses her lips together. "Remember I told you that my dad and I aren't speaking, that our relationship is messed up?"

"Yeah."

"He's done some illegal things and he's probably going to prison for a long time. Before you ask, yes, I'm shocked and I'm saddened. But all this has put me in a really awkward position. People who knew and trusted me have turned on me. Even those I've worked with for years suddenly seem to have their pitchforks in hand, and they're coming after me."

"Guilt by association?"

"Pretty much. The guy in the loud Hawaiian shirt who keeps hounding me? He's a former client. I've known him for a decade."

The asshole's behavior makes more sense now, but it's still not okay. He doesn't get to verbally or physically harass Bethany for answers.

Is what you're doing any better?

I shove aside the nagging voice. "What does he think you can tell him? Do you actually know anything about what your dad was busted for?"

She sighs and rises, clearly uncomfortable with the conversation. "I can't really talk about it."

I try to tamp down my disappointment. It was unrealistic to hope that after one night she was going to spill all her secrets. But I want like hell to end this subterfuge, tell her who I am, admit my unexpected feelings so we can move past this. Maybe she cares enough about us to stay with me.

"I'd like to help you, but I can't if I don't understand."

"I appreciate that, but there's nothing you can do now. I just thought you should know I'm kind of off-balance and I have been since my professional life fell apart. I'll figure it out, but everything happened so recently. It's been a lot."

"Off-balance in what way?"

"Men who once worked around or under me used to call me ball-buster and ice queen and all the other unflattering, misogynistic terms for a smart, confident female. That's how I see myself. This shy, stuttering, uncertain person you know? I'm not her."

That explains the hints of assertiveness she showed me last night. And I feel good about that because she wouldn't have demanded anything she wanted sexually if she didn't feel comfortable with me. "I think you're awesome, even if you are feeling a little uncertain right now. If you ever want to talk, I'll listen and help you however I can."

Bethany smiles gently. "Thanks. I just wanted you to understand. I should also tell you that I might have to leave suddenly."

That makes me panic. "Leave?"

"I'll be called to testify, but I have no idea when. It could be next week or two years from now."

"As a witness for the prosecution? Or the defense?"

"Either. Both." She shrugs. "Anything is possible. Can we change the subject?"

I grasp all her reasons for being secretive, but I can't stay in limbo. I need answers. I'll need to deal with Bret's shit soon. I also need to get back to my life. I'd like to stop lying to Bethany. And I'm going to have to deal with the unexpected attachment I'm feeling to her somehow.

"Sure. Just...if you leave, don't forget me." I caress her face. "I'm not going to forget you anytime soon."

"Believe me, I won't." She bites her lip, this time to suppress a smile. "You have another condom, right?"

Despite all the problems, I grin. "Yes, ma'am. I do."

"And we don't have to be to work until four this afternoon."

"Yes, ma'am, that's right." I clasp her hips and drag her closer.

"I promised I'd help Britta's mom serve breakfast for the inn's guests, but I've got an hour or so. What do you say we put that condom to good use?"

I love the way she flirts—and lets me part her robe to see all her naked skin underneath gleaming in the morning sun. "I always like to make a lady happy…"

AFTER BREAKFAST IN bed that was way more bed than breakfast, I leave Bethany's ohana with a big smile on my face. Unfortunately, during the drive back to Ash's place for a shower and a change of clothes, reality intrudes.

Bethany is slowly opening up to me, but at this rate it might be weeks or months before she divulges everything. I don't have that long. Sure, Howie, who's running my business back home, is reliable and capable. But I'll have to return to North Dakota and oversee operations again soon, or the reputation of the oil services business I've spent more than five years building will all swirl down the toilet.

That means I need to start digging around to see if I can uncover any dirt myself.

From the console of Ash's crappy sedan, I grab my phone. While I'm idling at a stoplight, I scroll through the device until I find the picture I took of the card I uncovered in Bethany's wallet. Trying not to register the tremor in my hands, I dial the FBI agent's digits. I'm almost positive I'm going to get voice mail.

Trevor Forsythe answers on the first ring. "Hello?"

"Agent Forsythe, my name is Clinton Holmes. My father was one of the victims of the Reed Financial fiasco."

He pauses. "I'm listening."

"I'm calling for some information. I know Barclay Reed was arrested and is currently out on bail…"

"Yes."

"I read an official statement a few weeks back that you've arrested all suspects in the case. Is that still true? Do you have any additional suspects you're now pursuing?"

As soon as the words are out of my mouth, I wince. This guy doesn't know me at all. He can't even verify that I am who I say I am. He's not going to tell me a fucking thing.

"I'm not at liberty to discuss this case beyond the statements we've already issued."

Of course not. "Look, my father only ever had contact with Reed's daughter, Bethany Banks. I understand she was his right hand for a decade. She kept a full list of clients and supposedly managed their money, yet all their funds—in addition to those of Reed's own clients—disappeared. I watched my father fucking die of a heart attack the day he realized all his money was gone…" My voice is getting louder, and have to choke back the desperation in my tone. "Sorry. I'm personally impacted by this case, so I'm trying to understand her involvement and if there have been any inroads in recovering the money. And I'd like to see *all* the perpetrators brought to justice."

Getting Dad's savings back would at least be a consolation prize. But I'm far more focused on Barclay Reed—and anyone else responsible—going to prison.

"I'm not at liberty to discuss that either, sir. Parts of the investigation are still ongoing."

"But you've already determined Ms. Banks is innocent?"

"Mr. Holmes, I really can't say anything beyond the statement we've already issued that indicates Ms. Banks won't be charged with a crime. When the case goes to trial, the prosecution will lay out its case. Then you and the rest of the public will hear the details. Until then, I'm afraid I can't offer you any other information."

"But—"

"No. You want answers. I don't blame you. But I have a lot of victims to look out for," he points out. "I'm sorry for your loss."

The line goes dead.

With a snarl, I smash the button on my phone and resist the urge to hurl it into the windshield. I don't need another goddamn dead end.

The next twenty minutes of traffic, coupled with an impromptu rain shower, don't brighten my mood. Sure, I had a great night with Bethany. I'd like to have more. But I'd like to do it with a clear fucking conscience. I don't know how or if I can make that happen.

I shove the key in the lock, surprised to find Ash standing in the kitchen, chowing down on some Cheerios.

"Hey! Have a good night?" he asks with a waggle of his brows. "Since you didn't come home, I figured something good happened."

I pocket my phone, rake a hand through my mussed hair, and intentionally ignore his question. "I didn't expect you to be here."

"After work last night, Montana and I came here for a while. But early this morning, we decided that we've scratched our mutual itch, so she left about seven, waved sayonara…and we're done."

"You cool with that?"

"Yeah. She was fun, but there was nothing else between us."

I get that. "You know Samantha likes you, right?"

Ash looks surprised. "Why would you think that?"

"Are you kidding? Every time you left with Montana, she gave you longing looks as you two walked away."

"Huh. I totally missed that. I must be off my game." He shakes his head. "But now that I know… She's cute, not my usual. I might be interested. So what's going on with you and Beth?"

With a frustrated huff, I plop down on the cheap living room sofa. "Dude, I don't even know. I'm being pulled in so many different directions… What if she's guilty? What if she's not?"

"None of that would matter if you didn't like her."

I nod. "I more than like her. I think there's something real between us. As much as I've fought it…"

"You didn't expect to give a shit about the enemy."

"Yeah, and she's not at all what I expected. Besides being fucking sexy, she seems really sweet."

"Got any ideas what to do next?"

"Keep searching for information wherever I can, I guess. But it looks like I have to be patient until something gives."

I hate this plan, especially since I worry what Bret will do. He's not going to let our fight this morning go. And what happens if Bethany finds out I've been less than honest? She's been burned. She finds it hard to trust. She'll hate me if she learns the truth before I'm ready to tell her.

"Wish I had something brilliant to say, but you're right," Ash says.

I nod. "Maybe day drinking is the answer. Vodka is sounding wise right about now."

He barks out a laugh. "I don't know, man... I've asked tequila for advice, and when I've listened, it's been shitty."

"Good point."

With that, Ash tosses on a clean tank, says he's out to the gym, then disappears. I spend most of the day either Googling, napping, or pondering. Finally, it's time to head to the bar. After a quick text to Bethany, she assures me that Griff is giving her a ride to work since he's already headed in that direction. I arrive a few minutes before our shift. Despite all the doubt and uncertainty, the anticipation of seeing her again is way stronger. Excitement tightens my gut.

Right or wrong, I want to be near this woman. I want to see her smile. Hell, I want to give her reasons to smile—and not just for the sex, though that's amazing, too. I want her to smile because she's with me.

God, I have it bad.

When I duck into the bar, I expect to see Bethany setting her purse down, grabbing a tray, and wiping tables clean as she gets ready for what's sure to be another busy night of tourists partying their way through a holiday week in paradise. Yesterday's hangovers are a memory now, and a lot of these visitors know they only have another day or two here, so they're likely planning to make the most of them.

What I don't expect to see is Bethany sitting in the quietest corner of the place, holding hands with a stranger.

I stop. Stare. Scowl.

Who the fuck is he?

"That's a development I didn't see coming," Ash mutters in my ear.

A million things run through my head. Bethany said she wasn't into relationships right now. She said she'd only had one decent sexual experience in her life, so the odds of her reconnecting with an ex seem slim. I've already met all her siblings. Even if I hadn't, these two aren't looking at one another like family.

What pisses me off even more? She's crying.

Clenching my fists, I charge toward the far end of the bar.

Ash grabs my arm and holds me back. "Don't march over there and throw around accusations. It won't end well."

"Who is this fucker? Why is she letting him touch her?" I hiss. "And why the hell is he upsetting her?"

"I don't know, but you need to calm down. Did Beth promise you exclusivity?"

"No, but—"

"Then there is no but. You two spent a night together. That's it. That entitles you to nothing."

He's right, but that only pisses me off more. "I can't let him upset her."

Or put his hands on her.

"I get that. So why don't you make your way over there and ask in a friendly-like way if everything is all right. Anything else is likely to sound like an accusation and upset her more."

"Fine." I jerk my arm free and suck in seething breaths, trying to calm myself as I head closer.

It's a long twenty seconds, and they seem so wrapped up in their conversation—and each other—that neither even looks my way.

Until I clear my throat.

Bethany blinks up, spots me, and jerks her hands from the other man's. She looks pale. Though she's wiped away her tears, I still see the hint of wetness on her cheeks.

Whatever the fuck is happening, I feel like ripping this dude's head off.

"Clint." She jumps to her feet. "Hi."

This other guy is practically crawling across the table to put his hands on her, and that's all she says to me?

Maybe Ash is right. Maybe there's some explanation. I can't act like a jealous, overprotective prick…even if I feel like one.

"Everything okay?"

She lets out a shuddering breath. "Yeah. This is Stephen Lund." Then she turns to the tall, rangy guy with blond movie-star looks and a placating smile I want to punch from his face. "Stephen, this is Clint Dietrich. We…work together."

I shake his hand and glare directly into blue eyes a few shades lighter than mine. "Nice to meet you. Just to be clear, we're also dating."

Lund busts out laughing. Not exactly the reaction I was expecting… He's not surprised? Or pissed? Or wondering what the hell is going on? I sure am…

"I kind of guessed that. Bethany has always had a habit of keeping her personal life and thoughts private. I learned long ago to read between the lines." His grin widens. "But let's just say you made it a lot easier."

She rolls her eyes and slaps at his arm in a gesture that almost looks brotherly. Now I'm confused. What *is* their relationship?

"Glad we cleared the air," I say. "How long ago?"

"What?"

Since you fucked her? "Did you learn to read between the lines?"

"Oh…" He nods. "About two decades ago. I probably would have learned sooner, but we were just kids."

They grew up together? But they're not together?

"You two can stop talking about me as if I'm not here." Bethany scowls. "I'm going to clock in. I haven't done that yet. Stephen, be nice," she admonishes. "Clint, I'm fine. Don't worry."

With that, she disappears into the employees-only area.

I turn back to her supposed pal. "So you've known Beth a long time?"

He nods. "Her whole life. You haven't, and my guess is you'd like some dirt?"

Obviously, he can read me. I hate that, but it's not going to stop me from asking questions and hoping I get answers. "That would be helpful."

"How long do we have?" He glances toward the hallway where Bethany disappeared.

"Maybe three minutes."

"How serious are you about her?"

"It's new, but I definitely have feelings I didn't expect."

He flashes me a wide smile. "Good. She deserves some happiness."

"She told me there's a lot going on with her father." I fish for information.

"Yeah, it's a shit show. Look, I'm just here to talk to her. I've been on the island for a couple of days, staying with Harlow and Noah—where she would have crashed if she hadn't found out I was coming. It's a long story; I'll let her tell it. Bottom line is, she knows I'm not mad. Nothing is her fault."

Was he somehow impacted by the Reed Financial scam? I can't ask. If Stephen mentions the question to Bethany, it will give everything away. Instead, I bite my tongue.

"What's she like?" I ask instead. "I've only known Beth for a few days, and she says she's not herself right now. She's had some reservations because of her situation and the fact I'm a few years younger. I'm falling fast," I admit. "So I'd appreciate some help."

His eyes narrow. He's assessing me, gauging my authenticity. "I think she's figuring out who she really is. She's lived a very structured life until recently. She's always had a lot of expectations heaped on her shoulders. She was constantly overloaded and had to shove aside her personal life. Now, she's feeling her way through a new reality. But underneath all that, she's caring. Sensitive." He frowns. "She needs friends, and I'm trying to be here for her. So don't fuck with her. She's had enough of that to last her a lifetime."

I open my mouth to ask him what the hell that means. How is he trying to be here for her?

But Bethany appears beside us, a little frown knitting her brow. "You're not still talking about me, I hope."

"Maybe a little." He winks. "Like I was saying, I've got a car on the island and when I find a rental I like, you can crash with me if you want. In a spare bedroom," he adds hastily. "And I'll be happy to drive you home tonight to save Maxon the trip."

"I got it," I cut in.

Yeah, I don't exactly have a car of my own, just like I know who she rides with is her choice. I also understand she and Lund are "friends." But I don't know anything about this guy except that he's roughly her age, he cares about her, and that I see some sort of intimacy between them I don't like.

"You sure you don't mind?" she asks me. "It's so far out of your way."

"No problem." I'll figure out the details later.

"All right." The other guy shrugs. "Call me if you change your mind."

"Sure. My next day off is Sunday. If you still have time for dinner then, I'm up for that."

"Let's do it. I'll call you." He gives her a dazzling grin, then enfolds her in his arms and kisses her cheek like he has every right to touch her. "Good to see you again, shorty. Nice to meet you, man." He waves at me. "Talk to you."

Then he's gone. I don't dislike him. He seems okay. But he knows far more about Beth than I probably ever will, so in that moment I despise him.

Still, I can't do anything except grind my jaw, count backward from a hundred, and try not to sounds like a possessive asshole. I've never felt this way. I don't even know where this animosity is coming from.

"Hey, guys!" Andy shouts across the bar, and all the waitstaff comes running to the hallway.

Trying to shove down my annoyance, I follow, then listen as our mostly absent manager regales us with crap about a stopped-up toilet, a fraudulent string of credit cards, the wine shipment that's late because of the holidays, and the fact that Terry is still out with the flu.

I can't even grab a word with Bethany before an unexpected rain shower becomes a downpour. Drenched tourists rush in and the crowd suddenly goes from easily manageable to utterly insane.

By the time I look up again, it's nearly ten p.m. Hours have passed in a blur. I've seen Bethany, but I haven't been able to focus on where she is and if she's all right.

A quick glance tells me she's bustling from one table to another, dropping off the drinks I just mixed, before she wipes her hands on a dishtowel hanging from her waistband, grabs her tray like it's a shield, and heads to the back corner.

Mr. Loud Hawaiian Shirt is waiting, and she looks nervous as she approaches.

I can't hear them, but I can see he's agitated, and she's defensive. My gut says this is going to get out of line fast.

"I'll be right back," I tell Ash as I storm out from behind the bar.

Stephen's drop-in agitated me, but this guy's bullying is sending my temper over the edge.

As busy as we've been, Ash doesn't argue. Or maybe I don't hear. Whatever. Former client or not, this guy isn't manhandling or bruising Beth anymore.

"—the fuck happened," he spits. "I'm entitled to—"

"Beth…" I put a protective arm around her. "Go. I got this."

She turns to me, startled. "That's okay. I can do this."

"You can, but you don't have to."

There's that indecisive little nibble on her lip again. She's weighing the situation, probably her sense of responsibility, which is great, versus her fear and loathing, which seem pretty mighty, too.

"You sure?" she says finally.

"Oh, that's it," snarls the asshole. "Run away. Get your knight in shining armor to protect you. He must think you're a helpless little damsel in distress. Ha! He doesn't know the teeth and claws you have. He doesn't know that pretty facade he probably likes to fuck holds an ugly bitch inside."

"That's enough," I growl at him, urging Beth away from the confrontation. "Tell me what you'd like to drink or leave. Beth is a waitress, not a punching bag."

The guy slams his beefy fist on the table. "You don't get it. You look at her and you see a pretty piece of ass. I see a hustler. I see a criminal. Watch your money, pal. If you have any, she'll fuck it out of you, too."

He scrapes the chair across the floor and lurches to his feet, almost knocking the table over.

My heart freezes in my chest. What is he saying? That Bethany has had sex with him? When? Why?

Before I know what I'm doing, I'm chasing him to the exit—and barely keeping my hands off his throat. "What the hell does that mean?"

"Exactly what it sounds like. That sweet little thing you keep defending? I got ten minutes of pleasure out of her. And nothing but endless shit in the last six months."

He's talking about *my Beth* like she's one step above a whore. "Who the hell do you think you are?"

"If you have to ask, you might try paying attention to the news, kid."

I resent this guy on so many levels right now. But he's a former client. He has a story if he's here night after night, trying to get some sort of restitution or pound of flesh out of Bethany.

"I'm not a fucking kid. And I'm a lot more familiar with the news than you think. What the hell do you think she can give you at this point?"

Surprise bounces across his face, then he stares back in speculation. "She can return the money that belongs to me."

I swallow. I have to be careful here. I can't let on too much in case he says something to Bethany, and he's hardly an ally. But there are two sides to every story. I can't ask my dad his side anymore. This fortyish windbag is the only other client of Reed Financial I've ever met face to face.

"What if she doesn't know where it is?"

"She damn well should. I trusted her with my money for five years. Hell, I handed her a check for seven million dollars two days before Barclay Reed was arrested. She promised to personally see to it. You keep thinking she's innocent if it makes you feel better about fucking her. But I'm telling you, she's not the sweet thing you think."

Then he's gone. And I'm so angry I'm shaking.

Yes, this guy was a victim of the financial scheme, just like my dad. Instead of succumbing to the shock, he chose to fight back. He's entitled to be angry. Seven million is a lot of money. And I get that he's looking for someone to blame. I was once, too.

But what he's doing isn't cool.

This asshole will be back, I have no doubt. He wants his money, of course. But he's full of righteous, pent-up rage and seemingly desperate for revenge. I need to protect Bethany because I have a feeling he's capable of far more destructive things than hurling insults.

Why did she ever let this man touch her? He might not be terrible to look at, but he's an angry, vile misogynist. The way he talks about her, as if he sees no value in her… She *is* smart and kind. He thinks I don't know her? Ha! He's the one who doesn't.

That knowledge is my only consolation, because I don't understand anything else that's happened in the last ten minutes.

The only other thing I know is that I need to talk to Bethany ASAP.

CHAPTER EIGHT

"YOU'RE QUIET," BETHANY remarks on our drive back to Maxon and Keeley's inn.

As I steer through the inky night, away from civilization, I tap my thumb against the steering wheel. The silence during our ride feels sharp. It's ratcheted up my tension. I don't want to hurl accusations at her, and I don't want to argue while I'm driving. But waiting hours to get this off my chest has pushed my mood someplace ugly.

"A lot on my mind," I say finally.

"You're wondering about my relationship with Stephen."

"Among other things, yes."

He's not the first problem on my mind. I'm also deeply disturbed by everything her former client spewed. But since she brought Lund up, maybe I've cooled down enough to talk about him. The asshole? How do I deal with the knowledge that she had sex with someone who feels nothing but contempt for her? How do I even ask why?

She sighs. "When you walked in and saw Stephen holding my hands, you probably thought we seemed cozy and romantic. But it's not like that."

"So you've never been to bed with Lund?"

I'm hoping like hell she says no. Instead, a flush steals across her face.

"He's been a good friend my whole life. His father and mine were cronies and golfing buddies. Sometimes, all of us spent weekends together and had barbecues… He's comfortable."

I grip the wheel harder. There's a whole lot she's not telling me, including the fact they—at some point—fucked. No, I don't own her. But I want to understand what's going on between them now.

"Then why did he think you weren't speaking to him? Why did you stay with Maxon and Keeley to avoid him at Noah and Harlow's place?"

She rolls her eyes. "Of course he told you."

"He said you would explain."

"All right. Remember I said that my father had gotten a friend's daughter pregnant? I was talking about Douglas Lund. Amanda is Stephen's younger sister. That wasn't the only terrible thing my father did to his supposed bestie, but it definitely started the bad blood between them."

"Why would you assume Stephen would blame you for your father's sins? Because everyone else is?"

She nods. "I knew the affair was going on. I knew what my father is like. If I had said something… But I didn't because, despite the age gap, they're both adults and seemed happy, and I never thought he'd treat her like a piece of ass. But maybe I could have stopped it if I'd made my father's business my own." She gives a bitterly ironic shake of her head. "Then again, that's true of a lot of things."

"What do you mean?" Is she talking about the financial scam, too?

"Long story."

One she's not ready to tell. Another dead end.

With a frustrated sigh, I pull up at the inn. It's dark except for the light shining from the window in the nursery. So unless Bethany invites me in, the evening—and my chance to get answers—is over until tomorrow.

I stop the car and put it in park. "I know you and Stephen dated at some point."

She unbuckles her seat belt. "It's late, and I'm not up for this conversation, Clint."

When she opens the door, I grab her arm to stay her. "Please."

With a sigh, she settles back in her seat. "All right. We didn't date. He understood my life and he comforted me when I asked him to. I needed to know what sex with someone I actually cared about would be like. I needed to know if I could feel anything for someone I wasn't screwing for the wrong reasons. He was the only decent sexual experience I had until you. I'm not going to apologize for it. I'm thirty. I've made choices you'll probably never understand. My past isn't up for negotiation. If that's a deal breaker for you, then it's better for me to know now. I'll find another ride home tomorrow."

Her words ping in my head. I don't like her answer, but…she's right. I have no moral high ground. In the past, I've taken women to bed for way less righteous reasons than needing solace or affection. Hell, my intentions with Bethany are definitely less than pure. Or at least they started that way. Some people would argue that I'm fucking her for the truth. That I'm using her. While that might be a smarter choice for my heart, that's not what's happening at all.

"I'm sorry, Beth. Your past is yours, and you owe me nothing. I was…" *Jealous as hell.* "Out of line."

Under the sedan's overhead lights, she bounces a soft gaze my way. "Honestly, I didn't think it would matter to you until I saw your face. I'm—"

"Annoyed with my behavior? I don't blame you. I'm pretty fucking annoyed, too."

"No. In an odd way, I'm flattered. What I did has never mattered to any of my past lovers. I'm not looking for a caveman, but it's nice that you care."

Thank god she's not totally pissed. "Is it asking too much to not let someone else touch you while we're together?"

"Would that work both ways?"

Right now, I can't imagine being interested in anyone else. And I definitely don't need any more complications. "Yeah."

"Don't you want to think about whether you'd like to be exclusive?"

"No."

She glances over at the dark ohana beside the house, then back to me.

"Is Ash expecting you back at his place tonight?"

"I think he's trying to see what's between him and Samantha."

"Do you want to stay with me tonight?"

The smart choice would be to walk away until I have my head screwed on straight. Until I've got some perspective. Until I'm not jealous that someone else gave her the comfort I want to shower on her. But I need every moment with Bethany. I need her trust. And I need her attention. The truth is, I wonder if I'm coming to need her.

Jesus, I put myself in the stupidest, shittiest position.

Still, there's only one answer. "I would love to stay with you. I'd love to get those clothes off you, my hands on you, and hear you scream my name again."

A blush steals across her cheeks again. "Now that Maxon and Keeley are back, we might have to be a tad quieter than last night."

Fuck that. "They have a newborn, so I think they know all about sex."

"They just don't need to know my business. No one does."

Not even me. Bethany isn't going to make getting information from her easy.

Together, we cross the yard and traverse the stone steps to the little cottage. She opens the bright door and reaches for the light switch inside.

I grab her wrist. "Don't bother. We're not going to spend any time in the kitchen."

Her breath catches. I can't see her face in the dark but I hear her excitement. It probably shouldn't and I wish it didn't, but her gasp sets my blood on fire.

With a tug, I pull her body against mine. We crash together. I lower my mouth to hers and shove her lips apart with my own. I'm not patient. I *need* this woman in a way I don't understand. I want to be the one to give her pleasure and comfort and whatever else she requires.

When Bethany melts against me and surrenders herself to the kiss, I wrap my arms around her and lift her from the floor, urging her legs around my waist. She all but climbs my body, tightens her grip on me, and deepens our kiss.

Fuck yes.

The minute we reach the bed, I set her flat on her back, crawl onto the mattress above her, and strip away my T-shirt. "All I could think about all evening was replacing the memory of Lund's touch with mine."

She pauses unbuttoning her short-sleeve sweater to caress my face. "I wasn't thinking of him at all. I only want you."

Her admission does something to me that I can't ignore or fight.

Swallowing, I shove her sundress up her thighs, press my entire body onto hers, then grip her hips and lift. I strain to get closer, my cock notching against her sex. At the feel of my erection against the soft pad of her sex, I toss my head back and groan. *So, so good.* And she's already damp. I saw the little wet spot on her panties. I swear I can almost feel it through my strangling jeans.

With a snarl, I stand and tear into my fly, yanking a few condoms from my pocket and slapping all but one on the nightstand.

Around us, the sounds of the night—frogs, insects, and waves—resonate in the distance. But my breathing is the loudest. It tangles with her gentle pants, which ramp up to a little gasp when I rub my fingers directly over her lace-covered pussy.

"Take them off."

Bethany doesn't argue, simply shimmies the silken undergarment off her body and lets it fall to the floor. She peels the sweater off, too. The only things between me and her naked body are two spaghetti straps and the soft gray dress they're holding up.

"Does this zip in the back?" I tug at the cotton.

She shakes her head. "It stretches."

Even better.

I flip the strap off of one shoulder. As she shrugs out of the other, I'm aware of her bare pussy inches away. My entire body's imperative is to be there now—and never leave. But I want to see her nipples, too. I want her breasts bare for me.

I jerk down on the bodice. The soft cotton strains until her breasts spring free and the dress gathers around her waist. She's not wearing a bra.

I suspected it the second she ditched the sweater. Now that her taut, candy-sweet nipples are inches from me and her naked pussy is even closer, I'm not sure where to start.

Decisions, decisions…

I roll the condom on, ignoring my shaking hands, then dive onto the bed beside her, latching onto one of her hard pink crests at the same time my fingers find their way to her clit.

Bethany whimpers under me, fingers tugging at my hair, hips moving in needy wriggles.

Her arousal spikes my bloodstream with savage triumph. I'm driven not just to give Bethany pleasure but to surround her, to make her feel wanted and adored. Vital. I want to fill her up so thoroughly that she'll never seek out Stephen Lund or any other man for comfort. She won't find it in their empty touches. And I will make damn sure she thinks twice about having a meaningless fling with a client—or anyone else—again.

Yeah, that's lofty and irrational. I know. But I can't control my urges right now. I'm not even going to try.

"Beth…" I breathe against her skin before I pluck her other nipple with my lips and teeth, then follow that up by sliding excruciatingly slow circles around her clit.

"Clint…" Her breath hitches. "Oh… What are you doing to me?"

"Making you feel good. Do you like it?"

"Yes."

She sounds breathy, aroused. It turns me on more.

"Good. Tell me when you're close to coming."

"I'm almost there," she admits. "I don't understand."

"What?" The explosive chemistry between us?

"I hardly liked sex before you. But today, I thought of almost nothing else."

Oh, fuck if that doesn't flip my switch even more. "I thought about you, too, sweetheart. Your lips, your soft skin, the way you toss your head back when you're trying to fight the rising need to scream, the way your eyes turn so green before you come. Like now."

I can see her under the moonlight streaming in. The silvery beams illuminating her also show me how dilated her pupils are and how hazy her expression has turned.

"Clint!"

"I'm here. God, you're so fucking sexy." If my brain could focus on something other than arousing her, maybe I'd be more eloquent about the soft, slick pad under my fingers and her nipples stabbing desperately in my direction. But all my body knows is that she's ready for me to sink into her. "I want to put my hands and mouth everywhere."

"No." She shakes her head frantically, nails digging into my shoulders. "Inside me. Now."

I'll never turn down that invitation.

I vault over her thigh, between her legs, and grip her knees, settling them around my hips. Then I'm pushing my way inside her. The hot, slick walls of her pussy threaten to dissolve my self-control. But I'm spellbound by more than the physical pleasure of sex. Her arms encircle me, opening to me, welcoming me. Wanting me. As I penetrate her, Bethany presses kisses across my jaw until she catches the corner of my lips with her own.

All bets are off then. I slant my mouth over hers and slide deep inside as I surge forward the last few inches and take complete possession of her body. She arches up and cries out, legs spreading wider under me, silently begging me for more.

I clutch her hips, hoping like fuck I won't leave bruises, then I crash into her in every way possible, stroke after long, rapid stroke. My skin is burning. My libido is lit up. Every part of me is utterly on fire for this woman. I hate to put a name to what I feel for her…but I'm more than a little worried I've fallen in love.

Seconds later, she's tightening and bucking underneath me, clutching me as if she can't get close enough, and calling out to me in shrill cries that send shivers skittering across my skin. With a growl, I grip her hair, force her to stare into my eyes.

As I watch her come, ecstasy implodes me.

With a chest-deep groan, I bury my face in her neck and let go of everything, especially my sanity. I ride her through an agonizing, clawing climax that's the most fucking intense thing I've ever felt. My head is swimming, my senses reeling. And still I pound and press my way deeper, shaking and growling and holding her like I'll never let go.

When it's over, I'm panting, blinking. Stunned.

Son of a bitch.

I look down at Bethany—and freeze when I see tears seeping from the corners of her eyes.

"Sweetheart?"

She squeezes her eyes shut and shakes her head. "I'm fine."

"You're crying."

"You make me feel things…" She gives me the most heartbreaking smile. "You don't know how amazing and confusing that is."

I don't.

Swallowing, I smooth the hair back from her face. "Tell me."

"Don't you want to get up, get dressed…"

And put space between us?

"No." I'm still inside her, still connected to her. "Is this too intimate for you?"

She hesitates. "I'm not used to it. I'm not used to any of this. Where have you been for the last ten years?"

The humor she tries to inject into her question is unmistakable, but I hear it for the plea it really is. Something is going on in her head. In her heart. If she's half as caught up in me as I am in her… Yeah, that makes me want to celebrate. But it also terrifies me. What happens when she finds out why I sought her out in the first place?

"Wishing I knew you," I tell her softly. Until I can find a way to be honest about everything else, I can be honest with my feelings.

Her smile that turns into tears rips at my chest. "If I'd known you all this time, it would have saved me a lot of pain."

Bethany is so open right now. She wants to tell me things. The yearning to share is on her face. I feel guilty as hell for even encouraging her.

On the other hand, if I had zero agenda other than to love this woman, I would still be coaxing her to spill everything to me.

"You keep saying these things that break my heart. Tell me why. Let me take some of the pain."

She shakes her head. "It's not your problem, and you don't want it."

"I do." I press a soft kiss to her mouth. "Tell me what hurts you. I'll hold you. We'll work it out."

"I don't want you to look at me differently afterward."

"Beth, you aren't your past. You are your heart."

As soon as the words are out of my mouth, I stop. My world tilts on its axis in a dizzying sway before slowly righting itself. What I just admitted to her—and myself—is that I no longer measure her by what happened before we met. Whatever she was involved in previously doesn't define my feelings for her. I might not know every single thing about Bethany Banks, but I know her on some deep level that I'm not sure many do. Past transgressions, if she's even guilty in the Reed Financial scheme—that wasn't her. This woman who's still holding me and doing her brave best to fight tears is.

Gently, I withdraw from her, dispose of the condom, then return to gather her in my arms.

"You're amazing," she whispers. "You're the first man I believe genuinely wants to know how I feel."

"You're so warm and beautiful, and I'm struggling to understand how every man you've ever spent time with didn't see that and didn't care."

"It's…complicated. Dalton? My first…"

"Your father set you up on a date?"

"It wasn't a date." She swallows. "It was a business transaction. I was fresh out of grad school. Dalton was thirty-five. A new tech billionaire. Dad sent me to dinner with him, told me to be friendly, give him whatever he wanted, and not to come home until he agreed to invest with us. I was naive. I thought Dad meant let the man order lobster and for me to laugh at all his jokes. I thought he meant to be persistent."

Sick, roiling nausea slides through me. I know exactly where this is going.

"Your own father pimped you out?"

Her tiny nod is full of shame. "I felt flattered by Dalton's advances. Well, at first. I had a crush on him when Dad introduced us. The fact that someone obviously well-respected and urbane liked *me*? I was thrilled. When I say it now, I sound stupid, but I grew up sheltered."

"It's not your fault. He took advantage of you."

"Maybe, but I let him. After all the wining, dining, and conversation, he took me to his hotel room. The sex was horrible. It hurt. He thanked me for my virginity, then rolled over and called my dad to give him the account. Even then, I didn't get it. After that, he dialed his wife, told her that he loved her, turned out the lights, and rolled over. I was so stunned. I didn't know he was married."

"What a dirtbag." I'm completely furious on her behalf.

"As soon as he fell asleep, I cried. I eventually slept. But when I woke up, he was gone. The next time I saw him was at a big holiday bash we threw for our clients. He brought his beautiful wife and shook my hand as if he barely knew me. I was so humiliated."

Forget furious. I want to kill this guy. What an absolute prick. But he's a symptom, not the problem.

"I'm so sorry, sweetheart. What did your father say?"

"That I did a good job. In fact, he patted me on the back for being smart enough to know that business and sex mix just fine. He chastised me for letting silly emotions get in the way, of course. Then I got the speech about how there was no such thing as love, just power and control and having the balls to use the weapons at your disposal to wield them."

What kind of man uses his daughter's innocence and self-respect to make a buck? "He sounds like a goddamn monster."

She gives me a little shrug. "He is who he is, driven and detached. Since Dalton brought a ton of prestige and cash to the organization at a time we needed it, it was hard not to see Dad's point. So I buried how I felt and carried on." She closes her eyes. "Dalton was the first. Unfortunately, he wasn't the last."

Oh, my god. How many random VIPs did her father coerce her into getting naked with? How has she coped? I can't imagine what letting people use her did to Bethany's psyche. No wonder she never felt real pleasure. I'm also not surprised she sought Lund out. Who could blame her for wanting sex on her terms? Or wanting to know if being with someone she at least liked would be different? I'm thrilled she responds so totally to me. That must say something about her feelings, right?

If I don't find the gentlest way possible to explain why I pursued her and why I've completely changed my mind, the enormity of my betrayal... *Fuck.* It will crush her. And I doubt Bethany will never forgive me.

"What do you mean? There were...others?"

"Yeah." And she doesn't sound proud of that. "Dad occasionally asked me to close deals with other reluctant investors. Anytime I hesitated, he would tell me how much he needed me and how proud he was of me. So I didn't always say no when I should have." She winces. "It sounds horrible. I never wanted you to know because I didn't want you to lose respect for me. I swear, it didn't happen often. And it's been years since a client touched me. After a while, I became less naive and more savvy. I figured out ways to persuade a potential investor to sign without crawling between the sheets."

"Oh, my god..." I'm astounded by all the ways this man used his daughter. And I hate that she ever let him get away with it because it's clearly taken a toll on her. It's also probably why she developed a thick outer shell that I've had trouble cracking—until now. "Oh, sweetheart."

"I hope that also explains why I had sex with Paul Daniels," she murmurs.

"Who?"

"Mr. Loud Hawaiian Shirt."

"He didn't tell me his name," I say numbly.

"But he told you we fucked, I'm sure." She wrenches out of my arms and rises to pace. "He was a big prick when we met. I knew my dad was going to ask me to 'finesse' him. Turned out he had a little prick when it counted. But he also had hundreds of millions of dollars. That's all the reason my father needed to unleash 'his secret weapon.' That's what he called me, you know."

Dumbfounded, I sit back. "Your father deserves to die."

"He'll probably spend the rest of his life in prison. That's some consolation."

"That's not enough for the shit he put you through."

"Well, I should have refused, and I'm hardly the only one he hurt. In the last couple of weeks, I learned he's heaped misery on all my siblings. I don't know if prison time will be justice, but at least he'll be away from us. Hopefully, we'll all find solace in that."

She sounds torn and a little sad.

I don't understand. "You're not going to miss him?"

Her hesitation shocks me.

"I miss the man I thought I grew up with. He seemed to nurture and praise me. I was so starved for attention as a kid that I soaked him up like a sponge. Looking back, I see that he cultivated my intelligence because he always intended to put me to work. He was just waiting for me to grow up and finish school so I could be another tool in his box to expand his wealth and power."

The way she describes him, I can't imagine that she knew or had anything to do with his financial scheme. It sounds as if he was perfectly capable of screwing any and all of the people around him. No doubt he was happy to have a variety of pawns, including his own daughter, to shuffle in whatever way benefitted him most. The anger and disillusionment she must be feeling… It's no wonder she's been closed and guarded. It's a shock she's opening up to me at all.

And I feel like an utter shit for not being honest with her in return.

I've got to be. Now isn't the time. It will sully this moment where she's finally allowing herself to purge her hurt. She won't remember that I'm trying to console her or that I'm in her corner. She'll just hate me—with good reason.

Could this situation get any more fucked up?

I gather Bethany against me and hold her protectively, silently telling her that I'll be her buffer from her dad and the users who took advantage of her for a moment's pleasure. "I'm so sorry, sweetheart. I can't imagine what you've been through. I was always close to my dad, so to wake up one day and realize he's not who I thought... How did it not shatter you?"

"The one useful thing he taught me is how to compartmentalize. I've cried. I'm sure I'll cry again." She sniffles. "Maybe now if you don't stop making me so mushy. But I won't let him prevail. That's the other valuable lesson I learned from him. The last person standing wins. This time, that's going to be me."

"You're so strong. I'm proud of you. Never forget, you're better than that son of a bitch. I have no doubt you'll beat him. And I promise I'll be beside you."

"Thank you. I needed to hear that. I was so afraid that if you knew the truth, you would judge me." Her voice drops. "That you would rebuff me."

For the first time, she initiates affection by throwing her arms around me. My heart wrenches. Fuck the past. From now on, I'm going to take care of her. I'm going to live up to my word. And when I tell her the truth, I'm going to hope that she'll show me understanding and empathy. Then I'll tell her what I've been suspecting all day.

I'll tell her that I'm in love with her.

TWO DAYS LATER, I stand across the kitchen from Maxon, who's glaring at me. For the third morning in a row. I'd like to believe he's just grouchy because he's suffering from new-parent sleep withdrawal, but I'm pretty sure he's pissed at me. After all, I disregarded all his warnings about Bethany's fragility and took her to bed anyway.

If he knew the truth, he'd probably punch my face. And I feel so shitty about deceiving Bethany I would let him.

"You doing okay?" I venture. "Surviving fatherhood so far?"

"Yeah. You stayed over again last night, huh?"

I nod. "Beth is still sleeping, so I thought I'd bring her coffee." It occurs to me that maybe Maxon thinks I'm freeloading off of his sister—and therefore, off of him. "Look, I can pay for the room if you'd feel more comfortable."

Her oldest brother scowls. "I don't want your money. I gave my sister a place to crash. She can do whatever she wants while she's here. Have you thought about what you'll do when she moves out?"

"Technically, I'm staying with a friend." Hell, if I wanted to get a place of my own, I could. "But I know Beth has plans to move out. She'll find the right place eventually."

Maxon raises a brow. "She told me yesterday that she'll be leaving on Sunday."

No shit? Where is she going? Why didn't she tell me?

"She didn't mention that."

He gives me a judgmental arch of his brow. Since he's not happy with me, I'm sure he thinks there are at least a dozen good reasons why Bethany didn't loop me into her plans. But I can't think of a single one. Despite telling me her secrets, is she pulling away?

Clearly, we need to talk.

I'm about to gather a carafe of coffee for Bethany, along with a plate of fruit, when Keeley enters the kitchen holding baby Kailani, who's dressed in a white onesie that reads I FOUND MY PRINCE. HIS NAME IS DADDY. She's also wearing a pair of pink pants and a matching flowered headband.

"Morning," I say to break the tension. "She looks precious."

Keeley smiles. "Isn't she?"

Maxon kisses the baby's head, then looks at his daughter with an adoring grin. "You would be cuter if you'd sleep more at night, but I love you anyway."

His wife laughs. "Good luck, buddy. Britta assures me we have weeks, if not months, of two a.m. feedings in our future."

"That sounds terrible." But Maxon doesn't look upset. He's still wearing that loopy grin that says he loves his baby girl.

"Well, you signed up for it, big guy." Keeley winks, then turns to me. "Would you mind holding her for a minute? I haven't had a chance to say good morning to my husband yet."

"Sure," I mumble before Keeley hands me the infant and shows me how to support her fragile head. Once we're good, the redhead wraps her arms around her husband and kisses him soundly.

They're in love. It's obvious she's ecstatically happy with her life. Maxon looks damn smitten, too.

I want what they have. I mean, I always knew I would want a wife and kids eventually, but I saw that in my thirties, when my business was more established and I felt ready. Looking at the two of them, I feel the itch for that future now. I was ridiculous for imagining love would wait until it was convenient for me to fall.

Could Bethany ever let herself fall for me? Is happily ever after something she's even ready for?

I stare at the pink-cheeked baby who peers at me with slitted blue eyes. She's soft and smells good. She yawns as if she's already ready for a nap her parents won't be getting. She sticks her tongue out, lunging toward Keeley as if she's seeking her mother for some breakfast. But she wraps her little fingers around one of mine. Her nearly translucent fingernails are sharp as hell but she's absolutely adorable. I've never spent much time with a newborn. Suddenly, I'm fascinated—and a little envious.

Does Bethany want children someday? And why am I thinking about this before I even know whether we could possibly have a future?

Keeley ends the kiss with a squeeze of Maxon's biceps and a saucy grin, then picks up a little remote on the kitchen counter. Suddenly, Pharrell Williams's "Happy" floods the room. Bethany's older brother gives his wife a smile full of devotion. My parents used to look at one another like this.

When Keeley cradles her daughter in her arms again, I load up a tray with the hot coffee and bites of breakfast.

"Want some vegetarian quiche to take with you? I can also whip you up a watermelon-kale smoothie that's amazing."

She means well, but that sounds terrible. "No thanks. This will be plenty for now. We'll grab something more substantial before we head into work."

"Okay. Well…if you change your mind—"

"He won't, sunshine." Maxon wraps an arm around her. "Just like I'm not going to. Most men want more than seeds and sprouts for breakfast."

"You're just stubborn and have the palate of a four-year-old." She looks my way. "Come on. Back me up. You like kale, don't you?"

I wince. "Sorry, no. I have to side with your husband."

She gives me a mock huff. "Then out of my kitchen. Both of you! Neither of you are welcome back until you try my smoothie."

"Does that mean I don't have to do the dishes anymore?" Maxon teases. "Hot damn."

As I head for the back door, I see Keeley swat Maxon with her free hand, then both of them dissolve into laughter as their daughter falls asleep, cocooned between them safely.

Yeah, I definitely want that. Bethany and I need to talk.

At the top of the stairs, she surprises me by opening the door, wearing that robe that keeps me from her naked body too often. Not that I didn't enjoy her last night—more than once. But every time I'm with her, it's like I've never had her. Or like I'll never have enough of her.

"Coffee. Thank you!" She pours two quick mugs. After doctoring hers up in seconds, she sucks down half the mug in big, caffeine-deprived swallows.

Her moan of enjoyment is almost comical.

"Like that, I take it?"

"I *need* it. Someone kept me awake half the night."

"Are you complaining?"

"Not right now. Ask me how I feel at midnight."

We'll both be dragging ass then, but being with her was totally worth it.

Since I like my java black, I start gulping it down, savoring the hint of bitterness and burn on my tongue. "So...Maxon says you're moving on Sunday?"

She quickly turns sheepish. "I forgot to tell you, didn't I? My bad. Stephen called me yesterday morning. While he was looking for a rental on the island for himself, he found one within walking distance of the bar. It's not what he wants, but he sent me pictures. I checked it out yesterday on my way into work." She searches around until she finds her purse, then digs inside, finally pulling out an envelope. "I'm going to sign the lease today. It's only a three-month term. Granted, it's not a great place, but if I'm frugal, I should be able to afford it. I hope. But Maxon and Keeley will have their inn back. I can't impose anymore."

Everything she says makes perfect sense. But I'm not happy. I don't like that she intends to walk to and from work alone. And I don't like that she intends to live there without me. I want to be closer to her, both for my investigation and our future. If I'm with her nearly twenty-four seven, she'll keep feeling closer to me and open up even more, right? It should also give me the perfect opportunity to tell her the true reason we met. After that...I'm hoping she'll be able to forgive me.

But if, like the cynic in my head suggests, she's actually guilty of playing a role in stealing her clients' money... Well, if I'm living with her, she'll be hard-pressed to hide it for long. Then I can figure out how to make sure justice is served—without hurting her more than she's been hurt.

"What if we pooled our resources and moved in together?"

"Seriously?" She looks stunned. "Y-you want to live with me?"

"Hell yeah. I mean, first off, I need a place to crash, too. When I'm at Ash's apartment, my bed is his sofa, which could double as a torture rack. Making rent on your own in Maui can't be easy. Hell, I remember months in North Dakota when I was first starting out. Despite working multiple jobs, I could barely afford rent there, where it's way less expensive. We both need a place to crash, and it would be good to save some money." I set my mug down and approach, wrapping my arms around her and brushing my lips over hers in a kiss of good morning. "And I'd get to spend a lot more time with you. That's a bonus in my book."

"Are you sure?"

After everything she told me about her past, that's what she's asking. Does she somehow think that whatever her dad conned her into doing makes her less worthy or less desirable?

"Yeah. Admittedly, I've never moved in with anyone, but I think we'd do better than all right, Beth." I stroke her cheek and stare into her eyes, hoping she sees my sincerity. "In case it's not clear, I'm falling for you."

She sucks in a shocked breath and stares mutely.

I understand. It's the first time we've said openly that what we have is more than a fling. That there's more involved than our bodies.

"I'm falling for you, too," she finally murmurs. "Hard. Fast. It scares the hell out of me. But I don't want to stop."

Smiling, I draw her closer. "Good. Don't. I'm right here. I'm not going anywhere."

The tremulous smile that lights up her face enflames my body. An hour later, our coffee is cold, but I don't care. In the most eloquent way possible, she said yes.

In the back of my head, I know our cohabitation will be good for a lot of other reasons I haven't already considered. I can watch over her in case Paul Daniels comes around again, because the asshole still hasn't let up. Of course, once we move in together, I'll have to figure out what to tell my brothers. It's been three days since Bret hung up on me. I need to deal with that soon, and he'll flip shit when he finds out that I'm doing more with the "enemy" than sleeping. But I can't live my life to make my brother happy, and he doesn't know Bethany the way I do.

I've got so many reasons why this move is a great idea. But if Bethany found out who I actually am, would she see it as anything other than an epically underhanded betrayal?

No.

MORE THAN TEMPT YOU

Shit, my subterfuge is getting deep and difficult. I'm not sure I know how to dig my way out anymore. I'll have to figure it out soon. I don't have a choice because, for us to have any sort of future, I'll eventually have to tell her the truth.

CHAPTER NINE

MY FEET ACHE like a bitch. I've worked five straight days slinging drinks, each day seemingly busier than the last. Finally, our Saturday night shift is blessedly over. So is the New Year's rush. Most people who lingered this holiday week will be flying home later today.

In a few hours, Bethany and I will be moving in together. Despite all the secrets and lies between us, I can't wait to be closer to her.

"Hey." Ash slaps me on the back as I make my way out of the bathroom, shaking my hands dry because Andy has been too busy playing Candy Crush to order paper towels.

"Hey." I nod his way. "Crazy night, huh?"

He falls in beside me as we trek down the employees-only hall. "Yeah. I'm really hoping next week isn't so insane."

"I'm with you on that, man. You heading out with Samantha for the night?"

"Yep."

"How's that going?"

"Well, I'm not getting any, but—"

"Really? Even though you've spent the last few nights with her?"

He nods. "Crazy, right? But we talk. A lot. About anything and everything. It's not like being with Montana. She only wanted to fuck. I actually like that I'm getting to know more about Sam than her erogenous zones."

This is the first time I've ever heard Ash say that waiting for sex isn't a deal breaker.

"That's cool. So it's going well?"

"Yeah. Once she got past the shyness, I found out she has this quirky sense of humor I dig. Her mental Wikipedia of movie knowledge is damn impressive, too. What about you and Beth?"

"We're moving in together today, so I'll be off your sofa. Sorry I haven't had a chance to tell you before now. It happened fast."

He turns and blocks my path, stopping me. "Are you getting information from her? Or falling for her?"

I can't bullshit Ash. He'll see right through me. "Dude, I already fell. I never realized what I wanted or needed in a woman until her."

"How does she feel about you?"

"She says she's falling, too. I think she feels something. We haven't put labels on it yet." I blow out a breath. "I sound crazy, don't I?"

"Sound?" He barks out a laugh. "We both know you are."

I give him a good-natured grin. "True enough."

"I've known you awhile, bro. You wouldn't have feelings for Beth if she wasn't worthy of them. Does she know…everything?"

"Who I am?" I shake my head. "I need to figure out how to tell her without killing her trust. She's been through a lot."

"What happened to finding your dad's money and figuring out her role in the scam?"

"I don't know anything right now." And I need to for our future. For my brothers' sanity.

"You can't just forget about it. I get that you're really into Beth, but she's your only hope of learning—"

"The truth. I know, and I'm not letting that go. But if I don't handle this situation right, I'll lose her." I rake a hand through my hair. "I've wedged myself between a rock and a hard place, and I don't know how to get out. Any ideas?"

"No. Just be sure you know what you're doing. But if it turns out she's innocent and you want a future with her, my advice is to be as honest as possible—quickly. Every day you wait is just another day she'll think you've betrayed her."

I hate it, but he's fucking right.

After he sends me an apologetic shrug, he turns to find Samantha, purse in hand, waiting by the back door.

As Andy shoos everyone out, I notice Montana looking cozy with a buff tourist. Apparently, he'll be filling Ash's vacancy beside her tonight. Terry is finally back at work, but his energy flagged as the evening wore on, and he spent the last couple of hours in the back, rather than behind the bar.

I don't see Bethany anywhere.

With a frown, I poke my head into the break room. Her locker is open and empty, so she probably grabbed her purse and went outside. Sure, it's a nice evening, but I've warned her that Paul Daniels is likely coming back for his pound of flesh. Andy finally addressed the issue today and forced Montana to wait on him, but I worry that roadblock only motivated Bethany's former client more.

She shouldn't be alone outside.

Fishing my buddy's car keys from my pocket, I jog out to the sultry night. Ash and Samantha are already in her car and heading out of the lot. Andy locks up behind me, then makes a beeline for his truck. Montana and the tourist have disappeared already, probably on foot to his hotel nearby. Terry slumps to his beat-up VW, looking nearly ready to fall over in exhaustion.

No sign of Bethany.

Alarm sets in. I'm just about to shout for her when I hear her voice drift around the corner of the building. "What do you want?"

"To see you. I've been trying to find you for weeks. Why did you come to Maui?"

She's talking to some guy, and it's definitely not Paul Daniels. I've never heard this low, polished voice before.

I creep closer, careful not to alert them I'm listening.

"You're here, aren't you?" Bethany responds, her voice sounding as hard as armor. I've never heard her talk in this assertive, rapid-fire tone.

"Besides, I had to get away from the bad press back home. Too much negative attention."

"And I guess you're working in this shithole to lie low. Good cover."

Is that why she's working here? I've been wracking my brain for an explanation that made sense...

"Where are you staying?" he goes on.

"With a guy I met last week."

Technically, she's spent her nights with me, but we're not staying at my place. Did she misunderstand the question or is she trying to mislead this guy?

"And saving your money since your accounts are still frozen. Good. You've always been the smart one. Now I need you to do something for me."

"Tell me."

"We've taken a lot of damage. But you can put a stop to Reed Financial's bleeding and make this whole case against me go away now."

I freeze. Is she talking to Barclay Reed? He's *here*? Holy shit. Why does he think he has any right to talk to Bethany? He must have balls the size of fucking Jupiter.

Since he knows what happened to the money people invested with him, I have no compunction about eavesdropping. Besides, if Bethany needs me, I'll be here to protect her.

"What's your plan?" she snaps.

"Bring me that video, Bethany. You know the one I mean. It's critical. Tell me you were thinking ahead and got it out of the office before the feds descended."

"Where's the money?"

"Safe. I can't get to it now, but you know me..."

Is that supposed to be some kind of assurance? From a man who would cheat his clients and use his own daughter for profit?

"But it's accessible?"

"Are you second-guessing me?" he snarls. "I'm your *father*. I paid for your very private, expensive education, including that Harvard MBA. I gave you a position as my right hand in one of the most profitable organizations of the last decade. I've never doubted you. Don't you dare repay me like this. Do you have the video or not?"

God, he just laid an ugly fucking piece of manipulation on her. I want her to give him a verbal beatdown or, better yet, punch his damn face. She doesn't.

"Of course," she assures.

His sigh of relief is audible. "This is why I handpicked you to work by my side. Brilliant, brilliant girl. I need you to make a copy of it, then return to San Diego and deliver it to the AUSA."

"Timeframe?"

"What kind of question is that? Tomorrow. Hell, now. And I don't mean pop it in the mail, Bethany. I mean deliver it, along with a very personal reminder. You've never disappointed me. I know you won't start now."

My jaw drops. Is that asshole really insisting that she give her body to some other dude in order to save his ass? I hope she tells him to go fuck himself.

"I have no money for a plane ticket," she points out.

"Here's two thousand dollars." I hear the rustle of bills. "It should get you to the mainland and back."

"All right, but let's talk this through. We have to be smart. We can't overplay our hand."

Our hand?

"We're not," he insists. "You play a royal flush when it's time to crush the opposition. Now's that time."

"It's not. The case isn't going to trial for a while, but rumor has it our mutual friend will be promoted up the food chain in the next couple of months. If we wait until just before his new position is announced, he'll have far more incentive to heed your demands."

Bethany is *helping* her father? She's plotting with him?

I stagger back against the wall of the building. Please fucking tell me I'm misunderstanding this conversation.

But logic tells me I'm not.

Has she been lying to me all this time?

"Clever…" Reed praises. "You have a point." He sighs. "I don't like the idea of waiting. It inhibits our ability to start investing again, but it's all for nothing if the charges aren't dropped. All right. I'm relieved you're monitoring the situation, but I expected nothing less. Keep up the good work. I'll be in touch soon."

The click of his dress shoes as he walks away resounds in the night. His cadence steady, confident. I prop myself up against the wall since disbelief threatens to take me down.

I can't move. Hell, I can hardly breathe. What the fuck am I going to do?

Suddenly, Bethany appears around the corner. When she spots me, she gasps, palm pressed to her chest. Her whole body goes tense. "You're here. You heard."

"Yeah." I try to keep the accusing note out of my voice even though I'm livid that she's apparently conspiring with her asshole of a father. And like the possibility of that isn't ripping me to shreds.

"It's not what you think. Please, please believe me."

Under the overhead lights in the parking light, I see the vulnerable plea on her face that I hear echoed in her words. The confident ballbuster I heard only moments ago is gone, replaced suddenly by the shy, withdrawn Beth I first met over a week ago.

Who is the real Bethany?

"Then tell me what's going on."

"Can we please not talk about it here?" Her voice trembles.

When I look at her closely, I see that her body is, too.

She genuinely looks rattled. Whether I want it to or not, my anger softens. But confusion still has me reeling. Will whatever explanation she gives me really make everything okay?

"Fine. I'll take you back to the inn."

I'd rather head to Ash's place since he won't be there and it's so much closer. But doubt about her—and about our future—creeps in. If she can't explain everything I overheard away, I'm not going to want to be in the same room with her. I'll want to be alone, where I can wonder how the fuck my heart got everything so wrong.

On some level, I hate fresh mistrust creeping in. But maybe I shouldn't be surprised. She *is* her father's daughter. It's possible she's conned me in a different way than she conned my dad. It's also possible I was snowed by her sob story and so blinded by lust that I didn't see the truth.

"Thanks," she says quietly, then doesn't speak again until she's in the passenger's seat and we've left the lot.

As I drive down the mostly empty road, Bethany surprises me by wrapping gentle fingers around my arm. "Everything you overheard must have been confusing."

"That's putting it lightly."

"Will you listen to my side of things?"

That takes me aback. Does she think there's any way I don't want to hear this? "Of course."

"Thank you. That's all I ask."

Her fingertips drag slowly across my skin, as if she's reluctant to withdraw her touch. Once she does, she clasps her hands in her lap again, not saying another word until we reach the inn.

When I roll into the parking lot and shove the car in park, I turn to her expectantly. "Go ahead. I'm listening."

"Come upstairs with me? Please. The explanation is long."

I tap my thumb against the wheel, but what is there to decide? I want to hear how she'll talk her way out of this. I need to hear her side of the story I've been chasing for weeks. Now that she finally seems willing to give it, I'm anxious it will change everything between us. I'm dreading she'll tell me she's guilty…and I'll realize it doesn't matter as much as it should.

Because I'll still be stupidly in love with her.

Regardless, I can't run away. This is my responsibility. She might be a cheat and a liar, but I doubt she's capable of doing me bodily harm, so

I've got no reason to decline.

"All right."

In silence, I follow her up the stairs. I hear her keys rattling as she inserts hers in the lock with trembling fingers and enters the dark ohana. She doesn't bother with the lights.

Instead, she turns as I shut the door behind me and throws herself against me, barreling me against the portal. "Clint?"

Her nearness throws me into a tailspin. My head tells me to watch myself, but my body is seemingly wired to respond to her. All she has to do is brush against me and turn her face up, stare at me with those wide green eyes, and I'm more than aching for her.

Fuck.

"What, Beth?" I manage to get out gruffly. "Spit it out."

"I know what you heard sounded awful, but my father is a manipulative bastard. I told him what I had to in order to get away from him. I'll explain more. Everything. I promise. Just… Would you make love to me one more time? In case you hate me after I've told you all I know. Please."

I SHOULD SAY no. Her assurance helps some. Still, I shouldn't let sex cloud our discussion. But Bethany rarely asks me for anything, especially closeness, affection, or sex. And like her, I'm afraid of how the truth will change us. I don't know what I'll think or believe after I hear her side of the story. I also don't know where we'll stand after I tell her my secrets.

This may be the very last time I touch Bethany.

Swallowing down my desperation at the thought, I cup her nape, urge her body closer, and plaster every inch of her against me, then slant my lips over hers. She meets me halfway with a cry, clinging to me.

Under the press of my mouth, she opens eagerly. As I dip inside, I taste the need in her kiss and I can't help but groan.

In the past, she's always been more assertive in bed than in conversation, almost like she felt compelled to perform for my pleasure. Given what I know now about her corporate sex life, that makes sense. But what we have feels different. Real. Not like she's trying to coax or dazzle me, but more like she simply wants to be close to me.

Right or wrong, smart or not, I want the same.

Time turns meaningless when I pull her T-shirt over her head. The yellow bikini top she wore all evening distracted me each time I caught a glimpse of the strappy, suggestive thing. Now it's just in my way.

When I tug on the string at her back, the two triangles of fabric fall away from her breasts. I break the kiss long enough to pull the rest of the bathing suit top over her head. Bethany barely has a moment to gasp before I'm back her mouth again, eating at her like I'm starved, and cradling her perfect breasts in my hands, thumbs stimulating her nipples.

She encourages me by deepening the kiss and dropping her hands to my fly. With a few snaps of her deft fingers, she opens my shorts, shoves my underwear aside, and wraps her fingers around my aching length.

"Beth." I can't stop the moan. "Fuck, you do this to me…"

"What?" she whispers as she presses her lips up my neck and dusts them across my jaw.

"Turn me on and inside out. No woman has ever done to me what you can."

Shit. I'm giving her power over me, handing it to her on a silver platter. If she's only taking advantage of me for cover or merely having a fling for her amusement, I shouldn't make using me so easy. But her touch is like that favorite song I'll never stop wanting to hear. It calls to me, excites yet comforts me. It gets stuck in my head until I'm unable to think of anything else.

"I never really enjoyed sex until you," she admits. "And now all I want is to spend time with you, block out the rest of the world, and learn every part of you. I want to know how much better it feels when I pleasure you because *I* choose to."

What is she saying? My muddled mind can't quite untangle her meaning while her fingers glide up and down my cock.

My flesh is on fire. I can't stand clothes between us. I don't want anything separating us—especially not the dubious past or our uncertain future. I only want right now and the two of us naked.

"Jesus, Beth…" I hiss when her fist pulls its way down my length again. Her free hand tugs at my shirt in impatience.

As soon as I yank the cotton over my head and cede my bare torso to her, her lips are all over me. She nips at my shoulder, strokes my arm, laves my nipples. Her every touch makes me shudder. There's no stopping this or worrying about sanity. It's as if we both want to wring every ounce of pleasure possible out of this moment.

In case it never comes again.

When I reach for her shorts, Bethany dodges my grasp by sinking to her knees. I feel her hot breath on the crest of my cock, now aching and straining for her. The cynic inside me tells me she's offering me a blow job to distract me. She's sucked other schmucks like me to make them compliant, not to make love.

Then she takes me in her mouth, cradling my dick on her tongue, then draws her lips around me in a slow, sensual tug. An electric zap charges up my spine with primal need to have her—possess her—in every way possible. God, this *feels* like it means something.

"Oh…yeah." I tangle my fingers in her hair, tug away the elastic band holding it up, then grab the silky skeins by the fistful. "Beth!"

As I ride her mouth, she hums around me, seemingly greedy to have all of me. I hold nothing back because nothing else happening between us matters in this moment—not my suspicions, my worries, or my fear of heartbreak. Our connection matters. The woman I've fallen for is touching me, and I swear I feel her giving me something far beyond a mere blow job. She's giving me all of herself.

The nagging cynic inside me shouts that I'm romanticizing this moment because I want her to be innocent and every swipe of her tongue feels so good that my eyes are rolling in the back of my head. Yes, what she's doing to me feels epic, but that's not why I'm refusing to listen to that nasty voice in my head right now.

I'm choosing to listen to my heart. It urges me to pull her closer, melt into her, give her every bit of me.

I do.

With another surge, I sink more than my cock into her mouth. I surrender to the worship of her tongue and the devotion of her lips. I silence the argument in my head to focus on her alone.

Her fingers dig into my thighs, then curl around my hips to pull me even closer. She eases back to heap pleasure and adoration on my sensitive crest, then slips down my length in a dizzying, suction-filled glide. I feel her nose against my abdomen, her hot breath against my skin. Through the shadows, I watch her, an open-mouthed siren, staring at me like she'd do anything to make me love her.

Bethany repeats the process, picking up speed until I'm gasping. I watch her lose herself in the moment, see her seemingly let go of all her inhibitions and focus on exalting me.

Not going to lie, getting head is always great. But the way she showers me with bliss and simply gives herself is the biggest turn-on of all.

"Beth…" My strangled yelp is all the warning I can give. I'm about to lose it.

She doubles her efforts to touch me everywhere, seemingly dedicating herself to my ecstasy. I know I'm not the only man who's ever been in her bed—or in her mouth—but right now I feel like the most important.

And I have no doubt this is going to be the most cataclysmic orgasm of my life.

Seconds later, it crashes down on me. I'm helpless to do anything but growl out as need overtakes me, jolts my body, then sends me hurtling into a euphoria that's the closest thing to nirvana I've ever experienced. I lose myself in its crushing throes, forgetting all sense of time, place, purpose. Of anything but her.

When the massive orgasm comes to its devastating end, I blink and pant, swaying on my feet, heart pounding. Somewhere along the way, I melted against the wall. I'm still holding Beth's silky hair in my fists, just as I did while she wrung every bit of pleasure from my body that I had to give.

Holy shit. What the hell has she done to me?

With a soft pop, she releases my cock from her lips and slowly stands, looking shy as she kisses my shoulder, my pectoral, my cheek. "Clint?"

"Beth." I manage to pull her closer, even though my legs threaten to stop supporting me. "Oh, my god..."

When she lays her head on my chest, I feel a hint of her smile. "Finally, I get the chance to make you feel half as good as you've made me feel. I've wanted to do that for a long time. It's the first time I've ever wanted to do that at all."

Really? "What else have you wanted to do?"

She blinks up at me. "Honestly? Give more than my body to you."

Does she want to be open and honest with her body before she's the same with her story? Or is she hoping to butter me up with what she thinks I want to hear so I'll be so happy and sated and, of course, believe whatever she tells me?

Fuck, I hate this suspicion and indecision. What if the truth pulls us apart?

"How?"

She peels off the rest of her clothes to stand before me in the dark. "I've never, ever surrendered complete control of my body to any man. I was always in charge. I pulled the strings and held myself separate, despite the physical closeness. You're different. I don't want to manipulate you by doing things *to* you. I want to do them *with* and *for* you. I want to yield myself and give you whatever you desire."

Fuck, I want to believe her so much the ache is a physical pang. If she's serious, then I'm staggered and humbled by how much she's allowed herself to become vulnerable with me in less than two weeks. On the other hand, she might be telling me what she thinks I want to hear. I can't discount that...no matter how I'm dying to.

Either way, I'm not turning her down.

After kicking away my flip-flops, shorts, and underwear, I take her hand and lead her through the darkened ohana, through the kitchenette, and beyond her bedroom. I fling open the doors to the little balcony that faces the ocean and urge her outside.

Immediately, the night air caresses our skin. It's cool, but not chilly. The wind is like a soft caress. Palm trees sway. Ocean waves break.

Her breathing grows choppy and loud. "Clint?"

I turn to her. "No one will see us. The inn's guests are asleep. If Maxon and Keeley are awake, it's because they're with the baby, so they'll be too busy to care about us."

"But—"

"You asked me what I wanted. I want your trust. I want you to believe that I will treat you exactly as you deserve."

Whatever that might be.

And maybe after she's divulged her story, it will seem like the perfect time to tell her exactly who I am and why I pursued her. Maybe I'll even believe her enough to confess how much my feelings have changed since we met. In a perfect world, she'll believe me in return and admit she loves me, too.

Or everything will blow up in my face, and I'll wind up both empty-handed and alone.

"All right." Her murmur is so soft the wind almost sweeps it away.

I drop an approving kiss on her shoulder. "Lean forward. Put your elbows on the rail."

She does, looking back at me over her shoulder with trembling trust.

The acceptance on her face revs me up again. "Are you on the pill?"

"Yes."

Even if I hadn't seen evidence of that myself less than a week ago, I would have believed her earnest tone. "Have you ever had sex without a condom?"

"No."

I spread kisses up her spine as I reach around her body to cup her mound. She's drenched, as she always seems to be for me. At my touch she gasps, then melts with a moan.

My hand shakes as I align my crest to her entrance. "I've never had sex without a condom, either."

Dad drilled the notion of safe sex into us, and I never wanted to be that guy who got a random girl pregnant, then paid for my carelessness for the next eighteen years. But I'm not asking her about this simply because I left my condoms on the other side of the cottage. I want this because everything inside me is driving me to take Bethany without any barriers between us. Am I daring her to prove that she trusts me? Am I trying to get as close to her as possible?

Probably. Yes. And I'm done questioning it. Right now, I'm just feeling.

Despite the orgasm I had a few minutes ago, my cock is hard and my body is primed. I want her. I want to imprint myself on her. No matter what happens, I'm never going to forget this woman. I'm going to make damn sure she never forgets me.

"Do you want me?" I nudge my bare cock against her so she knows exactly what I'm asking.

For a moment, she hesitates, then she nods—slowly at first. Soon, she's looking back at me with something desperate in her eyes. "Please."

"Fuck," I hiss, then drop my mouth to the sensitive spot between her neck and her shoulder. "I want you so goddamn bad."

"Take me." Her voice is a whisper in the night. "Don't stop."

I know a dozen good reasons why I probably should walk away, but none of them compel me more than the connection I feel with Bethany right now.

I grip her hips, bend my knees, then surge inside her in one long, rough thrust.

She gasps and tosses her head back. The sight of all her platinum hair spilling down her narrow back and flirting with my hands at her waist turns me the fuck on. The feel of her, hot and silken and without a single barrier between us, almost undoes me where I stand.

It's *so* good. I groan and surge deeper before I settle into a slow, grinding rhythm that has her gripping the railing like a lifeline and writhing with me in a silent plea for more. I give it to her as I settle my fingers over her clit and rub in soft circles. I've paid attention and learned her body. This is how she likes it best. So even though it's killing me to put the brakes on my cadence, it feels totally worth it when she tightens around me and her needy bud turns to stone under my touch in seconds.

"Clint..." she keens.

"Right here," I mutter in her ear. "Wanting you to feel so good."

"Oh, god." She clutches the rail like her legs are threatening to dissolve beneath her.

Eventually, I'll speed up and send her careening toward orgasm, but I want to make this moment last as close to forever as possible. So I keep it slow, each bareback stroke of my cock a steady press inside her, a nudge against that sensitive spot high inside her, coupled with a lingering touch of her pouting clit. The friction sizzles me with so much sensation I swear I'm going to lose my damn mind. But I keep it up. For her.

"No. No!" she begs. "More."

"I will, sweetheart. Eventually..." I taunt. "First, I want to feel you, see you, listen to you beg."

"Please," she pants. "*Please!*"

Loving the knowledge that I hold her satisfaction in my hands probably makes me a caveman, but there's nothing better. Sure, I love orgasm. Who doesn't? But I derive a thrill out of knowing she's lowered her defenses and allowed me as deep inside her body and soul as a man can get. I never really understood the importance of that until this moment. But her honest responses to my touch are totally doing it for me, even as they're turning me inside out.

I nip at her shoulder as I fuck her deeper...and lift my fingers away from her pussy.

Instantly, she wails. "Clint!"

With a grin, I slip my slick digits in my mouth. "Hmm. You're so sweet on my tongue."

She only manages to answer with another toss of her head and a high-pitched whimper.

Moving the cascade of her hair aside, I press my lips to her ear. "I want to lay you across the kitchen table and have you for breakfast. Coffee and your pussy—the two best things in life. I would never need sugar or cream for my java if I had you spread out in front of me."

Maybe that's over the top, but it fits my mood.

And Bethany likes what I'm saying if that heavy-lidded look she sends over her shoulder is any indication.

Fuck, this is so hot, and I'd love to drag this out endlessly—just stay with her—but unfortunately my restraint has limits. And this slow, flesh-to-flesh seduction is killing what's left of mine.

Settling my thumb above her clit again, I strum it in rhythm with my quickening thrusts. She moans and grabs my arm, nails sinking into skin as her walls grip me tight.

She's close—so, so close. I can't resist pushing her even closer to the edge.

"Your orgasm is right there, isn't it?"

With a choppy, indrawn breath, Bethany nods and jerks back against me, as if she's trying to speed up my thrusts.

"You want it?"

She nods more emphatically.

I grip her hip in warning. "Then stop trying to control my pace. Beg me for it. Give all of yourself to me."

Again, she whimpers. Not a protest, but as if the idea of relinquishing the last bit of power is terrifying. Still, she syncs up with my rhythm, softens against me, and allows me to take her exactly where I want her to go.

In seconds, her breath begins to hitch, her body tenses, her cries turn keening. She freezes for a long moment, then her entire body shudders with an involuntary spasm. The jerk of her clit against my fingers and the hard grip of her pussy match her hoarse groan of ecstasy as she gives herself over to me without an ounce of reluctance.

Her total surrender undoes me like nothing else, and I lose all semblance of mastery and coordination. I can't stop myself from pouring into her, becoming one with her. Falling even more in love with her.

A small eternity passes before my head stops swimming and I catch my breath. The second I withdraw from the swollen clasp of her body, she tears away from the railing and whirls to me, throwing herself into my arms. She presses an inexpert, anguished kiss to my lips. I feel wetness on her cheeks.

Worry kicks me in the gut. "Sweetheart?"

"I'm fine," she croaks.

I know she isn't. Nothing about this situation is, either. "Tell me what's wrong."

She nods. "I'm worried. I need to tell you everything. Just…please don't think the worst of me."

Bethany fears I won't like her confession, and maybe I won't. But the irony of this situation doesn't escape me. She's definitely not going to like what I have to admit in return. But I can't lie to her anymore. If she's really decided to share her truth with me for the good of us, I need to do the same.

By mutual agreement, we shower. We kiss slowly, heaping affection on each other as if we're both anxious about what will happen next. When the water finally turns cool, I reluctantly cut it off. Dread churns in my belly. What if this really is the end? What if she tells me a story that perfectly explains away all my doubts…but she can't forgive my deception?

After she tosses on a thin blue nightgown, she climbs into bed. I'd rather have her naked, the way we've been sleeping the past few nights, but I sense the garment is the security blanket she needs right now.

When I ease onto the mattress beside her, I resist the urge to close my eyes. Sure, I'm exhausted. No surprise after a long, busy shift and two killer orgasms, but what happens in the next ten minutes might decide the rest of my fucking life.

"Come here." I open my arms to her, glad for the opportunity to hold her. "Talk to me."

She slides in willingly and lays her head on my chest. "Please try to keep an open mind, okay?"

"Of course." *Will she do the same when it's my turn? Or if she says she's guilty, will it even matter to me anymore?*

"Have you ever heard of Barclay Reed?"

Here it comes... Everything inside me tightens. "Yes."

She doesn't look surprised, probably because this story has been all over the news. "He's my father, and he's probably going to prison for scamming people out of something close to a billion dollars. No doubt, Paul Daniels told you that." She draws in a quivering breath as she tries to brace herself.

I shrug. He didn't, but I don't want to derail what she has to say with a technicality that's not important now.

"Did he also tell you that I was Barclay's right-hand woman?" She nods. "I was the face of Reed Financial. Dad kept a few clients of his own, like Douglas Lund. Clients who had a lot of money and predated me joining the firm. But most he had shifted onto my plate. I managed the investment strategy for the entire organization. I looked at every client every week—sometimes every day—and made recommendations about what to invest, as well as when and where. I said when to buy, when to sell, and when to get out of the market and take shelter in bonds or other low-risk investments."

I gape. *She was in charge of everything?* "People trusted you with their money and... Are you telling me you had a hand in taking it?"

"No. God, no. I'm trying to explain how everything went so wrong. Our organizational roles are what allowed the theft to happen. I have a securities' license, but my father insisted on maintaining control of all actual transactions. He said it kept him familiar with where his clients were in their wealth-management plan and allowed us to have a system of checks and balances, which was especially important when I was fresh out of school and my knowledge about managing people's money was still mostly theoretical. So my job encompassed more of the day-to-day operations—client meetings, risk assessment, and trade planning. He managed the organization itself and handled the execution of the clients' investments. I could check the balance of any portfolio simply by logging in to the software we had built about three years ago. I didn't *see* the funds, just tracked their growth or loss electronically. So I had every reason to believe they were exactly where I suggested he invest them."

Is she saying her father duped her, too?

"So…you advised clients, took their capital, and recommended the strategy, but your dad actually handled the money?"

"Exactly. But ten months ago, I was working late one Thursday evening. It was, maybe, eight o'clock. Dad poked his head in my office and told me to leave. Not like he gently urged me to go home because it was past dinnertime, and I'd been working killer hours for months. He literally ordered me to get the hell out of the office. He looked nervous."

"So you left?"

She nods. "Even if I was his 'favorite' offspring, as he liked to call me, he never quite let me forget that I was the illegitimate one. Most of his clients saw me as his brilliant investment strategist, whom he was probably banging. A few knew the truth, the ones I liked and trusted. Some of them, I really miss. They felt like friends."

Does she count my dad among those few? If so, why didn't she answer her phone that fateful day?

Her expression turns sad. "But I knew how most people viewed me. Sure, it irked and upset me. Sometimes that perception even undermined me, but my professional life was tied to Dad's. Until I truly proved my worth in financial circles, no one was going to believe I wasn't his something-something at the office since he had a reputation as a man-whore and I couldn't prove my ancestry. It would have been my word against his. And I knew he could be a real bastard…but he was my father. I never thought he'd stab *me* in the back." Tears well in her green eyes. "He did. And I didn't see it coming because some part of me always wanted his approval, was always trying to overcome being his bastard daughter, even though that was his fault, not mine." The silvery drops fall down her cheeks in wet paths in the moonlight. "I sound pathetic, like a stupid girl with Daddy issues. But I was accustomed to him and I thought I knew him well enough to believe that, on some level, he cared." She drags in a breath. "Anyway, since bad moods were nothing new, I didn't question him. I just picked up my things and left. After that, things started getting weird."

"In what way?"

"He told me to cool down on the trades for a while, said he was flipping some funds around so he could protect them during what he thought would be a turbulent time in the market. When I pressed him, he admitted that he was moving money around because his wife was threatening to divorce him, and he didn't want Linda to have half of his wealth. It wasn't until a few months later, and only after he installed a safe in my condo and stuffed it full of his most incriminating files, that I realized he was actually offshoring not just his personal funds but the whole organization's. He'd moved ninety-five percent of it to the Caymans without anyone knowing. He was positioning himself to take the money and disappear. But then Linda tried to serve him with divorce papers before he could finish what he started. He fled to Maui to evade her. Somehow, the FBI got suspicious—I think Douglas Lund had something to do with that—and they started investigating." She laughs bitterly. "I defended my father for so long. I knew he was a selfish asshole, but even I was surprised he had so little compunction about stealing from clients. It hurt that he lied to me. But the worst part was that everything he put in my safe made it look as if I was the guilty one. He tried to set me up to take the fall."

Her voice trembles. Her face looks so solemn. Maybe I'm a stupid schmuck, but I want to believe her.

If she's telling the truth... God, the enormity of Barclay Reed's dirty deception hits me square in the gut. It's so horrific it almost doesn't compute. My father would have done anything to make me happy and help me succeed. I was stubborn and I didn't always want his advice. Sometimes I refused to do something his way without first trying my own, but he would never, ever have plotted to throw me under the bus to save himself.

The cynic in my head reminds me again that she could be lying...but if she wanted to con me into believing how innocent she is, wouldn't she would have spoon-fed me an elaborate story up front? Why would she have waited days and sobbed through the explanation that seemed equal parts blunt and self-critical?

I have a choice to make. But right now, I only see one. I'm putting my faith in Bethany. I'm choosing her.

As I hold her shuddering body against me, the implications of her tale hit home. He used Bethany's brain, pimped out her body, and took advantage of her need for his attention and approval—for a fucking decade—then tried to throw shade her way so he could escape both his wife and prison in one fell swoop.

Barclay Reed left a lot of victims in the wake of his appalling scam, but Bethany was the ultimate one. He betrayed her as a human being, a boss, and a father.

I wish I hadn't merely eavesdropped on their conversation earlier. I wish I'd killed him.

"Oh, sweetheart. I'm so sorry. That must have hurt so damn much. But the FBI cleared you, right?"

"They wanted to arrest me on principle, but the feds declined to file charges. It was touch-and-go for a while. I spent so much money on attorneys... Finally, they stopped viewing me as a suspect, but everyone else is still suspicious. *Everyone.* Paul Daniels? I can't convince him that I had nothing to do with his money disappearing because I was the face of Reed Financial. Whenever he'd call in the past, I could tell him at the touch of a button what was happening with his money. So in his mind, I not only knew the funds had been swindled, I was in on it. No amount of logic has convinced him otherwise. It's been that way with so many of my clients and their families..."

Including me. I'm part of the reason she's crying now. Paul Daniels approached Bethany head on. He demanded information and repayment...and yeah, he was an absolute insulting douche about it. But at least he didn't lie to her.

I did.

176

"I can't tell you how many desperate calls and emails I had to ignore on advice from my attorneys since anything I said could and would be used against me…"

Which probably explains why she never answered any of my questions or accusations.

"It's been a lot to handle. But I tried to do the right thing. An attorney friend of mine, Kathryn, helped me set up a nonprofit corporation for the victims and their families. I donated a hundred thousand dollars to the fund. I had to do something. The victims have suffered so much at my father's hands, and I didn't see what was happening in time to stop it. The money I gave isn't much in the face of what Barclay stole, but was all I had to offer. I'd love to give more once the feds unfreeze my accounts, but I don't have much liquid cash left."

I'm stunned. Despite everything Bethany has been through, everything she probably realized she would go through in the future, she gave up the financial security she had to help others. How many people would do that? How many would bother while they were having to work so hard to simply survive?

"That's an amazing gesture, Beth. Incredibly selfless."

"I had plans to do more, like fundraising with corporations I've worked with over the years. When I started soliciting donations before I left San Diego, I quickly realized that everyone viewed my attempts to help as either a stunt to deflect my guilt or another greedy money grab. So I stepped aside and let Kathryn manage the fund." She closes her eyes, looking as if she's fighting tears. "The investments are growing nicely since I'm quietly managing everything in the background, but donations have become a lot brisker without my involvement."

And Bethany feels rejected. I hurt for her. She's been used, betrayed, and snubbed at every turn. And still, she chose to give back to others. I'm not convinced I would have been half that altruistic.

I wish like hell I could erase all that for her and make her happy. But I don't have a magic wand, so I simply hold her tighter. "I'm sorry, Beth. Nothing has been easy for you."

She shrugs. "The fund is growing. That's what's important, not my feelings. Believe me, no one wants to hear that I had to leave everything and everyone I knew behind, rely on strangers I share blood with, and take a job where I can't use my education. The victims have been through worse. I get it. I live with the shame that all this horrible stuff happened on my watch. And disillusionment because the father I thought I knew didn't live up to the pedestal I put him on as a kid." She caresses my face. "But I'm bouncing back. This won't beat me. He won't because I won't let him. And some good has come out of all this. I've gotten to know my brothers and sisters. I feel like I'm actually a part of a family now. That's something I've never really had. And you…you're the brightest spot in my life. Thank you for listening and understanding. Thank you for believing me. I *need* the solace of a safe place, and I'm so blessed that I've found it in your arms."

Stab me in the heart. She couldn't have made me feel any more unworthy and guilty if she'd tried.

I can't confess now. She needs reassurance, comfort. I have to show her I'm someone she can believe in. If I tell her that my father was one of her clients and that I came after her for "justice," I'll only add to her sense of betrayal and disillusionment. I'll hurt her—maybe beyond repair. But I can't go on keeping the truth from her forever, either.

What the fuck am I going to do?

I'll work on that—after I've reassured her.

"I'm here for you. Whatever you need, sweetheart… I want to help you." I kiss her, a tender press of my lips to hers that's so bittersweet, and hold her tighter when she cuddles into my arms. "Will your dad be back for that video he wants? What is it?"

She tenses. "That's another way he used me, and I didn't want to believe it—until the obvious stared me in the face. Shortly after his arrest, he came to me and said Lund was being vengeful and bribing people to pin this crime on him. He swore his old crony had fabricated evidence, drummed up false witnesses, and poisoned the FBI against him. I believed it because after the man found out that Dad had gotten his baby girl pregnant, Douglas came screaming into the office and threatened to get my father back if it was the last thing he did. So, still believing Barclay was innocent, when he asked me to dig up blackmail material on the federal prosecutor, I should have said no…but I didn't. The video was supposed to be the backup plan to the backup plan. He swore we'd only use it if *nothing* else worked. But I know now that Dad's own actions have put his ass in boiling water, and he wants me to take that video to James Braden, the prosecutor"—she clarifies—"and deliver it…ahem, 'personally' to let him know we mean business."

"I can't believe he has the audacity to assume you'd lift a finger to help him, much less sleep with someone."

"Well, like you heard him say, I've never let him down. And Dad never likes a task done halfway." After an acid smile, Bethany turns quieter. "It doesn't matter, though. I don't actually have the video."

"Why did you tell him you did? And why didn't you cuss him out for everything he's done to you?"

She sighs. "Because if I told him I didn't have the video, he'd only berate me for failing him and hound me until I fix his problem. I don't want to deal with him, and since he never bothered to tell me the truth, I don't feel that I owe him any semblance of honesty in return. And I didn't cuss him out because, first, he wouldn't have heard it. Sociopaths don't feel guilt. They can pretend to, but they don't actually empathize with anyone else's emotions, you know? And second, I've been called a man-eating shark. Which I can be."

"I heard you talking to your father. You were so…snappy and forceful, almost commanding."

"With Dad you have to be, or he runs you over. But I can't outshark him when he's the one I learned from, so I didn't even try. Instead, I went with misdirection. By the time he realizes I lied to him about the video and about James Braden's upcoming 'promotion'—which will be an utter shock—it will be way too late."

And Bethany will have gotten a bit of revenge of her own.

I'm proud of her. She's slaying her dragon in her own clever way, and

I love that.

I love her.

After another gentle kiss, I hold her close. Soon, I'll tell her the truth, when the time is right. She deserves that. For now, I'm going to support her and believe in her the way her father should have. Once we get past the inconvenient truth about how we met, I will never give her a reason to doubt me again. Then I'm going to ask her to spend her future with me. If she's happy here in Maui, I'll give up my business in North Dakota. I'll also find some way to make my brothers accept her. I'm so in love with her I'll do just about anything to keep her by my side.

CHAPTER TEN

"**H**ELP ME," I say to Ash later that morning.

He and Samantha stopped by our new place to lend a hand, and now the ladies are in the kitchen, checking out the appliances. She's really different than Ash's usual squeezes, and they seem comfortable together. Vaguely, I wonder if the sex is happening yet. Interestingly enough, my guess is no. Sam is going to make him wait after the way he chased Montana's tail, and I kind of respect her for that. But that's not what I wanted to discuss when I dragged my pal outside to grab the last of Bethany's clothes.

"What's going on?" Ash frowns. "Did you tell Beth who you are?"

"No, and before you say anything, I know I've got to soon. But I have to find some way to make sure she doesn't completely hate me afterward. Yes, I created this stupid-ass mess, but I'm in love with her."

"I know. Do you think she's innocent?"

"Yeah." Mostly. I still have a few niggling doubts, but they're really unanswered questions. Things she was too raw to answer last night. Probes that would have killed the feels between us when we needed them. "She told me pretty much everything. She's been through a lot, man. It's beyond awful. So when I'm done confessing everything, I need her to know that I've really, truly fallen for her. There's nothing more important."

"All right. We can work on that. But I've been thinking since we last talked about this. Let me play devil's advocate for a minute."

"Okay, but Bret is already doing a damn good job of that."

He smiles grimly. "In his shoes, I would, too. Look, you've known this woman for…how long?"

"Ten days." Admittedly, it sounds crazy.

"I see you wincing. You get what I'm saying." He leans in and drops his voice. "Personally, I think she's a good human being. A really hard worker, too. But you told me yourself that she's used to playing corporate games and winning. She has to be at least a little bit good at crafting and floating cover stories or she would never have been able to swim in the same chum-infested waters as her father."

"She has a good poker face," I admit. It's still not easy for me to read Bethany. "But once she opened up, she was brutally honest about her past. It's not pretty. Everything she told me jibes with what I know about Barclay Reed and the events that led to his arrest. I even called an FBI agent assigned to the case and he reiterated that the feds have no intention of charging Bethany with anything. Besides, she has no idea who I am. Why would she bother to BS me?"

"That's a valid question. I don't have an answer, unless she's simply covering her tracks in general. But what I'm saying is, your brothers are going to suspect she played you. So will everyone else. I understand you don't want to alienate her when you tell her the truth. But I also want you to make *really* sure she hasn't duped you before you divulge your identity and lay your heart at her feet."

"Demanding proof before I tell her how I feel isn't a good way to start a relationship that requires trust."

He nods as if conceding my point. "There is that. And you've got your mind made up. Since I'm not going to sway you—and I'm not even sure I should—tell me what you want to do."

"Besides get the two-ton gorilla of guilt off my chest so we can figure out how to have a future together?"

"Yeah." He laughs. "What did you have in mind?"

"The whole picket fence, man. She's the first woman I've met who I can see myself with long term. She's smart as hell. Like you said, she's not afraid of hard work. She's gorgeous and surprisingly compassionate. We…click. Something in my gut tells me not to ever let her get away."

"Is that your motive for moving in with her? You're done digging deeper into her life and her past?"

"If I find out more about those things along the way, that's great. But exposing her isn't the reason I want to live with her. I'm sure it sounds crazy. If you were telling me you'd fallen in love with someone after ten days, I'd probably check your temperature, too. But everything I've done in life I did because it felt right, like moving to North Dakota and starting my business. Both decisions turned out good. I think the same might be true of my relationship with Beth. We just need to get to an honest place. So help me figure out how to do that, huh? In time, we'll convince my brothers. But I keep feeling like the stolen money isn't what's important. Bethany is."

"Then like I told you before, you just gotta do it. Rip off the lies like a Band-Aid."

I shake my head. "It can't hurt. She's had enough of that."

"What if tonight, after you're all moved in, you open a bottle of wine, sweet-talk her into bed, then tell her you have feelings for her and that you might have gone out of your way to meet her for the wrong reasons, but you're all in now. She's either going to believe you or she's not."

True, but that's asking a lot of someone who's been betrayed by a parent she idolized for most of her life. In fact, she's been disillusioned by men for a decade. Had her trust burned. She needs me to give her more than platitudes to believe that revenge is now the last thing on my mind.

"You're on the right track, but I think I have the perfect idea."

"Good. I hope it works out. I'd like to see you happy."

After lifting the last suitcase from Ash's car, I lug it toward the front door, where I hear the women chatting and the sports channel in the background informing me that the Jaguars beat the Bills in the first Wild Card game of the playoffs.

I glance over and notice the way Ash is looking at Samantha. "I'd like to see you happy, too. Any chance?"

A sly grin crosses his face. "When I first got together with Sam, I was thinking no-strings sex. But she's successfully—and creatively—put me off and forced me to get to know her. I'm digging the way she has this fun approach to life, but it's serious, too. And you know I've never taken anything too seriously. Her? She's different."

"I totally understand."

Ash claps me on the back, then drops his voice. "You got this. Just convince Beth that being with her has changed your mind."

I also have to convince her that being with her has changed my heart, that I came to Hawaii prepared to make her pay because I hated her. Now all I want to do is love her forever.

"Yep. I'll let you know tomorrow how it goes."

LATE THAT NIGHT, I'm about to drop over from exhaustion, but Bethany and I are settled into our new apartment. In truth, it's just shy of a train wreck right now. It's a studio apartment with less than five hundred square feet. I've never lived in a place so run-down and cramped. It came unfurnished, so after Ash and Sam left to start their shift, we spent the afternoon at thrift stores buying a second-hand futon, a coffee table, and a couple of folding chairs, along with some mismatched dishes. At a big-box store, we bought some must-have small appliances and groceries, then lugged it all back here to organize.

Finally, after hours of sweat-inducing work and a takeout pizza, we're settled in. It's a definite step down from the ohana Beth has been staying in. But our new place has a quirky charm I don't hate. And most important, it's ours—together.

While we were at the big-box store, I slipped two doors down to another store while she was perusing a small table and chairs for the dining area. In less than ten minutes, I found the one thing that should convince her I love her and, despite our twisted past, I seriously want to spend my future with her.

A gorgeous two-carat engagement ring. It's simple and elegant and looks exactly like her.

Hopefully, when I propose, she'll say yes. Then, thank god, I should be able to come clean so we can start our future together.

I'm also glad that will mean the end of my poor bartender act. I'm exhausted. Then again, who wouldn't be after a few hours of sleep, thanks to our late-night discussion and our early-morning lovemaking, followed by hours of lifting heavy shit and carting it up two flights of stairs—no elevator—all day? Bethany looked somewhere between weary and catatonic when I shooed her into the shower and told her I'd toss some of the new sheets we laundered in the communal facility downstairs onto our crappy little futon mattress.

And I will. Right now, I feel glued to my chair. I'm trying to muster the energy to move while staring at the black-velvet ring box in my grip, nervous as hell. Israel Kamakawiwo'ole's chill ukulele-rich version of "Somewhere Over the Rainbow" plays in the background, assuring me that dreams I dreamed of really do come true. I hope so. If all the clouds were actually far behind me right now, I could believe it more easily. When I close my eyes, I can picture Beth and me, hand-in-hand, under the swaying palms, all smiles living an amazing life here together. I believe it…almost.

But what if she doesn't say yes? What if she can't forgive me?

As I hear the shower spray turn on, my phone buzzes. Who the hell is calling this late? I glance at the display. Why is Bret ringing me past midnight his time? I shouldn't complain. At least he's calling me after hanging up, hopefully to listen to what I'm saying about Bethany.

"Hey, bro."

"Are you sitting down?"

"Yes."

"Don't be mad, but I did something. I needed to. I *had* to know."

That sounds ominous. "What?"

He hesitates. "I drove to San Diego and broke into Bethany Banks's apartment."

I vault to my feet, nerves and exhaustion forgotten. "What? Why the hell did you do that?"

"To prove you're wrong. She may give you good pussy, but she's a lying, thieving snake. I needed you to see that. And now I can prove it."

Foreboding gongs in my chest. I force myself to take a deep breath. He can't be right. Bethany told me herself that her father left incriminating evidence at her place for others to find, right? Bret simply fell for it.

But I have to hear my brother out. He doesn't understand how I feel and he doesn't know Beth. I have to prove that I'm listening and that I care. "First of all, are you fucking crazy? You could go to jail for breaking and entering. A conviction like that could be attached to every résumé you ever float for the rest of your life."

"Relax. I didn't take anything of value. And no one saw me."

"How do you know? Where are you now?"

"I'm heading out of San Diego now. I drove to a mall, then waited until well after dark to hire a taxi. I paid cash. No one should be able to tie me to anything. But I got two hours alone in your girlfriend's place."

I do my best to tamp down my fury. "You have no right to invade anyone's privacy. You don't see me snooping through your shit."

"Yeah, okay. So it's underhanded. I get it. But what's really important is the shit I found."

"And what is that?"

"Admittedly, nothing at first, except the fact her apartment is almost all white. It's so devoid of color that it's weird. Like she has no personality."

"I promise you she does." But Bethany definitely prefers neat and organized. She likes lines that are simple, colors that are crisp and unfussy. White suits her.

"Well, the place gave me the creeps."

I refrain from pointing out that Bret was predisposed to not like anything about Bethany. "Her decor isn't a reason to convict her of anything. If it was, I would have locked you up a long time ago for violating good taste with all those skateboard posters and bikini shots."

"Ha ha," he returns acidly.

"I'm serious. You don't know her. I do."

"Boning her doesn't make you an expert, either," he spits back at me. "You *think* you know her, but your dick is not the most logical part of your body. Stop being a chump. I saw the evidence of her guilt tonight."

He's clearly dying to tell me all about whatever "smoking gun" he's found. He's convinced it's going to change my mind. I'm not sure how. Bethany has already told me so much, probably more than going through her apartment ever would. But I'd pretty much figured out that truth when I searched the ohana. At the time, I thought prowling through Beth's stuff was simply being thorough and smart. But I didn't start understanding the woman at all until I opened my ears and my mind.

"Bret, look… I'm tired. It's been a long-ass day, and I have to work tomorrow night. I'm pissed as hell at you for taking a chance that might have flushed your future down the toilet, especially for a vendetta. As much as we hate it, Dad is gone. So is the money. But think about this: he was the last person who would ever want you to risk yourself, especially for revenge. Despite what you think you saw, Bethany has told me everything. And I mean *everything* about how the money disappeared. I get why she had nothing to do with it. Which is also why she hasn't been charged with a crime."

"Whatever she told you was bullshit. She wasn't charged with a crime because she fucked the federal prosecutor. I saw the video, bro. I found it tucked away in her apartment. I'll cut you some slack for being bowled over by a pretty face and a centerfold body. She looks like she'd be fantastic to bang. But get the right head in the game, bro. She's responsible for Dad's death. How can you let your dick get in the way of that? How are you living with yourself? Sleeping at night?"

The bottom drops out of my stomach. I gape. Is this the video Barclay hit Beth up for? "How do you know the identity of the guy in the video?"

"His name, James Braden, was on a sticky note in the envelope with the flash drive. All I had to do was Google."

The box containing the ring—the symbol of my future with Beth—drops from my numb fingers.

She fucked the prosecutor? Funny how she never mentioned that part… In fact, she lied and told me she didn't have the video at all. Did she film herself fucking the prosecutor to save her glorified sperm donor from prison, as Barclay seems to think? Or did she whore her body out to save herself?

It's an ugly fucking question, one I don't want to answer.

For months, I've been trying to fathom how she wasn't charged with embezzlement and theft. When she confessed everything and put her spin on it, I believed her. Her explanation sounded so real and she seemed so guilt-ridden and torn. But if I take emotion out of the equation, I gotta be honest…Bret's suggestion makes a lot more sense.

I let out a rough breath. God, this can't be happening. Please tell me it isn't. I close my eyes and try to process Bret's words away. The agony in my chest insists my brain find some other explanation. There must be a perfectly rational one, right?

Like what? And why didn't she tell you the truth about the video?

I have no answers.

Still, I refuse to jump to conclusions. I need to talk to Beth, hear her side.

See how she'll squirm out of this one.

"What did you do with the video?"

"Made a copy. I left the original there, in the envelope she used to mail it to herself. You want to check out the fine piece of blackmail for yourself?"

Do I want to see the woman I'm in love with fuck someone else to avoid being charged with a crime? Even the thought of it cramps my gut.

"Send it." No matter how much I don't want to, I have to watch. I have to see if anything on the footage indicates why she hopped into bed with James Braden.

"I'll do it when I get home." Bret sighs. "I get that you're really vibing with this chick, and she's obviously smart enough to feed you a believable story. But it's better to know the truth now, before you're in even deeper."

Like after we were engaged?

It feels absolutely shitty, but my brother is right.

Behind me, the bathroom door opens and Bethany walks out with a towel wrapped around her clean hair—and absolutely nothing else.

My jaw drops. My blood races. Guess what my cock is doing?

How stupid does that make me?

"Um, thanks. I gotta go."

Bethany sends me a catlike smile and revs my libido even more.

"Call me tomorrow, after you've seen the footage," Bret says. "Then we'll talk about how to nail the bitch to the wall."

"Later," I mutter, staring at the woman who seemed to be everything I needed and wanted in a wife…and staggering because my happy vision from mere minutes ago is now falling apart.

"I'm serious, Clint."

Bret is, and he has every reason to be.

"I know you're trying to help. I'll take it from here. And…thanks for looking out for me."

"I've always got your back, bro. Get your head out of her pussy and do the right thing."

With that, we hang up, and Bethany sways toward me. "Who was that?"

"One of my brothers."

"Everything okay?"

No. It's a fucking disaster. I want to confront her, but on the off chance Bret somehow got everything wrong, I don't want to accuse her before I've seen the video. Besides, I'm tired. I'm stupidly fucking emotional. And I also haven't found a way to be honest with Beth myself.

I can't deal with any of this right now.

As I hurtle myself out of the chair, I swoop down and clandestinely scoop up the little ring box before pocketing it. Then I turn to her. "Fine. I'm ready to call it a night. You?"

"Well…" She sidles up to me, pressing her naked body against my bare chest and dusting kisses up my neck. "I'm ready for bed."

If I take what she's offering, she'll only cloud my head. And if she lied to me, I can't let myself want her anymore.

Somehow, I manage to grab only her shoulders and ease her away. "Sorry. I need a shower and some sleep."

"Oh. Okay." Bethany tries to hide her crestfallen expression, but I see her hurt. "All right. Good night."

When she turns away, I hate to end our great—even momentous—day together on a sour note. I wish she could come clean and allay my worries, put this goddamn terrible suspicion to rest once and for all...

"Hey." I grab her wrist and turn her to face me again. "I meant to ask you, what was on the video your dad is after? How did you blackmail the federal prosecutor?"

"He hooked up with a suspect."

That's all she's going to say? "Who? Anyone you know?"

She blinks away. "No one important."

Her lie guts me. I release her quickly, as if touching her burns me. Fuck, if she was so easily dishonest about this question, what else was she dishonest about?

"Gotcha. Sleep well."

Shaking, I turn away and shut the door between us. That ring in my pocket? I might as well throw it in the trash. I'm still going to sleep on this and wait for Bret's video, just in case it contains something that changes my mind. But it's wishful fucking thinking. My broken heart finally agrees with my head. Bethany has played me, and I've just been too dazzled to see her for the beautiful manipulator she is.

So unless a miracle happens, I'm going to tell her who I am...and that I have the video that enabled her to escape prosecution. Then maybe I'll get what I came here for in the first place: justice for my dad.

Now that Bethany has torn my fucking heart out of my chest, ripped it to shreds, and spit on it, nothing else matters.

CHAPTER ELEVEN

THE FOLLOWING AFTERNOON, we drive into work. We've barely spoken since we woke on opposite sides of the bed.

I received an email with the video from Bret late this morning, along with apologies that he came home and fell asleep almost instantly because the drive was long and, because of a freak accident on I-5 in Santa Ana, traffic was a bitch. The footage is still on my phone, unwatched. I can't bring myself to open it and see beyond any doubt that Bethany has betrayed me. To know that I fell for someone and I now have the power—and the responsibility?—to destroy her because maybe that's what she deserves.

But I also can't bring myself to stop looking at her, wanting her, wishing she'd explain everything away so I could go on blissfully believing her.

What a fucking fool. I knew before I met her that she played corporate games to win. I thought if I didn't pit myself as her foe, if I approached her instead as a friend and a lover, that she would be human and honest. But no. Maybe she never learned integrity since her father used—and warped—her for his gain. Unless none of that is true, either.

Or maybe I'm letting suspicion get the best of me because it seems crazy that I could fall so hard and fast for a habitual liar and a heartless criminal.

I'm at a decision point now. What I choose next will either make or break us.

"You okay?" Beth asks softly as she stashes her purse in her locker at the back of the bar.

She's asked me at least ten times today.

"Fine," I lie.

"Do we need to talk about something?"

Everything. Make all this confusion go away so I can believe in us again…

But odds are, that isn't going to happen.

"I've just got a lot on my mind after my brother called last night. I need to sort it out. We'll talk after the shift, okay?"

She looks reluctant to let the matter go. "Sure. If you need some space to think, that's understandable. But if you want to talk, if you need a sounding board… You've been so good about that with me, I'd be happy to return the favor."

Because she means that or because she wants another opportunity to gather info and figure out a way to use it so she can keep screwing me over?

God, I hate this fucking uncertainty.

I nod her way, and she clocks in before leaving the break room. I can tell she's worried. Vaguely, I wonder if I actually matter to her or if pretending to give a shit is all part of the act.

Ash told me I had to rip the Band-Aid off and be honest with her. He was right; I do. I've got to force myself to sit down with the footage, take it all in—no matter how hard it is—then man up and let the chips fall.

"How did last night go?" my pal asks as he saunters in, low-voiced. "Did you tell her?"

"No." I close my eyes. I have no doubt he can see my misery all over my face. "I think she played me after all."

He rears back in shock. "What makes you think she's guilty?"

"Everything I was too busy falling for her to see."

"I'm sorry, man. Really." He claps me on the shoulder. "If you need an ear or a sofa, you know where to find me."

I nod, and he clocks in. Before he leaves the break room, he pauses. "I don't know if it matters to you, but as I came this direction a minute ago,

I noticed the dude in the loud Hawaiian shirt with the even louder mouth is back. He's already drunk. I think he's unstable."

Great. I don't need Paul Daniels adding another wrinkle to this mess. I'll keep an eye on him. Whatever Bethany's sins—and they might be plenty—she doesn't deserve his violence.

"Thanks."

With a nod, Ash leaves.

Finally, I'm by myself. And I'm out of excuses. I have to watch the video.

My hands shake as I shut the door. No one else should come in here since our shift is about to start. If I gave a shit about this job—or anything but the truth—I'd be out there helping Ash set up. But he'll cover for me since he knows I need a few minutes.

Finally, I launch my email, ignoring everything but the attachment from my brother. Before I see a single image, I already know this is going to hurt like hell.

Four sickening minutes later, I close the app, darken my phone. After watching Bethany use her moves on the suit she seduced, there's a gaping hole in my chest where my heart used to be. I'm in danger of throwing up what little lunch I managed to choke down. The emptiness of my future without her stretches out before me. Her perfidy is going to leave a scar for decades. God, she's an amazing liar. I believed everything, all the way down to the boo-hoo stories about how her father used her.

This video proves she's more than capable of using someone for her own ends without anyone coercing her at all.

I feel so fucking gullible and stupid.

But I've got to detach myself from her and turn over this evidence. It may burn her—if the feds choose to open the investigation against her again. But if I won't be walking away happy, then I should get the justice for Dad that I came to Maui for.

Slowly, I rise. Weariness beats me down. Fury bubbles under it all, simmering dangerously. I put a lid on it. Sure, I could be mad at her, but I'm far angrier with myself. Bethany was only being who she is deep down. I'm the dumb ass who fell for it.

When I make my way out of the break room, Andy is standing in the hallway, looking all too ready to point out that I wasn't behind the bar at four o'clock, which makes me late. Instead, he takes one look at my face and frowns.

"Do you need the night off?"

I drag in a breath. Even that's excruciating. My whole body feels ready to crumble. Goddamn it, I hate this thousand-pound weight of defeat crushing.

"I think…I need to quit. I wasn't really here to work. I was here for Bethany."

Andy heaves a sigh. "I kind of figured. You look like shit so I hate to ask, but can you stay for this shift? I'll get Terry to cover you tomorrow. He owes me some extra time after being so sick. After that, I'll find a replacement."

I'd like to help a guy out, and I hate to think I'm too whipped by one lying bitch to perform a function as simple as pouring drinks with a smile, especially when the bar isn't particularly busy, but I don't know if I have it in me tonight. "I'll do my best."

"Thanks. I actually came back here to tell you that the tall blond guy who visited your girlfriend—or maybe ex-girlfriend—the other day is back. And whatever he said made her cry. She ran down to the beach. He followed. They've been gone a few minutes."

I don't care what Stephen said to her. Well, I try not to care. Did she bamboozle him, too? Or are they in on this scam together? It would be a sly but clever move for her to take advantage of the fact that her father has a vengeful enemy determined to see him locked up. Once Barclay was in prison, then she could make off with her lover and all the money. And that would conveniently set them up for life. *Nice.*

I murmur a thanks to Andy, who nods and wanders off. When I look up, Ash motions me over with a frown.

"What?"

"You look terrible."

"It's even worse than I thought."

Watching Bethany work James Braden over with her mouth, then her lithe little body… Granted, she didn't look as if she was enjoying being naked with the pompous windbag. But that's neither here nor there. She's not the prey wrapped up in her father's web. She's the fucking black widow.

"Jesus. I'm sorry. What are you going to do?"

I shrug. "What I should have a long time ago. She's on the beach?"

"With that Lund dude, yeah. He came in all full of righteous anger and acted super protective of Beth. He murmured a few words to her in the corner, showed her something, then she fell apart."

The smart thing to do would be to leave. Turn and walk away from her drama and her lies. Not give her another chance to sink her hooks into me because I have this terrible feeling I'll take one look at her and my heart will ache to make excuses and I'll be too fucking weak to resist her. I can't let that happen. And I can't let her have the last word. I want to look at her, face to face, and tell her what she's done to my family. I want her to understand what an amazing man her greed killed. I want to show her pictures of my brothers so she'll know the faces of boys orphaned before they were ready to be men. I want her to feel some fucking guilt for once in her life.

Is she even capable?

That anger brewing in my belly starts spewing as I march outside the bar and spot Bethany pressed against Stephen Lund. Her entire body shakes with supposed sobs. He's holding her and stroking her hair, as if he's comforting her.

Is any of it real? Or has she conned this poor sap, too? After all, why take the money from the Caymans and split it with a lover when she can have it all to herself?

Vaguely, I wonder why she even bothered to make this pit stop in Hawaii and why she worked in this nowhere bar doing this dead-end job if she had nearly a billion dollars waiting for her in the Caribbean. Some part of her cover? An elaborate ploy to keep the feds off her trail? But doesn't she already have the perfect get-out-of-jail card with that video? James Braden won't want to lose his position of power. I'm sure he'd do almost anything to keep this secret buried.

Whatever. I'm done trying to figure out how Bethany's mind works. Time to confront her and end this.

"Hey," I call out to them.

She wrenches out of his embrace, nose red, cheeks wet with tears—and eyes blazing with betrayal. "Clint Dietrich, huh? How long were you going to feed me that bullshit, you son of a bitch?"

So she knows my identity? A glance over at Lund, sharp brow raised, tells me he's the snitch.

"Until I got the truth, which I apparently never did," I spit back. "But congratulations. Now you have the real name of the latest guy you fucked over so you can add me to your long and distinguished list."

Gaping, she lunges my way. "What the hell are you talking about? I believed in you. I told you some of the ugliest, most shameful details about my past. Things I've never really told any other human being because I loved you—"

"Aww, my heart is bleeding."

Her eyes flash rage, but her sniffles offset the menace in her expression. "And you never even told me your real fucking name. When you came on strong day one, hot and gorgeous and so focused on me, I should have known it was too good to be true, that all your talk about wanting to get to know me was just lies. You only wanted information. You wanted to use me." She shakes her head in self-recrimination. "I was the idiot who fell for how caring you seemed, how perfect we felt together. I'm genuinely sorry about your father, Mr. Holmes. I really liked your dad a lot. He was one of my favorite clients, one of the few who knew who my father really was. He told you, didn't he? You came here knowing. And you blamed me, like all the others, because I was the face of Reed Financial."

Is she really going to play the victim until the bitter end? "I watched my father die on my living room floor because *you* didn't call him back when the news broke."

Bethany recoils. "I didn't know that. I'm sorry. I feel terrible about his passing—"

"Save your empty platitudes, *Beth*. You were never going to call because you were complicit in stealing the money he'd earned with his life's work." It feels both good and horrible to finally say that. The rage growing and growling inside me pats me on the back for laying that at her feet.

But my stupid heart is still breaking.

"What? No! I couldn't call your dad—or anyone—back that day. The FBI was *interrogating* me. They thought I was complicit, too. I eventually proved them wrong."

"No, you proved calculating and cunning after you fucked the federal prosecutor. Congratulations. Did you do it to save your dad's miserable ass? Or were you planning all along to take the money and run by yourself?"

Bethany's jaw drops. She blinks, seems to reel, then shakes her head, looking beyond hurt. "Is that what you really think of me?"

I've got to hand it to her. If I didn't know the circumstances and hadn't seen the evidence, her crushed expression would convince me that I've got everything wrong and that my lack of faith is breaking her heart.

"That's what I *know*. And don't think I won't use it against you."

"Then we have nothing left to say. For the record, I slept with James Braden at my father's request—something I hadn't done to help him in over four years. Something I'd told him I would never do again. But I demeaned myself because, at the time, I thought Barclay was innocent. He'd convinced me the feds were on a witch hunt at Douglas Lund's request because the man knows big people in high places. The father I'd looked up to my whole life was seemingly being framed for a crime he didn't commit. His business—hell, *my* business—would undoubtedly crash down. Everything I'd ever poured my energy or soul into would be gone. First, I tried to talk to Braden, convince him using every other method I could. In the end, he told me he would look the other way, but only if I fucked him. You see, he was six weeks post-divorce after his wife left him for another man, and he was looking for revenge sex. He said I would do. So I let him use me. I wanted to cry the whole time. But what choice did I have? What would you have done, if you could, to save your dad?"

I think of the exhausting thirty-plus minutes of CPR I tried to perform—to no avail. I would have done anything, of course. Would I have let someone I didn't love use me? Yeah, without hesitation. I also took Bethany to bed way after it was too late to save my dad. Does that make me worse? No. By then I was falling for her…

What, if anything, does she feel for me?

Nope. I'm not asking myself any more questions where she's concerned. Every time I do, I just give myself mental wiggle room to let her fuck me over again, and she's way too good at covering her ass. I can't let myself believe a word she says anymore.

It's over. We're done.

"When all else fails, spread your legs and dazzle the poor schmuck, huh? You got that act down, sweetheart."

"Are you serious right now? I paid Braden for his silence with my body. I made love to you with my heart. But since you lied to me from day one, I don't expect you to understand how genuine my feelings were. And for your information, I had *no* idea my father filmed my encounter with Braden. When he told me later he had so he would have an 'insurance policy,' I was horrified. Oh, and he gave me pointers on how to improve my performance. You know, for the next time he needed my 'help.' I still didn't find out for months after that my own father was both lying to me and ready to let me take the fall for his crimes."

"Why did you lie to me about what was on the video and whether you had it?"

"I didn't tell you the contents because I was ashamed," she says as if it's obvious. "I whored myself out to help a man who will never know the meaning of love and never gave two shits about me except for the money I could make him and the favors I could do for him. And I didn't lie about the location of the video. I thought it was gone. How did you find it?"

"Why would I give you any clues to help you talk your way out of this one?"

She rolls her eyes. "I'm not trying to talk my way out of anything. I'm genuinely trying to understand how you got your hands on it. I found the video on my dad's laptop. I saved a copy on a flash drive in case I ever had to explain myself, then did my best to erase it from his machine. But Dad was paranoid at that point. He was having security monitor all emails and searching everyone's purses and briefcases before they exited the building. He told me it was because there was a corporate spy in our midst selling our secrets. I know now that he wanted to make sure no one could help the feds build a case against him. So I physically mailed the flash drive to myself. As far as I knew, no one was checking the mail room. But the flash drive never came to my apartment, so I assumed it was lost. Barclay destroyed his computer as the feds were rushing in to raid our offices. I'd mailed myself the only remaining copy—that I knew of. How did you find it?"

Bret didn't mention where in Bethany's apartment he found the video or how he located it. But he did mention an envelope… Coincidence? Shit, if there's any chance Bethany is telling the truth…

No, I can't let myself hope that. It screws me every time.

"It's irrelevant. I've seen the footage. And from my viewpoint, it sure looks like you took Braden to bed to avoid being charged with a crime."

"Well, you'd be wrong. And how do you think for one minute that you have any moral superiority? Everything you ever said or did with me was a lie." She huffs. "You know, I shouldn't be surprised that the first time I let myself fall in love, you turn out to be no different than most every other man. You used me. You never cared about me. You just wanted revenge. Well, you got it. I hope you're happy." She turns to Stephen, who stepped back and silently watched our exchange. "Can you take me somewhere? Anywhere." She sends another glare at me. "Away from him."

That shouldn't cut me to the quick. It does.

"Sure, shorty." He eases forward and moves to wrap a protective arm around her.

I step between them and clutch her arm. "It wasn't an act. Oh, it should have been. I wanted it to be. But if anyone is the idiot here, it's me. I loved you, and I have no reason to lie about that now. I was going to fucking propose to you." I grind out the words in fury. "I had the ring in my pocket last night when I found out about the incriminating video."

Why am I defending myself? Why do I think it will even matter to her?

She shakes her head, clearly fighting off new tears. "Stop! I can't handle more of your bullshit. Yes, I probably deserve this heartbreak for all the wretched things I've done in the past. Fine. I'll heal. I'll learn from this mistake and move on. At least I can live with the knowledge that I was genuine with you. But you know the really terrible part? If you had come to me and told me your actual name and said that you'd once wanted payback but had changed your mind, I would have believed you. I would have forgiven you. I still would have loved you. But that's my fatal flaw: blind loyalty. No more. I'm done being lied to and used. Fuck off." She wrenches free. "And don't come back."

I stand numbly as she dashes away and disappears into the bar. Through the open awning, I see her disappear down the hall. She appears a moment later under the bright lights, wiping her cheeks, purse on her shoulder. Samantha hugs her. Andy says something that has her shaking her head. Then she disappears out the back door.

"I fucking want to break your goddamn face right now."

Zipping around, I glare at Lund. "Because I fucked your girl, too?"

It's a nasty swipe, and I wish I could take the words back the minute they're out of my mouth. What if Bethany was being honest and Stephen really is just a friend? What if she genuinely gave all her body not to keep herself—but her father—from prosecution? What if she really loved me?

What if I was too fucking suspicious to listen?

That seems to break his calm. "No, because you fucked her over, just like I suspected you would the minute I started digging into you and nothing added up. You broke a good friend's fragile heart. Did I take Bethany to bed once? Yeah. She'd never known what it was like to have sex with someone she liked and trusted. So I tried to be there for her. It wasn't passionate. It never happened again. I tried to be good to her. And you're being an absolute shit for not grasping that the multimillionaire scumbags her father hooked her up with were strangers who saw her as nothing more than a piece of ass. Believe me when I tell you Barclay didn't give two shits what Bethany had to do to make his life better. He expected it of her, and she tried so, so hard to please that terrible son of a bitch. She had no one else. The worst of it is after Braden finished with her, she felt so dirty and terrible and worthless. She admitted to me years ago that's how she always felt after sex. I hated Barclay for putting her in that position. But you know what? I loathe you even more right now because you just made her feel a hundred times worse than her father ever did."

I flinch, but his words still flay me open. "Don't lecture me."

"You need to hear the fucking truth," he roars back. "Finally faced with overwhelming evidence that her father had swindled all their clients, Bethany did the bravest thing she could, you righteous motherfucker. She took everything Barclay had stashed in her safe, prowled through every bit of it, including his electronic records she accessed via his password records. Then she made sure it all reached the FBI. That woman you think took everything from you, including your father? When they first arrested Barclay, the FBI only had circumstantial evidence. Bethany changed that. She's the only reason Barclay Reed will be going to prison."

I stagger back. Stare. The words repeat themselves in my head.

Oh, my god.

"How do you know that for sure?"

"Suspicious till the end?" He shakes his head. "My half sister, Nia, told me. Her husband, Evan, confirmed since Bethany asked him to provide the feds access to Barclay's files on his private storage servers. I came to Maui because, like her, I'm having to deal with the sins of my father. And there are a lot of them, some I may never be able to forgive.

But I also came because I knew Bethany was here and because I suspected she'd be hurting and need a friend. I intended to convince her that I didn't blame her for Barclay getting Amanda pregnant. I'm pissed, but my sister is an adult. She knew exactly who he was. At least half this shit is her fault. My dad wouldn't hear any of that. He went all *V is for Vendetta* on Bethany's father. And now we're in this fucking mess." He shakes his head in disgust. "But I'll take her from here. You go back to North Dakota, though I'd rather you burn in hell. And stay the hell away from Bethany. I'll take care of her until the real Mr. Right comes along."

WHEN LUND TURNS and makes his way across the sand, I barely notice. It's all I can do to stay upright and process the bomb he just dropped on me.

Maybe she's duped him, too. It's possible Stephen has all his facts wrong. But if he was too smart to buy my act, it stands to reason that he wouldn't buy any Bethany put on, either.

And what if Lund is right? What if Bethany is telling me the truth? What if I screwed up by letting my "logic" deep-six the gut instinct that told me she's innocent?

Fuck. Right or wrong, stupid or not, I've got to talk to her before Stephen takes her away. Before it's too late. Before the woman I once swore was the best thing to ever happen to me leaves me for good.

I dart up the beach and into the bar. Inside, Andy looks less than thrilled. Samantha glares my way. Ash is giving me a what-the-fuck side-eye. Lund is nowhere to be found. Ditto for Bethany.

"Where did they go?" I look at my pal. If anyone will understand my need to find her and unearth the truth, it will be him.

"Out the back door, to the parking lot."

I pull his keys from the pocket of my shorts as I take off in that direction. "If she comes back, keep her here and text me."

MORE THAN TEMPT YOU

"Dude, I don't think she's coming back—ever."

Samantha's glare only turns more glacial. "I don't know what you said, but she looks absolutely devastated, you asshole."

If Bethany has been honest with me from the start, that makes perfect sense. If she hasn't, why would she bother to put on an act to convince my pal and his kinda-sorta girlfriend that I've broken her heart? The obvious answer: she wouldn't.

Oh, fucking hell. Tell me I didn't screw up this badly...

But I can't deal with Ash, Samantha, or any of the others right now. I have to see if I can catch Beth and Lund in the parking lot before they leave.

Shoving my way out the double doors, I stumble onto the porch, under the rusting overhang. It doesn't take more than a few seconds to scan the nearly empty lot. I never paid attention to what kind of car her guy pal drives, so I don't know whether Lund has already taken her away. But I don't see either of them hanging around.

But I hear a sudden groan of pain. What the hell? I can't see anyone, but it sounds as if it's coming from around the corner of the building.

"Shut up, Junior."

Barclay Reed. I'd know that patronizing voice anywhere.

What is the fucker doing here? Even if only half of what Bethany told me turns out to be true, he's a horrible father and an even worse human being. Ultimately, he had at least some hand—if not all—in swindling money that belonged to my father and all the other Reed Financial clients. I hate him. He deserves full punishment under the law. Since I came to Maui for justice, I should start with him.

I'll figure out how to feel about Bethany later.

"Oh, my god!" She sounds horrified. "What did you do to Stephen? You could have killed him."

"So what? Listen to me, you ungrateful bitch. I gave you half your blood. I raised you. I educated you. I gave you valuable life lessons on a silver platter. And how did you repay me?"

The wooden boards of the patio creak with someone's every step. I try

203

to ease closer silently.

"Dad, put the bat down." Bethany's voice trembles.

My eyes flare wide. Is the son of a bitch threatening her?

"Don't you back away from me," he snarls. "I'm not going to use it on you unless you make me. Lund Junior just needed his mouth shut. Stupid prick. He's soft and he's weak if he thinks his father's greatest sin is in not recognizing his illegitimate black daughter. As if anyone gives a shit about Nia… Stephen would be stupider than hell to disown his father and walk away from his inheritance because of one irrelevant female. If he does, that only proves he'll never make it in the real world, and I'd certainly be doing everyone a favor by offing him. But that's not why I'm here. You better explain why my attorney called me today to tell me the evidence the feds have against me is all the shit I stashed in your safe. Did you fucking turn me in?"

"You planted that evidence in my apartment so the FBI could find it on my property and think I was guilty," she returns incredulously. "What did you expect me to do?"

"I had to have a backup strategy. I would have gotten you the best lawyers on the planet. At the very least, you would have only served a few years. You're young. You could bounce back. I'm an old man."

"You're not even sixty."

"That's still too old to go to prison."

Holy shit. I won't even ask what's wrong with Barclay Reed. Obviously everything. Sure, he's seemingly confirming everything Lund told me on the beach. But one thing is crystal clear—and far more important—right now: Bethany is in danger.

I don't care about the rest of the conversation. Sure, I have more questions. Eventually I'll want to understand. But now I only care about keeping Bethany alive.

Barclay having a baseball bat concerns the hell out of me. I can't let him whack me unconscious like Lund or I'll be no good to Beth. I need the element of surprise. Or I need help.

Suddenly, I feel a heavy hand on my shoulder.

Startled, I whirl and find Paul Daniels and his loud shirt behind me, holding a finger to his lips.

He wants me to be quiet? Fuck that. I can't leave Beth to Barclay's mercy. He clearly has none because, just like she said, he's a sociopath. He cares only about himself.

I wrench from Daniels's grasp, ready to charge forward, focused on how I'm going to stop Bethany's father. This time, her former client wraps his beefy fingers around my arm and hauls me back and shoots me a silent, thunderous scowl before motioning me to be quiet again. Why? Is he looking to use the element of surprise against Barclay? Or Beth?

Then he withdraws a 9mm pistol from his pocket and flashes me a terrible smile. My blood runs cold.

Emphatically, I shake my head. He can't hurt her. He can't snuff Bethany Banks out of my life.

I'm not ready to live without her.

That realization blows me away, but I have to compartmentalize it for now and deal with the threat in front of me.

"Run, Beth! Go!"

Hoping like hell she can escape her father, I turn to face Daniels, prepared to stand between her and his bullet.

The shorter man pushes me out of the way with a snarl. "Stupid son of a bitch."

As I hear pounding footsteps thundering off the porch and into the dusk, my shoulder bounces against the wall. I whirl toward Daniels, as Barclay comes around the corner with a killing glare all over his face—directed at me.

Until he sees his former client holding the gun.

He pales and holds up both hands, shaking his head. "Paul... I'm glad you're here. You can help me make that little blond thief pay for all the pain she's put us all through. She wants everyone to think I tried to frame her but—"

"Fuck you, Reed. It's over. I overheard everything you said. If anyone was set up, it was her. After all, you had no problem offering her to me as incentive to invest. Everything you've done is even more appalling now that I know she's your daughter. What kind of father tries to destroy his own kid? And what kind of asshole steals the fortune a dying man wants to leave to his children? You deserve to rot in hell, you motherfucking scumbag." Daniels raises the gun.

"No!" Barclay pleads.

"Don't!" Suddenly, I hear Beth's voice and look up to find her standing ten feet past her father's shoulder. "He's done terrible things, I know. And I'm sorry about your cancer. But we can't take justice into our own hands."

The way I did.

"Believe me, I thought about it," she goes on. "Once I realized what he'd done to me, there were times I *really* wanted to, but his fate isn't up to you. Or me. I didn't want to throw away the rest my life for him. Do you? Honestly?"

"My life is already over," he growls.

Daniels is going to pull the damn trigger. I can hear it in his voice.

In that split second, I see Bethany lunging toward her father like she intends to do whatever it takes to save him. I can't let her. Daniels isn't going to mete out justice, but cold-blooded murder.

I have a single instant to choose, but there's no choice at all. I have to protect Bethany, even if that means her father dies. She must live.

With a roaring leap, I tackle her out of harm's way just as Barclay's former client pulls the trigger.

His shot shatters the quiet paradise. Nearby birds squawk and fly to the safety of the skies. Tourists in the bar scream. People charge out. And Bethany's father crumples to the concrete in a bloody heap.

CHAPTER TWELVE

"ARE YOU ALL right?" I ask Bethany.

It's been hours since the shooting. Since her father died right before her eyes. Barclay Reed was a callous son of a bitch who died faster and easier than he deserved. After all, he's the reason my own father is gone, and I'm fucking glad to see the justice I came to Maui for has finally been served. But that barely registers now. I'm focused on Bethany, on the horror and wrenching sadness she's struggling through after watching the man she looked up to her entire childhood unexpectedly and violently take his last breath.

"Fine," she murmurs, not meeting my gaze.

It's a lie. She's not fine. She's not merely exhausted. She is emotionally spent.

Besides Barclay Reed lying on a slab at the morgue, Stephen Lund suffered a blow to the head that resulted in a concussion. He's in the hospital for observation, but should recover in a day or two. The police arrested Paul Daniels for murder, interviewed Bethany and me at length, then left with assurances that they'll be in touch. I'm hoping she finds some consolation in that.

A glance at my phone tells me it's almost ten p.m. Through the evening, Ash brought us bottles of water. Samantha followed up with salads and appetizers, even a couple of scoops of ice cream, trying to tempt Bethany into eating. She refused every morsel and now looks ready to fall over. I'm worried about her.

The woman has been through hell. In the span of an hour, I broke her heart and she lost her dad. Despite all that, she answered the detectives' questions clearly and concisely. Her voice trembled, but she never succumbed to tears. I see them lurking now, needing release. Normally, I would put my arms around her and lend her my strength, encourage her to give me all her troubles. In fact, I'd love to. I'm desperate to. But she refuses to lean on me. Hell, she's barely speaking to me.

I have no one to blame but myself.

I fucking wish I had a do-over on this entire afternoon. If I could go back, be honest with her about my identity, then ask questions before I accuse her of playing me, remind myself there are two sides to every story… None of that would save her father, of course. Paul Daniels was determined to have his pound of flesh and, once he heard the truth from Barclay Reed's own lips, he was willing to go to prison to get it. Maybe that's not a surprise since his days are numbered anyway. But I compounded her sudden loss with my lack of trust and utter betrayal. I thought I understood the situation, so I opened my big mouth and said all the worst things. I was so fucking wrong.

How do we come back from this? Or can we? Did I destroy us forever?

Despite those anxieties, I can't not help when she looks so ready to fall over. "Sweetheart…"

When I cup her elbow to lead her toward a chair, Bethany twists away. "Don't touch me."

Sighing, I release her and step back, somehow managing to keep my hands off her. But it's a fight. Touching Bethany, comforting her, feels so right.

"I'm sorry for your loss," I say instead. "I know you and your father had a difficult relationship at the end, but it's always painful to lose someone you love."

She wraps her arms around her middle as if she's trying to give herself the fortitude to press on. "More than I probably should have. But he was a positive influence in my childhood. He made sure I never wanted for anything, he educated me well, and spent time with me. For that, I'll always be grateful. I'm just in shock now. I'm sure I'll grieve him and eventually accept that he's neither the man I thought nor here with me anymore. Forgiveness for everything he did—to everyone—will take time."

True. It's a small blessing that she's already considering absolving him. If I'd forgiven sooner, I wouldn't have been stupid enough to pursue Bethany under false pretenses. And I wouldn't have gotten my heart ripped out. I'm probably only getting what I deserve... But if she can eventually find mercy in her soul for her father, she'll find peace. Of course, part of me can't help but wonder if she might find it in her heart to forgive me someday, too.

"The healing will happen when you're ready," I murmur. "And I know it's a small consolation that he won't be able to hurt you anymore—"

"But an important one. At least now there will be no trial. Not having my name dragged through the mud anymore will be a relief. The truth can come out, and I can walk free from his shadow and move on with my life."

"Eventually, those will feel like positives."

Bethany turns to glare my way. "Yes, but don't act like you care. I've already heard enough of your lies. I don't need more."

"Sweetheart—"

"Don't call me that."

I sigh. "I'm really sorry, Beth. For everything I accused you of. For every lie I told you. For—"

She holds up a hand. "It doesn't matter now. You got the answers you came for. You got the justice you wanted. The will my father updated weeks ago in anticipation of his divorce becoming final leaves me everything. So hopefully, I'll be able to track down what's left of the victims' stolen funds and return them to everyone, you included. Beyond that, you and I don't have anything else to say. It would be best if you didn't contact me anymore."

Oh, fuck.

But I need to tell her so many things. That I feel like the most stupidly righteous idiot on the planet. That I regret not being honest with her. But most of all, that I love her. Bethany isn't ready to hear any of that now. I understand. I won't give up on us, though. I may have fallen for her because I orchestrated this giant lie to ferret out her "crimes," and I regret that like hell. But I don't regret a moment of the time we spent together.

"Did you call your siblings?"

She shakes her head. "I don't think the news of Barclay's passing is something I should deliver over the phone. It would be better to gather everyone together and tell them face to face."

"You're right. Grab your purse, and I'll take you—"

"No, I'll find my own way. I don't want to see you, spend time with you, or even be in the same room with you. I'm moving out of the apartment, so you can do what you want with the lease. It's over, Clint. We're done."

Her words hurt like a physical blow, but arguing is pointless now. I fucked up and all I can do is give her the time and space she needs while hoping I'll someday have the opportunity to put us back together.

"You don't have a car, and even if they've discharged Stephen from the hospital, he's in no condition to drive. I'll get you to Maxon and Keeley's place. I'll even help you tell your siblings what happened so you don't have to live through it again by yourself. Then, if you still want me to go, I will." I can't resist cupping her face. "But I'll be back. I meant what I said when I told you that I fell in love with you and I had every intention of asking you to be my wife."

Bethany hasn't cried all day, but now my words reduce her to tears. "Don't. Just…don't."

I'm pushing, and she can't take it.

Slowly, I drop my hand. "Okay. We won't talk about it any more tonight. Just let me get you to your brother's house safely."

She hesitates, then nods. "Only because it's the fastest way there, and they deserve to know what's happened."

We make our way out the bar's back door, probably for the last time. I already told Andy I wouldn't be back. No need to work this job now that my cover story is moot. I doubt Bethany will be back, either. She needs to grieve. And just like I can't stand to be in my North Dakota home anymore, I doubt she'll want to work in the place where she watched her father die.

The drive to the inn is tense and quiet. She texts Maxon and tells him to gather the family at his place. It's important, but she refuses to say why. He agrees, then she darkens her phone and zones out. Whatever she sees of the dark night out her window seems to hold her attention. Or maybe that's just her way of avoiding me.

We're drawing close to Maxon and Keeley's bed-and-breakfast, and I have this sense of a clock ticking away the last of my time with Bethany. I try to rationalize. She'll still be on the island tomorrow. I won't let her get too far from my side. I'll find small ways to let her know I love her and that I'm here for her without pushing too hard. She thinks she doesn't want me now, but someday she'll realize that she wants a lover who will care for her, who will devote himself to her. I'll be waiting. I'll be ready to prove that I'm sorry and that I'm worthy. I'll beg her forgiveness. Then I'll do whatever it takes to convince her that she's it for me. She's the only woman I'll ever love.

Still, what if that day never comes? What if these are the last moments I ever spend with Bethany?

Panic eats at my gut. If I don't say something, will she leave thinking she meant nothing to me except revenge? Will I regret staying silent in these final moments for the rest of my lonely life?

I reach for her hand. "I was proud of you tonight, Beth."

For once, she doesn't wrench away. She also doesn't reply.

Into the silence, I go on. "I know from personal experience that what you went through tonight with your father was one of the hardest things to deal with—ever. A father's death stays with you, and you constantly wonder what you could have done to save him."

Finally, she turns to me with a little frown furrowed between her brows. "I've already wondered that."

"The answer is nothing. Paul Daniels was on a mission, and you couldn't have stopped him. Just like I couldn't do anything to prevent my dad's heart attack. Your father made enemies. My father didn't take care of his health. Sometimes accepting that things are out of your control is the most difficult lesson of all. It's a lesson I wish I would have accepted before I lost you."

Bethany pulls her hand free. "Don't."

I back down. I have to. "You handled the police and their questions with poise and perfection. I'm not surprised. You're strong, Beth. Hell, you had the spine and the independence weeks ago to realize you had to cut ties with your dad. You'll carry on professionally now that he's gone and I have no doubt you'll succeed."

Slowly, she nods. "I'm not going to let my father take my future from me. He's already tainted too much of my past. I'm damn good at investment counseling, and I love what I do. Multimillionaires and Wall Street bigwigs may never trust me again, but that's okay. I'll face the future on my own terms. That's something I should have done all along."

"Where will you go?" I ask as we pull up at the inn.

My time with Bethany is almost up—and it's killing me.

She shrugs. "I don't know. There's nothing but terrible memories in San Diego. I'll probably sell my ridiculously expensive condo I can't afford anymore and find someplace else to call home. You?"

I'll be wherever Bethany is, but she isn't ready to hear that. "I'm going to leave North Dakota. The guy who's been watching my business back there wants to buy it. I'm going to let him. The sale of my dad's insurance agency should be complete in the next week or two. Both of my younger brothers are away at college. So I guess I'll be looking for someplace to call home, too. And a new job to go with it." Then I take a risk and grab her hand again. "But wherever that is, Beth, I'll be thinking of you. And only you. You may never believe me because I know I didn't show you the way I should have, but I love you. I love the way you make me think. I love the way you challenge me to understand you. I love it when you finally let me behind your walls and smile. I love that, when you give your body to me, you do it completely. Most of all, I love your strength and courage. I love the way you didn't let your father or anyone else defeat you. I love that you're real and true and that you taught me so much about ignoring my assumptions and listening to my heart."

She doesn't say anything, just continues to look down, occasionally swiping at her wet cheeks with a shaking hand.

"Beth…" I tilt her chin to face me.

Her big eyes, the pain twisting her mouth, and the silvery paths running down her face all rip me apart. She didn't let her asshole father break her, but I just might. I hate that—and myself for hurting her—more than anything.

If Bethany never gives me a second chance, I have no doubt she'll be my biggest regret.

She closes her eyes as if she can't take the intimacy of our stare anymore. I want to lean in and kiss her passionately, convince her I mean every word I say. We're only inches apart… But that's not what she needs now.

Instead, I press my lips softly to hers—a breath, a brush. A good-bye.

When I ease back, I see Maxon, Griff, Noah, and Evan all hovering on the lanai, looking grim. Just beyond, I spot the women gathered in the great room, heads bent together, hands clasped. I hazard a glance Bethany's way. She looks relieved to see everyone and yet more than nervous now that the moment is upon her.

"I'm here if you need me," I vow.

She shakes her head. "I've got this. It's something I need to do. It would be better if you left and didn't come back."

I'm hurt but not surprised by her answer. "Take care of yourself. If you need or want me for anything—ever—all you have to do is call."

"I'm done being blindly loyal. And you've proven that I can't trust you."

Before I can reply, Maxon and Noah are at my door, opening it. Bethany exits the car on the other side, and Griff pulls her straight into his waiting arms.

"We know," her oldest brother says somberly. "News travels fast on an island this size."

At least Bethany won't have to break the news or explain everything again. Instead, Griff and Evan lead her inside the house. All the women rise and greet her, Harlow the first to hug her and offer both affection and condolences. I'm so relieved that Bethany won't be alone tonight.

"Thanks for being here for Beth," I tell the other two men. "She's really broken up."

"We know she is," Maxon assures me.

"Not only is he gone, she watched the son of a bitch die…"

Noah winces.

Maxon lets out a curse. "I'm sorry for her. I hated my father, and I'm neither surprised nor upset that a former client offed him. But I wrote him out of my life to preserve my mental health long ago. Bethany only realized his true colors a few weeks back, and before she could even reconcile the reality with the fairy-tale father she thought had raised her, he's gone."

Exactly. "She's grieving. She needs people who care."

"She's got us. And she's got you, too."

I shake my head. "It's…over. I'll let her explain if she wants to share. I can't do anything right now except respect her wishes and go."

Noah scowls. "You're walking away from her?"

"Not by choice." And not forever. "She wants me to. And…I deserve to suffer."

"Whoa. Slow your roll." Harlow's husband looks at me as if I've lost my damn mind. "You're giving up? When she needs you most?"

I open my mouth to explain, but Maxon waves a hand in my face. "I get it. You're doing the altruistic thing for some reason. It's a mistake. Maybe that's my perspective because ruthless is bred into my veins. It's a Reed trait…along with not knowing your heart. That's where Bethany is at right now. If I had only listened to my head, I wouldn't be married to the best woman in the world and I wouldn't have a beautiful baby girl."

"Same for Harlow," Noah cuts in. "I can't tell you how often she tried to put distance between us. I'm damn glad I was pushy and tenacious."

Their admissions surprise me. I thought they'd always been deliriously happy. Nice to know someone overcame their differences and found happiness. Just not sure that's ever going to be Bethany and me...

"Did either one of you deceive your wives?"

Their identical scowls might have been comical if I was in any mood to laugh.

"No," Noah admits.

Maxon shakes his head. "But I did plenty of other shitty stuff. Trust me. Do you love Bethany?"

"Yes." I came for my pound of flesh...but I'm the one who lost my heart.

"Then we'll help you."

"Why?" It's a passing curiosity. His help or lack thereof isn't going to change the outcome. Bethany has to decide on her own that she wants me. "When we first met, you didn't like me much."

"I didn't. But the more time my sister spent with you, the more she came out of her shell. None of us had managed to get past her defenses. You did. If you give up on her now, she'll only retreat into herself. And since I've gone this route—so has Griff—she'll turn brittle. If you love her, don't let that happen."

I look up at Beth. The wives are reaching out to offer their comfort and support...and already I see her pulling away.

"Believe me, I have no intention of walking away forever, but she needs time to grieve. And she needs time to figure out if she can forgive me. I'm not going far, though. And she'll have to tell me that she'll *never* love me before I give up on her completely."

Maxon smiles his approval and claps me on the shoulder. "Perfect. Keep working on her. We'll help. She'll come around."

I can only hope.

Noah nods. "Why don't you crash for the night and come back in the morning when she's fresh. Right now, she's in no shape to make lifelong decisions. Things may look a lot different tomorrow."

I doubt it, but I nod and exchange digits with the guys. "I'll be back. Take care of her for me until then, huh?"

Maxon nods. "You got it."

As I climb in my car, I'm grateful to see the two men join the rest of the family to exchange condolences and hugs. They're not letting Bethany shy away from their comfort or support. As much as I hate leaving her now, I know she'll be in good hands until I can wrap my arms around her again and begin proving that I am the man she can count on. Until she believes deep down that I'm the same man she fell for.

I stop by the apartment we moved into only yesterday, when the day was bright and the possibilities were seemingly endless. But everywhere I look I see Beth now. I can't stay here. It's too haunted. I can't miss her this much without losing my mind. Instead, I grab a shower and a clean change of clothes, then head to Ash's, who welcomes me with a beer and an ear.

It's close to dawn when I finally find sleep on his lumpy piece-of-shit sofa. I wake up a few hours later, feeling less than rested but beyond ready to start winning Bethany back.

When I reach the inn a little before ten, Maxon greets me with his mouth pressed in a grim line. "She's gone. I'm sorry. We tried... She's leaving the island. And honestly, I don't know where she's going or if she's coming back."

CHAPTER THIRTEEN

Three months later
Los Angeles

BETHANY

MY HAND TREMBLES as I smooth my skirt, then press my fingers across my jittery stomach to calm it. Above me, the sunny spring sky wraps me in California blue. Behind me, my car door hangs open. Stay or go? But I know the answer. It's now or never. Do or die.

I'm a woman on a mission. This is it.

I shut my car door, press the fob to lock the vehicle, and stare straight ahead at the gorgeous but unfamiliar home in front of me. The now-familiar strains of Jason Mraz's "I Won't Give Up" float through my head, crying out that, although we have a lot to learn, we're worth it.

Today, I'll find out if that's true. I'll figure out once and for all if anything Clint Holmes claims he felt for me in Maui was real.

Would he have sent me the ballad about persevering, along with the handful of other songs encouraging me to give our relationship another try if he wasn't? It seems unlikely. He now has all the answers he sought about the Reed Financial scam. He got justice, too. What else could he want from me…except me?

No, Clint didn't compile the song list he sent a few weeks ago. Keeley did; he admits that. But he swears he feels all these sentiments.

I never thought of music as therapy, but apparently it's Keeley's way of navigating difficult emotions. It seemed silly at first, but I see why now. I've picked every song apart. Sting's "Fortress Around Your Heart" tells me he understands that he invented the battle between us inside his head and that he's well aware his lies caused me to raise my defenses. Bryan Adams's "Please Forgive Me" just melts my heart. How can I refuse a man who asks for forgiveness for loving me too much? Yesterday, "Dig" by Incubus was on high rotation. Yes, we all have a weakness that cleverly attaches and multiplies. I'm guilty, so I can't blame him for not being perfect.

But do I dare trust him again?

Do I dare not try?

I haven't been ready to tackle that question until now because the last three months have been hell. My final morning in Maui, I left Maxon and Keeley's place with tears and hugs and promises to keep in touch, then I took a taxi to the hospital, helped Stephen through the discharge process, and settled him into the temporary rental he's found. He had to be feeling better because he was already eyeing the property's caretaker, a pretty blonde named Skye. Before I hopped on my red-eye back to LA that night, he told me I was crazy to run from Clint because that man loves me. I was too shell-shocked by everything that happened the night before to hear it.

A week after my father's death, he was buried in San Diego. The service quickly became a nightmarish media circus. Thank goodness my siblings came, except Griff, who stayed behind with Britta for the birth of their second beautiful little boy, Grayson. But Maxon watched over me protectively. Harlow held my hand. Evan fended off the press.

My siblings came not to pay their respects to the man who sired us but to support *me*. I was beyond touched—and they haven't wavered since. If one silver lining has come out of the multitude of Barclay's lies and indiscretions, it's my family. We've grown closer over the last few months, despite me being back in California now.

But I miss them. A lot.

During the funeral, Maxon also made sure that Linda, Barclay's vengeful wife, didn't get too close to me. Once she found out I had inherited everything remaining in Barclay's estate and her boy-toy Marco left her for a wealthier sugar-mama, the woman threatened to kill me. Last month, she was found guilty of all charges in the Reed Financial scandal—conspiracy, aiding and abetting, money laundering. She's going to prison for the rest of her life. None of my siblings seemed surprised or broken up about it. How sad that the woman who met this tragic end was such a horrible human being that none of her children even shed tears. Then again, being married to Barclay for thirty-five years probably warped her into someone as twisted and self-serving as he'd been.

Clint came to my dad's funeral, too. That was the first—and only—time I've seen him since our breakup. I hoped laying eyes on him wouldn't affect me. After all, he lied to me. He betrayed me. He coaxed me into laying my soul bare when he didn't love me. But his expression as we stared at one another across the thirty feet that separated us said something very different. I felt him there, full of concern and remorse—and devotion I wanted to believe so badly it tore at my heart.

Still, how could I after his words and longing looks in Maui were all lies?

He sent a beautiful sympathy bouquet for the service. We talked afterward, but he didn't press me. He didn't touch me, either…though I secretly wished he had. Instead, he told me that if I wanted or needed him, he would come right away, no questions or expectations. Then he whispered that he loves me.

I wasn't ready to hear it. Though Barclay's passing no longer upset me, I left the funeral in tears.

Not long after, I flew to the Caymans. My trip there to retrieve the victims' stolen funds was long and frustrating. Weeding through all the documentation, bureaucracy, and legalities took weeks. Finally, the bank relinquished the funds to me—all seven hundred eighty million dollars of it. It took another few weeks for me to clear my plans with the feds.

And the entire time I was in the blue-ocean, palm-tree paradise, I couldn't stop thinking about my time in Maui with Clint. Was any of what we shared real? Did he fall for me, despite wondering if I was guilty? Does he really love me?

I don't know, and the battle between prudence and hope seems never ending.

Since returning stateside two weeks ago, I've dispersed all funds back to the victims and quietly let them know I'm here if they ever need a resource or help in understanding their investments. I recommended other well-respected advisors to them, of course. I was stunned that a handful of former clients insisted on sticking with me.

Though maybe I shouldn't be surprised. After Barclay's death and during Linda's trial, the facts of the case hit the news. I was exonerated in the court of public opinion when it became clear that I had no knowledge or hand in the scheme. The one day I had to testify, I barely held myself together as I described the moment I realized my father had utterly deceived me—and all our clients. Maybe those people now feel sorry for me. Maybe they believe in second chances. Either way, I've retained enough of these former investors to start my own financial services firm.

Stephen Lund hired me, too. Yes, probably out of loyalty and pity, but I appreciate his friendship. He still hasn't left Maui, and he's not spilling about what he's up to, much less when—or if—he intends to return home and resume his role as his father's second-in-command again at Colossus Investment Corporation. But he sounds happier than I've ever heard him. I wonder if that pretty blonde is the reason…

Noah and Harlow hired me to manage their money, too. Ditto Evan and Nia. It's above and beyond the call of sibling duty. But I'm working exceptionally hard to make the most of their investments and ensure they never regret their decision.

The only client whose stolen funds I haven't returned yet is Clint's. This, I wanted to do in person. Because honestly, every day we've been apart, the man has done his best to ensure he's never far from my thoughts.

I need to know where we stand—once and for all.

Shortly after my dad's funeral, he started texting me. Sure, he said he was sorry a lot. Every day, he reiterates that he loves me. I've never replied. At first, I had too much happening to expend mental energy on anything except Barclay and the mess he left. Now that I've straightened it up, I've started getting perspective. I'm wondering if Clint and I could ever be an us again.

In the last two weeks, I've thought of almost nothing else. I'm still not sure what to believe.

Recently, he started texting me about more day-to-day stuff, too—making me feel like I'm a part of his life. Bryson, his youngest brother, is apparently flourishing at college. Bret, the middle sibling, finally realized that his hate for me was misplaced. He's laid off the booze and started hitting the books again. I'm happy for them both. I've never met Bret, but I'm glad for his sake that he's moving on.

Not that I don't understand where he was coming from. Grief can bend a person in terrible ways, and while it's fresh, it's hard not to welcome any kind of comfort, even if it's wrong. Thankfully, my crutch was less destructive than alcohol. I devoted most every waking hour to the victims' fund I began, which has grown twenty-three percent in the last nine months. I'm proud of that accomplishment. I'm even happier that the funds I returned to the victims were sometimes even more than the amount they initially invested.

Clint sold his father's business, then sent me his third of the proceeds with the explicit request to add the amount to the victims' fund. To have him embrace my most near-and-dear cause touched me. It made me cry…and wonder if we could have forever.

A few weeks later, he surprised me again, this time by sending me the proceeds from the sale of his North Dakota business, along with a note asking me to invest it. Because he trusts me, he says. Because he wants to show me that he has utter faith in me. Because, despite what I think, he still loves me.

At the time, I didn't know what to say…so I've said nothing. All professional correspondence has been via certified letter or a temp I hired until I land my business somewhere and put down roots. Regardless, every single day Clint texts me his thoughts, his feelings, his hopes for our future, and his sincere apologies.

Why would he persist after three months if he didn't mean it?

In my purse, my phone buzzes. Speak of the devil… It's Clint.

`Good morning, sweetheart. I miss you. It's a beautiful day, but it would be even better if you were here. It would be perfect if you wanted to talk.`

I'm tempted to reply…but I don't. What I need to say should be said in person.

`Hey, good news. I got a message from Ash last night. He and Samantha are engaged! Happy for them… He's managing the bar now but that's temporary. Sam finishes her degree in finance in May and will be looking for an entry-level position. The wedding is in June in Maui, and I'm best man! If you'd like come, I would love to see you. Because I love you. Still. That's not going to change.`

There's no stopping the way my heart melts.

Right after I found out he lied and used me for revenge, I wanted to hate him. For a few days, maybe I even did. But it didn't last. He's made staying mad impossible. Now, I look forward to his daily texts. He doesn't know, of course. I've waited to see if his feelings were more absolution than lifetime devotion. But he hasn't wavered one bit since our separation.

So, it's time for me to finally figure out if we have any hope of a future. Because as much as I'd like to say I've fallen out of love, I haven't.

The phone in my hand buzzes again as I head slowly up the walkway, toward the door.

`What are you up to? I'm still at home in LA, working through what my next business venture will be. I've got some ideas… I wish we could talk about them. You might be surprised. I know you're probably still angry—and with good reason. But I won't stop texting you unless you tell me to. Maybe I won't even stop then. It's the only way I have to convince you that I'm beyond in love with you and want to spend my life with you. I want to marry you.`

He says that almost every day, more lately than when he first started texting. I'm finding it harder and harder not to believe him. I've questioned whether that makes me crazy. Maybe I should be holding a grudge. That might have been satisfying, at least for a while. But I've realized a few things through all of this. First, not forgiving is what started this mayhem. Second, the more I let distrust and negativity into my life, the more I risk becoming like Barclay.

That's something I never, ever want.

For the first time since our one-sided correspondence, I raise my trembling fingers to my phone and tap out a reply.

`Answer your door.`

As soon as the message is delivered, I shove the phone back in my bag and ring the bell.

Seconds later, footsteps pound through the house. The door wrenches open, and Clint stands there, tall and shocked and looking so good in jeans and a T-shirt, he makes me as weak-kneed as the first time I saw him.

I drag in a breath and brace myself. "Hi."

"You're here. Oh, my god. You're here! Come in."

When he lurches back, I step over the threshold and into his foyer, nervously clutching my purse. He leads me into the living room beyond. It's expansive, lined with bookcases, framed by a large sectional, comfy chairs, and a marble fireplace that's a statement all its own. This place is nice, but it doesn't look like him.

"Thanks. Did your mother decorate the house?"

He nods. "A few years before she passed, yes. Did you want to sit?"

I can tell he's nervous. Because he doesn't want to spoil the opportunity to convince me of his feelings...or is he worried I'm here to call his bluff?

"Thanks." As I perch on the edge of the sectional, he sits on the massive coffee table right in front of me.

He's mere feet away. My heart pounds. I wasn't sure if or when I'd ever be close to this man again...and now I can't think about anything else.

"I'm sorry." I assume he's apologizing to me again for what happened in Maui, but he takes my hands instead. "I can't not touch you. It's been so long. I need to be sure you're real."

When he squeezes my fingers, he squeezes my heart, too. I clutch him in return. It feels so good to touch him again. He's like welcoming warmth after three long months of emotional winter.

"What brings you here? Not that I'm not thrilled to see you. Not that I want you to ever leave," he rushes to assure me, scooting even closer. "But you haven't spoken to me since the funeral and…"

He's been trying not to give up. I see that on his face.

We have to figure out how—or if—we can put the past behind us. But first things first.

I reach into my purse and pull out an envelope. "Open it."

Clint tears into it and scans the check for just under four million dollars, then looks at me with a scowl. "You came here just to return my father's money?"

"It's something I had to do. I know money won't bring him back, but I'm hoping it gives you and your brothers some sense of peace and security."

"This is a nice gesture. Thank you for your honesty and integrity, but I haven't doubted you since you left Maui. In fact, I want you to invest this money. My brothers and I already talked about it." He presses the envelope back into my hands.

Is he for real? "You want me to manage the money he spent his life making? The money my father took?"

Clint nods. "I don't trust anyone else."

He's serious. OMG… My heart floats in my chest as if his face-to-face vote of confidence filled it with hope again. I can only think of one thing he's trying to say to me with this gesture: that he's put every reservation he ever had about me to rest. When our gazes connect, I see that same message in his blue eyes.

I smile. "You're sure?"

"Positive. What I'd like even better is to talk to you, try to alleviate your distrust in me, so we can be together again. Please don't say no."

I'm not surprised he's confronting this head on. We need to. I'm finally ready.

"Clint, what you did to me was deceitful."

"Horrible and unforgivable. But..." He slides his fingers between mine. "I'm hoping you can find some way to forgive me."

Now that I've been able to move past my own trials and reflect on what he went through, that no longer sounds farfetched. In fact, I almost don't blame him. Shock, grief, loss—they can do terrible things to anyone's psyche. And unlike my father, his did nothing to deserve a premature death. I understand why Clint looked for someone to blame— and I was the obvious choice. But we have to talk this out.

"You lied about everything."

He shakes his head. "Our meeting was a lie. My job at the bar was a lie. Initially, my attempts to be your friend were a lie. Everything else was totally fucking real, sweetheart—especially how hard I fell for you. Even when logic told me I was being selfish and irresponsible, I couldn't stop myself. I wanted you. I needed to be with you. I love you. I hope you can find some way to believe me."

He's been saying these same things via text the last few months. It's hard not to believe him now, when he has no more reason to lie.

"Tell me, in your ideal world, what would happen next between us?"

"Hey, bro. I'm out. I'll be back—" When I turn to the other man who just stumbled into the room, his eyes flare wide. "Holy shit. Bethany Banks?"

Standing, I nod, absently thinking how much he looks like his brother—and their father. "You're Bret?"

He approaches, hand outstretched. "Yeah. Hey, I'm really sorry for being a douche and breaking into your apartment."

Clint admitted that to me, too.

"It's okay. I understand." Honestly, he didn't destroy or deface anything. If Clint hadn't told me his brother had been in my place, I wouldn't have known. "Water under the bridge."

"Great. Thanks. I'll, um...leave you two to talk. It was nice to meet you. For whatever it's worth, I wish you'd put my brother out of his misery and marry him. He loves you. Bry and I would be happy to have you in the family."

My elation spikes. I expected it would take months—maybe years—for Clint's brothers to stop hating me. I worried they would resist any attempt we made to patch up our romance. But for Bret to practically beg me to marry his brother…

As Clint and his middle sibling exchange a manly shoulder bump, I can't stop smiling. Then his younger brother nods my way and melts out of the room.

"Sorry about the interruption," Clint says. "We're alone now."

"Your brother seems like a good guy."

"He's made progress lately. In fact, he came down from UCLA to spend the weekend with me. Bry may or may not show up, depending on whether he can tear himself away from his new girlfriend. But even if he does, I won't see him for hours yet. So let's talk about us and my ideal world."

"Please. I want to hear that."

"You would be the center of it, of course. The only part of our past we'd ever think about would be meeting and falling in love. You'd be wearing my ring. We'd be planning a wedding and finding a place to live together for the rest of our insanely happy lives. Soon, we'd start catching up with your siblings on the baby thing. I want a few of our own, and it would be great if all the kids were roughly the same age so they could play together. I'm glad you're starting your own financial services business, because I'd like to be working beside you eventually. I'm already registered to take the online classes to become a certified financial planner. Once I've completed those, I'd want to learn from you, grow our business together, while I finish my college degree. I would be your full partner—in business and in life. Most of all, I want to show you how madly I love you every day. And I want you to love me back. That world, to me, would be perfect."

I blink, utterly stunned at how far he's already gone to mesh his life with mine. More hope makes my chest swell until it's tight—but in a good way. The very best way, in fact.

"How do I know you mean it?" That's the last question I have, the one I haven't been able to get past on my own.

"Stay right here."

Before I can reply, he darts across the room and up the stairs. I hear him rummaging around up there. A curse follows, then he jets back into the living room winded, but looking surprisingly upbeat—and clutching something in his fist.

That hope expands even more until it fills up my whole body.

"You don't have any proof about me. Just like I never had any proof about you when we were in Maui. The truth is, I tried to apply 'logic.' I questioned everything and took each word you said with a grain of salt. It's what a cautious, rational person does, right?" He shrugs. "How much better would it have been if I had simply gone with my gut and believed you were exactly the woman you seemed? That you were the only one I could ever want or need, despite the apparent 'proof' otherwise, for the rest of my life?"

He makes an excellent point. Relationships don't come with guarantees. It's not a savings account or a municipal bond. There's no assurance this romance will pay the dividends I want. Cupid isn't the FDIC, who will insure a substantial chunk of my investment in his heart.

I'm willing to trust him—and us—or I'm not. It's as simple as that.

Granted, in the past, I was blindly loyal to my father. But I put my faith in the wrong someone. Clint took such good care of me in Maui—far better than my father did, even at his best. I can't shade Clint with Barclay's wrongdoings just because they're both men who told lies. I can't fall into the guilt-by-association trap. I have to believe that Clint is exactly the man I fell for.

Slowly, I nod. "What's in your hand?"

He smiles, looking both sheepish and a bit shy. "You never saw it, did you?"

"What?" But I'm pretty sure I know.

Suddenly, he's down on one knee. "Bethany Alannah Banks, will you—"

"You dug up my middle name?"

Clint laughs. "I knew everything about you before I orchestrated our first meeting in Hawaii. The only thing I didn't know was the actual you. So, yes. Bethany Alannah Banks, I love everything about you—the kind, the shy, the ballsy, the witty, the unsure—even your middle name. Please do me the extreme honor of being my wife and making me the happiest man on earth."

When he flips open the ring box, I gasp. It's everything I ever imagined an engagement ring should be. It's not big or gaudy. In fact, it's simple. It's elegant. It's…me. The marquise-cut diamond sits on a simple white-gold band, flanked by two smaller marquise-cut diamonds nestled on either side. No other embellishments. Nothing that jumps up and screams "look at me!" Just a pure, exquisite expression of the love he's been trying to give me for the last three months.

"Can I try it on?"

He doesn't hesitate. "If it gets you any closer to saying yes, then absolutely. All day long."

After yanking the ring from the box, he insists on sliding it onto my finger.

The moment he does, my equilibrium fixes itself. Everything feels right. My world is perfect.

Well, almost.

I blink up at him. "Want to hear my version of an ideal life?"

"Yes. Please tell me we can meet somewhere in the middle, Beth. I don't want to live without you."

Finally, I reach out and touch him. "You're the center of it. The only part of our past we ever think about is falling in love and learning from our mistakes so we can have an amazing future. I'm wearing this ring, and we're planning a wedding. And buying a place on Maui, where I can be near my family, and we can live an insanely happy life together. Yes, we definitely have to catch up to my siblings in the baby department. I want our kiddos to play with their cousins. Professionally, you and I would have this great home-and-work relationship, and we'd make an amazing investment team to help the financial dreams of others come true. And most of all, I want to show you that I love you, too. And that I never stopped. That's my perfect world."

"Seriously? For real?" Clint gapes, looking sucker-punched. "You're saying yes?"

I glance at the ring, then into the face of the man I never expected to love…and now can't imagine living my life without. "I'm saying an enthusiastic hell yes."

Instantly, my reply fills the chasm between us and builds a bridge across the divide. He pulls me close, crushing me against his chest, then swoops down to claim me with a kiss that feels like a tender, passionate start on our forever.

When we finally lift our heads long moments later, we're both panting. "No joke, right?"

"I love you. I have for a long time. And I think Bethany Holmes has a wonderful ring to it."

"My dad thought the same thing. In my last conversation with him, he tried to convince me that you and I would be perfect together."

I smile. "Your dad was a wonderful, wise man."

Clint kisses me again. This embrace takes even longer to tear ourselves away from. We'd both rather find the bedroom, but there are still things to settle…

"How do you feel about moving to Maui?" I finally ask between long bouts of lip locks.

"Actually, I was thinking of heading there anyway. Bret and Bry will be okay if I go. They're men now. They're both doing great. None of us want to sell the house here since it's full of our childhood memories. Thankfully, my aunt Sandra has decided to leave Kansas after a miserable winter. So she'll be moving here in a few weeks. We're going to rent her the house. She'll take good care of it. Problem solved." He gives me a big grin. "When I was on the island, I fell in love with it and the people, just like I fell in love with you. So all we have to do is choose a date to get married and a house in which we'll live happily ever after."

I'm beyond elated. When I first stepped foot on Maui, I never imagined the journey would change my life—and me—for the better. My heart feels like it might burst from my chest—in the best way possible.

Tossing my arms around Clint, I kiss my way across his jaw before brushing my lips over his and tugging up on the hem of his very inconvenient shirt. "We'll look at a calendar and real estate listings later. Right now, I can't wait to be with you."

He cups my face in his hands. "Oh, sweetheart. You have no idea how desperate I've been to get my hands on you, how much I want to show you in every way possible that I love you. I'm thinking we should get started on the rest of our lives now. We can call the family and give them the good news later. Don't you think?"

Smiling, I flash him my engagement ring. "I do."

The End

Read on for more from Shayla Black!

The More Than Words series continues later this year with…

MORE THAN PLEASURE YOU
by Shayla Black
(a 1001 Dark Nights novella)
Coming November 12, 2019!

Can I convince her our hot but temporary engagement should last forever?

I'm Stephen Lund, confirmed bachelor…and son of a successful billionaire whose sins I can't forget—or forgive. After he delivered an ultimatum to either get over his transgressions or get out of the family business, I put space between us with a temporary getaway to Maui. My rental's sexy caretaker, Skye Ingram, is a beautiful distraction. Yeah, it's a terrible time to start a fling, but I can't help wanting to give her every bit of pleasure she's willing to take.

When Skye needs a date to her ex-boyfriend's wedding, I'm game to play her pretend fiancé. The jerk should see what he passed up…and that I'm holding her now. But our pretend engagement begins to feel real. Our passion certainly is. So are the consequences. When I'm confronted with the reality that our lives are now irrevocably entwined, I have to choose between leaving Skye to return to the life—and wealth—I've always known or abandoning everything familiar to start over with the woman who awakened my heart.

MORE THAN WORDS SERIES
By Shayla Black

Sexy contemporary romances that prove sometimes words alone can't express the true depths of love.

Each book can be read as a standalone. You may enjoy them more in order, but it's not necessary for your reading pleasure.

More Than Want You
More Than Need You
More Than Love You
More Than Crave You
More Than Tempt You
Coming Soon:
More Than Pleasure You (novella) (November 12, 2019)

LET'S GET TO KNOW EACH OTHER!

ABOUT ME:
Shayla Black is the *New York Times* and *USA Today* bestselling author of more than seventy novels. For twenty years, she's written contemporary, erotic, paranormal, and historical romances via traditional, independent, foreign, and audio publishers. Her books have sold millions of copies and been published in a dozen languages.

Raised an only child, Shayla occupied herself with lots of daydreaming, much to the chagrin of her teachers. In college, she found her love for reading and realized that she could have a career publishing the stories spinning in her imagination. Though she graduated with a degree in Marketing/Advertising and embarked on a stint in corporate America to pay the bills, her heart has always been with her characters. She's thrilled that she's been living her dream as a full-time author for the past eight years.

Shayla currently lives in North Texas with her wonderfully supportive husband, her daughter, and two spoiled tabbies. In her "free" time, she enjoys reality TV, reading, and listening to an eclectic blend of music.

LET ME LEARN MORE ABOUT YOU.
Connect with me via the links below. The VIP Readers newsletter has exclusive news and excerpts. You can also become one of my Facebook Book Beauties and enjoy live, interactive #WineWednesday video chats full of fun, book chatter, and more! See you soon!

Connect with me online:

Website: http://shaylablack.com

VIP Reader Newsletter: http://shayla.link/nwsltr

Facebook Author Page: https://www.facebook.com/ShaylaBlackAuthor

Facebook Book Beauties Chat Group: http://shayla.link/FBChat

Instagram: https://instagram.com/ShaylaBlack/

Book+Main Bites: https://bookandmainbites.com/users/62

Twitter: http://twitter.com/Shayla_Black

Google +: http://shayla.link/googleplus

Amazon Author: http://shayla.link/AmazonFollow

BookBub: http://shayla.link/BookBub

Goodreads: http://shayla.link/goodreads

YouTube: http://shayla.link/youtube

If you enjoyed this book, please review it and recommend it to others.

OTHER BOOKS BY SHAYLA BLACK

CONTEMPORARY ROMANCE
MORE THAN WORDS
More Than Want You
More Than Need You
More Than Love You
More Than Crave You
More Than Tempt You
Coming Soon:
More Than Pleasure You (November 12, 2019)

THE WICKED LOVERS (COMPLETE SERIES)
Wicked Ties
Decadent
Delicious
Surrender to Me
Belong to Me
"Wicked to Love" (novella)
Mine to Hold
"Wicked All the Way" (novella)
Ours to Love
"Wicked All Night" (novella)
"Forever Wicked" (novella)
Theirs to Cherish
His to Take
Pure Wicked (novella)
Wicked for You
Falling in Deeper
Dirty Wicked (novella)
"A Very Wicked Christmas" (short)
Holding on Tighter

THE DEVOTED LOVERS
Devoted to Pleasure
"Devoted to Wicked" (novella)
Coming Soon:
Devoted to Love (July 2, 2019)

SEXY CAPERS
Bound And Determined
Strip Search
"Arresting Desire" (Hot In Handcuffs Anthology)

THE PERFECT GENTLEMEN (by Shayla Black and Lexi Blake)
Scandal Never Sleeps
Seduction in Session
Big Easy Temptation
Smoke and Sin
At the Pleasure of the President

MASTERS OF MÉNAGE (by Shayla Black and Lexi Blake)
Their Virgin Captive
Their Virgin's Secret
Their Virgin Concubine
Their Virgin Princess
Their Virgin Hostage
Their Virgin Secretary
Their Virgin Mistress
Coming Soon:
Their Virgin Bride (TBD)

DOMS OF HER LIFE (by Shayla Black, Jenna Jacob, and Isabella LaPearl)
Raine Falling Collection (Complete)
One Dom To Love
The Young And The Submissive
The Bold and The Dominant
The Edge of Dominance

Heavenly Rising Collection
The Choice
Coming Soon:
The Chase (2019)

THE MISADVENTURES SERIES
Misadventures of a Backup Bride
Misadventures with My Ex

STANDALONE TITLES
Naughty Little Secret
Watch Me
Dangerous Boys And Their Toy
"Her Fantasy Men" (Four Play Anthology)
A Perfect Match
His Undeniable Secret (Sexy Short)
HISTORICAL ROMANCE (as Shelley Bradley)
The Lady And The Dragon
One Wicked Night
Strictly Seduction
Strictly Forbidden

BROTHERS IN ARMS MEDIEVAL TRILOGY
His Lady Bride (Book 1)
His Stolen Bride (Book 2)
His Rebel Bride (Book 3)

PARANORMAL ROMANCE
THE DOOMSDAY BRETHREN
Tempt Me With Darkness
"Fated" (e-novella)
Seduce Me In Shadow
Possess Me At Midnight
"Mated" – Haunted By Your Touch Anthology
Entice Me At Twilight
Embrace Me At Dawn

Join the

*Shayla*BLACK

Book Beauties
Facebook Group
http://shayla.link/FBChat

Join me for live,
interactive video chats
every #WineWednesday.
Be there for breaking
Shayla news, fun,
positive community,
giveaways, and more!

VIP Readers
NEWSLETTER
at ShaylaBlack.com

Be among the first to get
your greedy hands on
Shayla Black news, juicy
excerpts, cool VIP
giveaways—and more!

238

CPSIA information can be obtained
at www.ICGtesting.com
Printed in the USA
LVHW041935200519
618483LV00018B/2083/P